ECHOES OF US

Also by Kat Zhang

What's Left of Me

Once We Were

KAT ZHANG

ECHOES OF US

THE THIRD BOOK IN THE HYBRID CHRONICLES

HARPER
An Imprint of HarperCollins*Publishers*

ECHOES OF US: THE HYBRID CHRONICLES, BOOK THREE

www.epicreads.com

ISBN 978-0-06-211493-8

Typography by Torborg Davern
14 15 16 17 18 CG/RRDH 10 9 8 7 6 5 4 3 2 1
❖
First Edition

To the readers who sneak books under desks and stay up long after dark. Our lives are all stories, in the end.

ECHOES OF US

PROLOGUE

I remember my childhood better than most. Usually, people gain freedom as they grow older; I lost it.

As the recessive soul, I was born weaker than Addie. She triumphed whenever we fought for control of our shared body. She was fated to win and I to lose, the promise of it written into our genes.

By the time we were twelve, I seemed ready to fulfill a recessive soul's other destiny: to disappear. I never did. But I did lose all my freedoms—the ability to speak, the power to move, the right to be acknowledged by anyone other than Addie, whose body I haunted.

So I remember my childhood well. Because however limited it was, for a long time, those were the only memories I had of liberty.

It wasn't until I met Lissa and Hally, Ryan and Devon, that I started thinking about my future, and not my past. They were hybrids, too. They knew what it meant to live in secret, and taught me how to regain control over my body.

But now, as we were all forced on the run again, moving from safe house to safe house, I returned to my childhood memories, seeking comfort in the worn softness of their edges.

<*What are you thinking about?*> Addie asked one night. We were all stuffed in a van, Peter driving, Dr. Lyanne beside him. The rest of us sat cramped, shoulder-to-shoulder in the back two rows, the windows rolled up tight against the autumn chill.

<*Pyxis*> I said.

All my memories of childhood were Addie's memories, too. We lived cleaved to each other, hybrids in a country where our very existence was outlawed.

The memory of pyxis came from before we understood all that, which made it all the more precious. Addie and I were three or four years old. Our family had gone camping. Our little brother, Lyle, hadn't been born yet, so it was just the four of us—Mom, Dad, Addie, and me.

I remembered that first sight of the stars in the crisp mountain air. We'd been a child accustomed to city nights and city lights. The enormity of all those stars had awed us.

<*Remember?*> I said. <*How Dad used to tell us about the constellations when we went camping? Only he couldn't—*>

<*Couldn't think of any stories about pyxis*> Addie said. Her smile wasn't just a physical thing, a curve of our lips. It was a warmth at the edge of my mind, where I felt

her presence with the same assurance I felt our heartbeat. *<I remember.>*

We fell into the memory, calming each other with the past as the road raced by.

All too quickly, a week passed. Then another and another. Addie and I started walking again, the pain in our ankle and the bruises on our body fading along with the sharpest recollections of our last few days in Anchoit. The bombing of Powatt's hybrid institution—the police raid—the frenzied escape through darkened streets—they'd never stop haunting us completely. But we tried to bury their pain with happier memories.

Addie and I drew everyone into the storytelling. Living at safe houses in the middle of nowhere, there was little else to do. We'd watched the news religiously at first. But the screen spit images of our faces and names, blaring our crimes: the "explosions" at Lankster Square, the Powatt bombing. After a while, the fear and upset crept into our insides and rotted them. Emalia said, *They're just saying the same things, over and over. Can we please turn it off?*

So we did. We gathered, instead, in the upstairs hallway, or around the dining table, or on the threadbare couch. If Ryan and I were in control, we sought the warmth of each other's touch, the press of my cheek against his shoulder, the comfort of having somebody there.

I told them about the day Lyle and Nathaniel were born. Addie and I had only been four, but I hadn't forgotten the happy, nervous chaos. The baby wrapped in blue and the momentary disappointment I'd felt that it wasn't a girl.

I didn't tell them about the day Nathaniel faded away, and it was considered normal, because he was the recessive soul. Or the day Lyle fell sick, and they rushed him to the hospital—a pale little boy too frightened to speak.

That was one of our unspoken rules. No sad stories.

There was too much of that already.

I knew a lot about Ryan's past, but it was nice to hear it again. The enormous old house in the country, where the Mullans lived before moving to Lupside. The creak of the ancient floorboards, the ever-dusty library, the stretch of field where the grass grew waist-high, perfect cover for war games at dusk. Hally or Lissa interrupted when they had something to add, or a complaint that he wasn't being entirely truthful. Ryan protested, but he smiled, and I knew he didn't really mind. His sisters' interruptions made us laugh, and laughter was a rare commodity now.

Dr. Lyanne had to be coaxed into the storytelling. At first, she talked only about her youth—snippets of a lace-and-satin childhood. I watched the sharp lines of her face and tried to imagine her two decades younger: not a woman, but a little girl named Rebecca who made the adults laugh with her grown-up sensibilities and too-serious face. Who knew the secret her brother, Peter, carried, but protected it fiercely.

Eventually, we wheedled out anecdotes about medical school. But we had to be careful. Dr. Lyanne's studies in medicine linked too closely to her specialization and interest in neurology. In hybridity. It all led to her work at Nornand Clinic of Psychiatric Health, where she'd met Jaime, then the rest of us. Where Addie and I had convinced her to betray her fellow doctors and help us escape.

Everyone liked Henri's stories best, because he'd seen the world. Jaime, especially, pored over Henri's remaining maps as he described the places he'd been, the things he'd experienced and written about.

"Have you written about us?" Kitty asked in the middle of a story about the Middle East. Henri had spent two months there, following a border war between two countries we'd never heard of—that hadn't even existed on the outdated maps taught in our schools. "About *us*, specifically, I mean."

Henri smiled. "Not by name. It's safer that way, in case anything gets intercepted."

Somehow, the notion hadn't struck me before. I'd known Henri had traveled here to cover the hybrid plight in the Americas, sending back articles and information through his satellite phone—more miniature computer than phone, in my mind. But I hadn't imagined his stories would be anything but general.

The thought of it didn't leave me. Somewhere out there, someone might hear our story, and it might just be that—a story over morning coffee, or playing in the background during dinner. Nothing more.

<It's weird, isn't it?> I said to Addie.

<You think too much, Eva> she replied.

But I couldn't help it. For years, before I regained control of our body, I'd done nothing but think and imagine. Now, I imagined what life might have been like if Addie and I had been born in one of those countries across the ocean, where hybridity was accepted, and normal.

Or what if Addie and I had settled when we were five years old, right on schedule? I would be gone, and Addie would have lived so differently. No doctor's appointments, no therapists, no medication. No sideways looks in the playground. No whispering teachers. No Nornand Clinic of Psychiatric Health.

No Hally and Lissa, or Ryan and Devon, or any of the people we'd met since then.

It had been less than a year since Addie and I had left our home for Nornand, but already, it was hard to imagine what our life would have been like if we'd kept the secret of my existence. Addie's ghost-in-the-head, who shouted too loudly to be contained.

We had a lot of time to sit and think now. But it was sweeter to focus on the good times. To remember the people I cared about at their best.

My mother and father, who I was convinced still loved me.

My brother, Lyle, who I told myself had gotten the kidney transplant our family had been promised.

I chose to remember Sabine and Josie for the steadiness of their eyes, the confidence they'd instilled in me with a look. I pictured Cordelia and Katy when they'd laughed, head thrown back, their short, bleached-blond hair feathery in the light. I decided to think of Christoph only in his softer moments, when a crack in his angry armor revealed the broken fragments of his past, still digging into his insides.

Jackson—Jackson and Vince I saw as the delivery boy at Nornand Clinic who told us there was hope of escape.

I wasn't supposed to be thinking about the things we'd done with Sabine's group. The chaos we'd inflicted on Lankster Square with our homemade firecrackers. The plan we'd aided to bomb the institution at Powatt—not knowing Sabine wanted to rip apart not just steel and concrete, but the lives of the officials touring that night.

The fight among us when we'd found out, and tried to stop everything.

The price we'd paid.

No sad stories. That was the rule.

ONE

On the day Henri was supposed to leave us, Addie and I woke to a news anchor's quiet murmuring. We crept past Kitty and Hally, both still asleep, and slipped from our shared bedroom.

Devon sat downstairs in the semidarkness of just-before-dawn, his eyes fixated on the tiny television. The screen cast strange, flickering shadows in the living room. There was no one else in sight.

"They haven't left yet, have they?" Addie whispered as she joined Devon on the lumpy couch. He didn't take his eyes from the television, but shook his head.

<*Where are they?*> I asked, and Addie was about to repeat my question aloud when Henri's bedroom door opened. That was answer enough.

Henri smiled at us, his teeth a flash of white against the darkness of his skin. "I thought we said our good-byes last night so you wouldn't have to get up this early."

He carried only a small suitcase with him. Most of his

things had been abandoned when we fled Anchoit. I imagined the police stumbling onto them, rifling through his notes and half-written articles. They'd know to be on the lookout for him now. A foreign reporter living in the Americas was in a lot of danger, and Henri had finally given in to pressure from friends and family overseas to fly home while he still could.

He leaned over the back of the couch to get a better look at the television. "Jenson again?"

Devon nodded. It was an old clip. Mark Jenson had given so many speeches and interviews over the past few weeks. About hybrids. About Powatt. About the safety of the country at large.

It was hard to reconcile the presence he broadcasted to the world—calm, sleek confidence—with the man who'd tried to carry Addie and me from Powatt after we sprained our ankle. The man who'd dug us from the wreckage after the explosion, his eyes frenzied, his shirt bloodied.

Every time I saw him, I felt a phantom pain in our shoulder—his nails digging into the bruised skin. *Where's the boy?* he'd shouted at us. *Where is Jaime Cortae?*

"He's trying to take control of the situation." To someone who didn't know him, Devon might have seemed bored by the whole thing. But I caught the sharp way his eyes followed Jenson's movements. Devon was often the most perceptive of us, for all he acted like the world was only a vaguely interesting shadow play.

"Doesn't seem like it would be Jenson's job to control

things. But I guess he is supposed to be an expert on the hybrid issue." Henri straightened, and Devon finally looked away from the television. His face held its usual lake-water placidity, but something rippled through it as Henri said, "Well, I guess it's time to go."

Devon and Ryan were early wakers, but four a.m. was a bit extreme to just get up on a whim.

"Here—" Henri reached into his pocket and took out his satellite phone. He handed it to Devon. "You remember how to use it, right?"

Devon was already turning the phone around in his hands, checking the nearly palm-size screen, the miniature keyboard, the port where it could connect to a computer. He nodded as he fiddled with the antennae, then looked back up at Henri. "You won't need it?"

Henri shrugged. "It shouldn't take me more than a few days to get home. I've let my people know to expect no calls until I arrive. Besides, I need a way to stay in contact with all of you." He smiled a little. "Be careful, though. These things aren't impossible to track, if the government starts getting suspicious. Limit call times. And don't let Ryan take it apart. He might not be able to put it back together."

Devon—*Devon*—almost grinned. "I could put it back together."

I laughed silently in the corner of my mind and wondered what Ryan had said to that.

The back door opened, revealing Emalia and Peter. Emalia

didn't seem surprised to see Addie and me up, though Peter raised his eyebrows.

"Are we ready to go?" Emalia said, pulling her jacket tighter around her. She and her twin soul, Sophie, had volunteered to drive Henri to his contact in the next state, arguing that they were the best choice since the news broadcasts lacked their face. Only Kitty and Nina had likewise escaped exposure.

Jaime's information, of course, had been circulating in the media for months. Out of all of us, he was the one Jenson most desperately sought—the one child to survive the operation when Nornand's doctors stripped away his second soul.

But Jenson had also seen Ryan and Dr. Lyanne at Powatt, when they came to rescue Addie and me after we'd tried to stop the explosion. He must have intuited that Hally would be with her brother, and the police raids would have found enough incriminating information about Henri and Peter to label them as suspects.

It pained me to have them all share blame for the bombing.

"Be careful on the road," Peter said. He and Dr. Lyanne would stay here at the safe house with us in case anything went wrong. That was the phrase hanging over every second of our lives now: *in case anything goes wrong.*

Henri looked at us and Devon one last time, like he wanted to memorize our faces.

"Stay safe," he said, finally, and joined Emalia at the door.

They left, leaving the rest of us watching after them.

* * *

"I can't believe you didn't wake me up," Hally said hours later. She sat next to Addie and me on the indoor balcony, overlooking the living room and the foyer. Our legs swung over the edge.

Ryan, on our other side, reached through the balcony rungs to steal half of Hally's peanut butter sandwich. She snatched her hand away a second too late and settled for looking aggrieved.

"It was four in the morning." Ryan offered me a bite of the sandwich. Peanut butter oozed onto his finger, and he put it in his mouth, muffling his next words. "You don't like to get up before ten."

"I would have gotten up if the rest of you were up," she complained.

I could hardly believe that once, Addie and I had passed Devon or Ryan in the hall at school and barely noticed. That we'd gone out of our way to avoid Hally, because we feared her foreign looks might bring us more trouble.

Now, they counted among the most important people in my life.

Ryan's eyebrow quirked up when I stared at him just a little too long, his mouth softening into a smile. *What?* it said, and I shook our head with a smile of my own.

We'd gotten good at communicating through glances—through a touch, and the slant of the mouth. Small gestures were all we had. The safe houses were rarely large. Even if both of us weren't sharing bodies, we'd have trouble finding time and space to be alone together.

Sometimes, Addie would offer to temporarily disappear. But guilt usually made me turn her down. Addie's thoughts were filled with a boy, too. One who wasn't even there to steal kisses with her at the end of darkened hallways, laughing and ignoring the knowing way Emalia looked at us when she passed.

Hally finished off her sandwich and stood, brushing crumbs from her blouse. "Well, if—"

The doorbell rang.

Hally's mouth snapped shut. Addie whispered <*But no one—*>

No one rang the doorbell. This house was a little less remote than the first two we'd lived in, but it was still almost an hour from the nearest major town. People didn't just stumble onto our doorstep.

Dr. Lyanne emerged from her downstairs room, her hair damp and braided after her shower. There was something naked about her expression as she looked up and motioned for us to be quiet.

Peter joined his sister in the foyer. The windows were all curtained. Our remaining van was in the driveway, so we couldn't pretend the house was abandoned, but we could pretend there was nobody home.

For a long moment, no one spoke. No one made to open the door.

The doorbell rang again.

Then the knocking started. Sharp raps against the door.

A woman's voice rang out.

"Excuse me," she said. "My name is Marion Prytt, and I would like to speak with Addie Tamsyn."

TWO

Dr. Lyanne gestured for us to clear out, and we retreated to our bedroom with the others, our heart thudding. I sank onto a bed, hands fisting around the worn patchwork quilt.

Hally was the last one in. "Who do you think it is?" she whispered as she shut the door. Ryan stood beside us, his body tense with confused worry.

Of course, no one had any idea. With our pictures circulating, anybody might know about us now. *Keep calm,* I told myself fiercely. I focused on our breathing. *Don't freak out.*

Addie and I were no strangers to panic attacks—hadn't been since we were seven years old and learned the fear of small spaces. But in the weeks since Powatt, other things had begun to set us off—sudden noises; flashes of heat.

Sometimes, just the thought of the darkness, pain, and fear of oblivion under a fallen chunk of wall, our remains eaten through by flames.

<If the woman wanted to arrest us> I said to Addie *<she wouldn't need to knock on our door.>*

<God knows what her plan is, Eva. Jenson knew we were in Anchoit—knew we were planning something—and he kept his distance until he knew he could do the most harm.>

Hally set her hands on the windowsill.

"She's got a nice car." She squinted, brushing her black curls away from her face. "Can't see the license plate—*oh*, there's a girl in the backseat—"

Ryan hurried to the window with us. As we watched, the girl opened the car door and climbed out. She looked maybe twelve, a little older than Kitty and Nina. Her overcoat flapped in the wind as she hurried toward the house, her shoulders hunched against the cold.

<If the woman wanted to arrest us> I said with slightly more conviction *<why would she have a kid with her?>*

"Do you think they're hybrid?" Hally said. Before everything had gone to pieces at Anchoit, people had often come to Peter for help. They'd hear about him from a friend of a friend—whispers of a man at the head of a network of hybrids and hybrid sympathizers who might be able to steal a child away to safety, or even break him out of an institution. Who was proof that there was hope out there, somewhere.

The girl outside the window looked straight up at us.

There was something familiar about her face.

She, certainly, recognized ours. Her eyes went big, and her mouth dropped open. The wind had whipped a blush to her cheeks.

<*How do we know her?*> I whispered to Addie.

Ryan twined his fingers through ours. "What is it?"

"I've seen her before, I think." Automatically, I squeezed his hand. "I—I can't remember where."

Peter walked into view, beckoning the girl toward him. Then his gaze followed hers, focusing on us before turning back to the child. She kept trying to steal glances upward, but he ushered her inside.

I flipped frantically through my memory.

<*Not from school*> Addie said. I hadn't bothered to think that far back. Our memory of this girl's face was more recent.

"From Anchoit?" Ryan asked, but he sounded doubtful, and I shook our head. The memory hovered at the edge of my mind—

"She wasn't at Nornand." There was a certainty in Hally's voice, and no one argued with it. I remembered the face of every patient we'd known at Nornand, even if the finer details had blurred after so many months. This girl hadn't worn a blue uniform with us.

A quiet knock sounded on the bedroom door.

"It's me," Peter said, and only waited a second before coming inside.

He looked much as he always looked now. Like he was trying to hold the world together in his fists. Sometimes I wished I could still see him the way I had the night he'd rescued us from Nornand. When he and Jackson had materialized in the darkness of the clinic hallway like heroes in a fairy tale, guiding us toward moonlight and freedom.

I knew him better now. He was only one man—who wanted so much, but could only do so much.

"Eva," Peter said. "Can I speak with you?"

Ryan was reluctant to release our hand. I gave him a reassuring look as I followed Peter. We only went across the hall, to the room he shared with Emalia. Like much of the house, it bore the smell of sawdust and wood varnish.

"I've seen that girl before," I said as soon as Peter shut the door. "I can't remember where, but—"

"Her name is Wendy Howard," Peter said, and I frowned. The name rang no bells in our memory. "I don't think you've met her before."

"I have," I insisted. "I recognize her face—"

Peter reached into his pocket and drew out a folded sheet of paper. He smoothed it open on his desk. "You're sure you're not just remembering this?"

I stiffened. Addie's reaction was more visceral, but she wasn't the one in control, and it didn't show. But I felt it—icy knife-edge sharp—against me.

The paper was a flyer. That's what we'd called them when we were making them. When we cast them over the edge of the buildings around Lankster Square.

Peter was right. We'd never met Wendy Howard. Just drawn a likeness that was so similar it sent a chill dancing down our spine.

“Wendy brought it with her,” Peter said. “It’s yours, isn’t it?”

I nodded. I was still staring at the flyer, at the drawing of the girl our hands had painstakingly sketched.

“We made them for . . . for Lankster Square,” I said quietly. We’d already told Peter and the others about it. How Sabine had recruited us to help her create a distraction during the rally so she and Devon could sneak into Metro Council Hall and uncover the government’s plans for the Powatt institution. “All the flyers had hybrid kids on them . . .”

I ran our fingers over the words printed across the face of Anna H., 15.

HOW MANY CHILDREN HAVE DIED FOR THIS CURE?

It was strange to remember how hopeful we’d been then. How desperately relieved and happy I’d been to be a part of something. To be a force of change.

<You did a spectacular job with the drawing> I whispered. Addie hadn’t had anything to go on but Cordelia’s description. Anna and Cordelia had been in an institution together. *<It looks just like the girl downstairs.>*

Addie shuddered. *<But that can’t be Anna.>*

Anna H. was dead.

We’d only chosen dead children for our flyers.

Peter folded the flyer back up. Maybe he’d caught the way I was staring at it—knew that as long as it was splayed out on the desk, I could think of nothing but the hours Addie and I had spent in that attic above Sabine and Cordelia’s photography shop. The day we'd snuck from Emalia's apartment and took, with such a dizzying sense of responsibility, a sheaf of these flyers and a homemade firework to a rooftop overlooking the Square.

How had one of those flyers made it into Wendy Howard's hands? Had she been there that morning? Or had the flyer passed from hand to hand, until it reached hers?

"Wendy claims she's Anna's sister," Peter said.

"Hybrid?"

He shook his head. I struggled to shed the memories of Lankster Square. The thunder of the fireworks when they went off. The terrified roar of the crowd. There wasn't time for sad stories. Not even in my own mind. "The woman with her? Marion?"

"A reporter," Peter said. "She says she wants to do a *human-interest* story about Anna and Wendy. About hybrids in general. She wants to help our cause."

A *human-interest story.* The words lost meaning in my mind, shattering into fragments that didn't collect into a comprehensible whole. Human interest. Did that mean she thought our story would be interesting? Or did she mean it was a story about the human interest? Our interests? Our need for the gifts of freedom and safety that for so many others were not just *interests* but rights?

<It could be a trick> Addie said. If the last few months had proved anything, it was that so few people could be trusted. *<The government and the media are so closely*

entwined. Why would she be on our side?>

"Why did she come to us?" I asked.

"Because she knows the risks she's taking." Peter stared at the musty shelves lining the bedroom walls. His palms were flat against the desk, his muscles tensed. "If she's discovered, the government's going to be after her. She's going to need people to hide her, and protect her."

"You think she really wants to help us?"

He hesitated. "Perhaps. Or she just wants to help herself. If things . . . if things end well for us, she'll have the story of a lifetime."

"Can we trust them? I mean, Wendy . . . Wendy might really be Anna's sister, but . . ."

"But that doesn't mean much," Peter said. "Just because Wendy's sister was hybrid doesn't mean she's beyond using that fact to help persecute other hybrids."

He said it so blandly, so simply. Wendy Howard barely looked old enough to be a teenager, but perhaps that just meant she could be easier to manipulate.

"Why're they still here, then?" I said wearily.

Peter laughed. Quietly, tiredly, but laughter all the same. "Marion came prepared. She has something we want, and she knows it."

There was something off in the way Peter looked at us. Something that sent warning bells thundering in our chest, knocking against our heart.

"What?" I said.

He paused. As if he needed a moment to convince himself that Addie and I could handle whatever it was he had to say.

"What is it, Peter?" I demanded.

"It's Jackson," he said. "She says she knows how to rescue Jackson."

THREE

Jackson's full name was Jackson Montgomery. But Addie and I didn't learn that until months after we met him. Our first day at Nornand Clinic, he'd been nothing but a delivery boy who stared at us with too much curiosity. We'd been the new hybrid in a psychiatric ward; there was plenty to wonder about.

We didn't discover Jackson's real purpose until he pulled us into a janitor's closet and whispered the truth: he and Peter were going to rescue us. Later, after the escape, we learned about Vince, the other soul sharing his body. We learned, through them, how to temporarily disappear from our body. They introduced us to Sabine and her group. Gave us a purpose. Delivered us from the suffocation of our own safety net.

In the midst of all that, Addie fell in love with the boy with the pale blue eyes and the too-long hair and the match-strike smile. Then he betrayed us both, and while she was still figuring out the pieces of her broken heart, officers arrested him brutally in the streets.

We still had the footage Kitty accidentally recorded of Jackson's arrest. We hadn't watched it—hadn't even taken it anywhere to be developed. But the cartridge sat buried at the bottom of our suitcase.

"Jackson?" Addie said. The rush of her emotions manifested themselves in the cramp of our stomach, the aching in our chest.

Peter had caught the switch in control. It wasn't always visible, especially to someone who wasn't looking for it. But Peter was hybrid. He knew the signs.

"That's what she's claiming," he said.

"Does she have proof he's alive?"

"She says she does." Peter studied us. Weighed us. "She says she's met with him. She says she has a message from him. And she'll only give it to you."

Addie and I found Marion Prytt in the kitchen, standing at the counter with Dr. Lyanne and Wendy. The three of them nursed mismatched mugs. No one actually drank.

Marion was about Dr. Lyanne's age—late twenties. There was a starkness about her narrow face, a lack of color. But her eyes lit up at the sight of us.

"You must be Addie." Her voice was oddly breathy, with a rasp to it. When she moved toward us, Dr. Lyanne twitched as if she wanted to intercept her. She didn't, and Marion smiled as we shook hands. "I'm Marion Prytt. It's lovely to finally meet you."

"Finally?" Addie said. Our eyes flickered to Dr. Lyanne. "You've heard a lot about us?"

From what we'd heard about ourself on the news, it seemed impossible anyone would think it *lovely* to meet us. But if Marion really was a reporter with the government connections it took to know of Jackson's whereabouts, perhaps she knew more about Addie and me than what the television broadcasted.

"Well, not a lot, of course." Marion's delicate features flexed with every expression she put on and shed. "But enough. Some from the information that the government's released about you. Some from Jackson."

Peter wedged himself in beside us in the small kitchen. "You said you had a message from him."

I hesitated. <*Addie—*> I didn't know how, but I wanted to protect her from whatever Marion was about to say. Shield her from the pain it might cause.

Addie was nothing but a wire of nerves, stretched to breaking.

Marion spoke as if there were no one in the kitchen but her and us. "He wanted to tell you to keep hope. And to remember when you went sailing."

<*We never went sailing—*> I started to say. But our fingers tightened around the edge of the kitchen counter, and Addie barked out a helpless, breathless laugh.

<*I did*> she whispered.

The phone rang.

"I'll get it," Dr. Lyanne said, and slipped past us, out the door.

"Does that sound like Jackson, Addie?" Peter's expression was gentle. As far as I knew, no one had told him about Addie and Jackson. But close quarters and high tensions weren't conducive to secrets. They shuddered through cracks, seeping from one person to the other.

Our teeth ground into our bottom lip. But Addie nodded.

I didn't say anything, not even in the shared privacy between our minds. I understood the message to *keep hope*. It was what Jackson had told us at Nornand. It was something I'd said back to him during our mission to save the officials at Powatt from Sabine's bomb.

But in all the months we'd known each other, we'd never gone sailing.

I'd never gone sailing. Apparently, Addie had.

"Peter." Dr. Lyanne stood in the doorway. There was a brightness in her eyes, and her cheeks were strangely flushed.

Peter took one look at her and left our side, motioning for us to stay put. He and Dr. Lyanne disappeared into the living room.

<Something's wrong> I said. Addie glanced over our shoulder, but Peter and Dr. Lyanne were too far away to see. *<I can feel it.>*

Something was always feeling wrong, nowadays. The sensation itched like a woolen cloak against bare skin. I couldn't throw it off.

"Has he told you?" Marion said.

Addie looked back toward her. "Sorry?"

"Peter." Marion spoke too softly for her voice to carry beyond the kitchen. "About Darcie Grey. About the footage."

Our expression must have been answer enough. Marion took a small step toward us, like we were some wild animal she might startle into fleeing. "There's a fourteen-year-old hybrid girl named Darcie Grey. She lives a few hours east of here, near Bramfolk. She's just been discovered."

I almost laughed at her choice of words. Back in Lupside, there had been a girl in our class who wanted to model. In eighth grade, she was chosen for some fashion show in Bessimir City, and came to school beaming about how she'd been *discovered*.

She'd moved away the next year, so I didn't know how things turned out for her. Probably a hell of a lot better than they would for Darcie Grey.

"I think your people could help her," Marion said.

"My people?"

Marion shifted her weight. Her crisp, seafoam blouse wrinkled as she shrugged. "It's what Peter does, isn't it? And I'm sure he has a lot of help. He can't possibly be doing all this on his own."

Addie frowned. "All what?"

"All, you know . . ." Marion made some vague hand gesture at the house around us. "This—"

"He saves kids," Wendy said. It was the first words Addie and I had heard her say, and they sent a shock through our body. Wendy fiddled with her short, dark hair, tucking it behind her ears. "He saved you, didn't he?" she said.

When Addie didn't immediately answer, Wendy set down her mug. It clinked against the counter. "You never met my sister?"

The question had a practiced air to it, like it was something she'd rehearsed asking.

"No," Addie said tightly. We'd used Anna as a symbol, but Anna had been a flesh-and-blood girl with flesh-and-blood family. A member of it stood in this kitchen in an oversized winter coat and a dark purple sweater.

"But you knew someone who did," Wendy said.

Maybe we should have denied it. Probably, it would have been safer to deny it. But staring at this girl, we couldn't.

"Yeah," Addie whispered. "I did."

Wendy's entire body stiffened. Then she smiled. Just a tiny bit. This was all it took for her to have a little happiness: to know a girl who knew a girl who knew her sister after she was taken away.

It was better than nothing at all.

"I'm sorry," Addie said, looking from Wendy to Marion, "but I don't understand what this all has to do with me. Or Darcie Grey."

Marion drew a small envelope from her purse and held it out to us.

"Wendy wants to help people like her sister." Marion sounded earnest enough. A little too earnest. There was something overly shiny about it. "So do I. Maybe you can't tell, stuck in this house in the middle of nowhere, but the country is getting riled up. People are questioning things they haven't had to doubt in decades. They're searching for answers. Things could go very badly for hybrids. But they could also go very well, if the right cards are played."

Inside the envelope was a photograph. We could only see the white backside, where someone had written, in neat cursive: *Darcie. Soccer championships.*

"A story like the one I want to tell about Wendy and Anna—about what happens to hybrid children in this country—it's something that's never been done before. No one's ever dared to. But it'll be worth it. People need concrete pictures, Addie. They can't just be left to *imagine* what it's like in an institution. They have to *see* it."

Addie flipped the photograph over and stared at the glossy image. Marion hesitated. "I need someone on the inside."

Darcie Grey had wavy, light blond hair and brown eyes. Darcie Grey had freckles and a small nose and thin lips.

Darcie Grey looked like us.

FOUR

Darcie didn't look exactly like us, of course. She seemed younger. Her eyes were bigger, and had more hazel in them. Her face was a little wider, her hair shorter and several shades lighter than our dirty blond. But we might have been sisters. Cousins, at least.

And Marion needed someone on the inside.

"Darcie has a heart condition," Marion was saying—her words had turned into a breathy tumble of syllables as Addie and I realized what she was asking of us. "Nothing too major, but sending her in to gather footage in the institution—such a high-stress situation seems unnecessarily cruel."

<Unnecessarily cruel?> I laughed bitterly. *<What about all the other hybrid children locked away? Is that necessary cruelty?>*

Marion was still talking. "Besides, Darcie doesn't have your experience. I can't know how she'd handle herself in the institution. She might go to pieces, or trust too easily, or not know how to lie well enough. But you . . ."

"I'm practically a criminal mastermind?" Addie said dully.

"You've proven able to keep a level head in precarious situations," Marion said. "I can't send an adult. All the caretakers are highly vetted now—it would take ages to get anyone through the necessary background checks, and . . ." She seemed to realize Addie was too dazed to listen about background checks. Our eyes fell back to the photograph of Darcie Grey, this girl with the minor heart defect and the soccer uniform and the face that could possibly, possibly be confused for ours.

"That was taken just before her fourteenth birthday," Marion said. "She doesn't have a driver's license or a permit. She was homeschooled, so there are no yearbook pictures."

"She was on a soccer team." The words slid from our confused mouth.

"She was," Marion agreed. "But all things considered, Darcie has lived a life off the record. And to be honest, it isn't as if they'll check too closely, if you put on a good show. Her parents aren't even supposed to know their daughter's been discovered—they still wouldn't know, except that I told them."

She paused, as if she thought this piece of information might endear her to us. Did it? The night Mr. Conivent came to collect us from our home . . . we'd had a few hours' notice, even if our parents hadn't. We could have run, or tried to warn Mom and Dad. We'd done neither. We'd been naive, still.

"If you get me this footage," Marion said, "I'll free Jackson Montgomery."

Addie looked at her narrowly. "I thought you wanted to help us. Help the hybrids."

Marion nodded. "I do."

"Jackson is hybrid. He's eighteen. He's never done anything wrong—"

"I'm sorry," Marion said, and she really did look it. As if she was explaining a game we didn't quite understand, and the rules said we'd lost. "But he helped orchestrate the bombing of a government building. He's an accomplice to attempted murder."

"That's not true," Addie said automatically. "You have no proof of that."

Marion leaned against the counter. Her long, straight hair pooled against the countertop, fawn brown. "It's been more than three weeks since the bombing. They've held Jackson for that long. They've investigated for that long. You really think they haven't had time to come up with any proof?" Her voice softened. "That's not the point. I know where he's being held. I know when he's going to be transferred. I can help you free him."

"Then do it." Addie stepped toward Marion, as careful as when the woman had done the same. The distance between us was fast disappearing. "An act of good faith."

"I can't."

"Then how can I trust you?"

"If I'm going to help Jackson escape," Marion said, "the timing is crucial. I can't just waltz in there tomorrow. And I'm going to need help from people I know on the inside—people who will be a lot more willing to help if *they* have some kind of proof that in ten years, they're going to be remembered as heroes, not traitors." She glanced toward Wendy. Smiled a little. "Not everyone is willing to put so much on the line, just blindly hoping for a brighter future."

There was admiration, of a sort, in her voice. But also a note of pity. Or even condescension—but perhaps that was just my irritated imagination. Wendy smiled hesitantly back.

Anger rushed through me. Did Wendy's parents even know what she was doing? Had Marion convinced her to run away from home, to join her on this complicated, uncertain quest? Maybe Wendy had a simple, genuine need to help. An unadulterated hope for change.

But such things were rarely enough.

I wanted, so badly, to tell Wendy to be careful. Of who she trusted. Of the decisions she made with nothing but good intentions.

Marion put out her hands, palm up. "We're on the same side. Please, help me, and let me help you."

Addie laughed bitterly. *<Where have we heard that before?>*

We're on the same side.

This is me looking out for you.

They were all things Sabine had said to us while she betrayed us. We wouldn't fall for pretty words again.

A hand brushed against our shoulder. Dr. Lyanne. She

glanced at Marion, then back to us.

"Give us a moment," she said as she directed Addie and me toward the kitchen door. She didn't let us stop walking until we'd reached the far end of the living room. Peter was already there, standing stiffly by the stairs.

Dr. Lyanne's grip tightened on our shoulder. "We have to leave. Go tell Jaime and the others. Get everyone to pack."

"What?" Addie said. We hadn't even recovered from the shock of Marion's proposal. Now we were being hit with something else. "Why? What's happened?"

"It's Emalia," Dr. Lyanne said quietly. Her eyes bore into ours, forced us to keep steady. "Something's wrong."

We'd prepared for this. We'd hoped it would never happen, but Peter was Peter, and we'd prepared.

Ryan met us at the top of the stairs, appearing from the darkness of the unlit hallway.

"We have to go," Addie said before he could speak. "Emalia never made it back from dropping Henri off. She should have checked in with one of Peter's contacts more than an hour ago."

I saw him swallow down questions. We'd never physically drilled what we would do in case Something Went Wrong, but the steps had run through our minds more than enough times. Extraneous questions were not on the list.

He allowed himself one: "And Henri?"

Addie shook our head. "Can't be sure. Peter's contact

checked out the area. There was some kind of investigation going on. Both Henri and Emalia are missing—together, separately . . . we don't know." She swallowed, throat tight. "Go get Kitty and Jaime. They're probably in the attic."

With Emalia and Henri possibly detained, there was no telling what the government might already know—or find out. This house was no longer safe.

In less than half an hour, we wiped the place clean of our existence. It wasn't hard. Each of us had arrived with no more than a single suitcase. The nuances and necessities of our lives folded right back where we'd stored them. A few changes of clothes. Some toiletries. A small notebook Addie had found at a bus station and doodled in.

Almost everything had been given to us by people in Peter's network. Men and women we'd never met who helped us sneak from city to city, state to state. Addie and I had a small shoulder bag, denim and old-fashioned. We packed the most important things in there now, so we could always have them with us: Henri's satellite phone, copies of our false identifications, some spare cash for emergencies, the little round chip Ryan had given us before leaving for Nornand. Addie slipped Darcie Grey's picture inside as well—and, after a breath of hesitation, the cartridge containing the footage of Jackson's arrest.

"Are they coming with us?" Hally whispered as we carried our luggage out to the van. "The girl and the reporter lady, I mean."

Addie shrugged. The others were already stacking suitcases in the van's trunk. Peter stood a little ways down the driveway, speaking with Marion. Wendy lingered beside them. Her eyes found ours as soon as we approached.

<I wish she wouldn't look at us like that> I said. *<Like—>*

<Like we could perform miracles> Addie said quietly.

"We have our own car," Marion was protesting. She had her keys in hand. "We'll just follow behind."

"No one's following behind," Peter said. "Give us a number, or some other way to contact you."

Marion frowned. Next to Peter, she seemed young, and slight, and faint with her pale looks and breathy voice. "How do I know you'll call?"

Peter held out his hand. His expression had gone rigid, his eyes stony. "I'm asking for a contact," he said. "That's the best you're going to get."

They faced off for a moment, neither looking like retreat was an option. Finally, Marion nodded. She scribbled a number on a business card and handed it to Peter. But when he was busy loading the last of the luggage, she brushed by Addie and me and pushed another card into our hands. We didn't need to look to know what was written on it.

"Call me," she said over her shoulder.

FIVE

After the rush and frenzy of packing, being on the road again was strangely anticlimatic. For the first half hour or so, we all sat in rigid silence. Peter seemed focused on nothing but the stretch of highway in front of us and the steering wheel he gripped with both hands. We'd left the farmhouse behind, were encroaching now on the edges of small towns, the narrow highway threading between them.

Addie hugged our arms around our purse, like it might protect us.

<*Do you think he's all right?*> she asked. <*Jackson.*>

I hadn't been thinking about Jackson. I'd been worrying about where Peter was taking us next, and how safe it would be, and whether Emalia and Henri had really been captured. I'd been noticing every time Ryan shifted in his seat, the way his shoulders were tensed, even when he tried to smile at us.

But Addie had been thinking of Jackson, and so I felt a pang of guilt that I hadn't been doing the same.

God only knew what he'd been through since the night we'd last seen him.

<*He spoke with Marion*> I said. <*That means something, doesn't it?*>

She nodded absently. Held the purse a little tighter against our stomach.

<*What if . . .*> Her voice faltered. <*Do you think he's waiting for us to do something? To help him?*>

The words were accompanied by a dagger-sharp jab of pain. It slipped in between breaths. Made our lungs hitch.

Jackson had told us about the years he'd spent in an institution, before Peter rescued him. The windowless rooms. The terrified children. The hopelessness of it all.

I couldn't help imagining him somewhere similar now. Or someplace even worse. If they threw innocent hybrid children into horrific institutions, what would they do with a hybrid criminal?

I was still searching for the right thing to say when the siren blared.

We dove to the floor. Yanked Ryan down with us, crouching in the space between our seats. Our fingers were vises on Ryan's arm. He squeezed our shoulder, then rose slightly to check the backseat. Hally had ushered Kitty and Jaime down, too.

Addie and I glanced through the back window. It wasn't a normal-looking police car. This was a van, like ours, but smaller. Sleek and black. It was still a few cars behind us.

The siren wailed. Lights flashed.

I found myself in control of our limbs, our tongue. "Peter?" I said tightly.

His eyes met ours in the rearview mirror. "Stay low."

"Are we going to stop?" Hally whispered. Beside her, Kitty had curled around her knees, her small hands clasped tightly. She stared at the scruffy floor of the van, her mouth thin.

Dr. Lyanne spoke just loudly enough to be heard. "We don't know if it's for us."

Ryan and I looked at each other. The police van gained, the other cars slowing and pulling out of its way.

No one else was going to say it, so I did. "It's for us."

Peter didn't slow. He didn't speed up, either.

The police van was right behind us now.

"Peter," Dr. Lyanne said. His eyes flickered to her. Then, finally, the car began to decelerate.

Sixty miles per hour.

Fifty.

Thirty.

"Don't, Peter." Ryan kept one hand wrapped around our wrist, but pressed himself forward, toward the front of the van. "Don't stop."

We pulled over onto the side of the road, hitting the rumble strip. Then the sparse grass. Peter put the van in park, but didn't kill the engine. The police van rolled to a halt behind us, wheels crunching gravel.

We hadn't been speeding. Even in his rush, Peter wouldn't

take a chance like that. Why had we been picked out?

Was it Marion? Had she been sent by the government, after all? She could have memorized our license plate. Peter switched vehicles as often as he could, but we hadn't gotten the chance since leaving the farmhouse.

Our heart thundered.

<There's only one direction to run> I said.

The highway was on our left. If we had to escape, we could only go right, through the tall, brittle grass. There wasn't cover for a good dozen yards or so, until the edge of the trees.

"Peter," Ryan said. His grip was crushing—I would have wrenched away if I weren't so focused on the police van. Its side door swung open.

A man stepped out. He wore the pressed black pants and collared shirt of a businessman. But we saw the gun holstered at his hip.

He moved toward us slowly. His partner stayed behind.

He was three feet from the back bumper when Peter threw the car into drive.

We screeched from the curb, lunging in front of a car. The driver blared his horn and stomped on the brakes just in time to avoid impact. Hally screamed.

The sirens wailed again. Peter's knuckles shone white on the steering wheel. He swerved left. Cut off another car. Put as much distance as he could between us and the police van hot in pursuit.

Horns bellowed up and down the highway.

After Hally's initial scream of surprise, no one in the van made a noise. No one shouted or said, *Peter!* or asked him what the hell he was doing—we were going to die, we were going to *hit* someone—

"They're gaining," Dr. Lyanne whispered, and that was all.

The police were only two cars behind us. Then one. Then none at all. The road ahead of us cleared of cars.

The black van drifted left, straddling the center lane. It was still gaining speed, though Peter gunned our engine for all it was worth. The van started to pull up beside us, its front bumper aligning with our back wheel well.

I saw the collision coming the second before I felt it.

Metal shrieked. We flew against Ryan. Tumbled against the car door. Something rammed into our shoulder. Luggage.

The world spun. Wheels skidded. Everyone careened in the opposite direction, Ryan's body slamming into ours even as he fought to grab on to the seat. Our head cracked against the window.

The pain blinded. It took us what seemed like minutes but was probably seconds to realize the car was no longer moving.

Something choked us—our purse strap. Dizzily, we tugged at it. Then Ryan was there, helping us wrench the purse free from a pile of suitcases.

"Eva," Ryan was yelling in our ear. "Eva, get up!"

The blow had jostled my thoughts beyond comprehension. But I understood the terrified urgency in his voice, and I understood *get up* and I went where his arms pulled me. He yanked the side door open. A suitcase tumbled out, smashing into the grass.

Grass. We'd spun back to the curb.

I tried to shake my head clear. Groaned as the nausea increased. Where was everyone? Was everyone okay?

"Jaime," I gasped. I turned, searching for him. The others could all run, but some days Jaime had trouble just with walking.

"Peter's got him," Ryan said. "*Come on*, Eva—"

He dragged us from the van, both of us tripping on the uneven terrain. I glanced back. Saw Peter pull Jaime from his seat. The boy wrapped his arms around the man's neck. We were almost to the line of trees, but we were leaving them behind—the others were gone, must have run ahead—Peter and Jaime had to catch up—

A gun fired.

Addie clutched at me.

Gunfire split the air again.

Split more than air.

Smashed through a window, and Jaime screamed. Peter fell. His back hit the ground so fast, so hard. So sudden. Jaime fell with him, limbs crumpling. He struggled to rise again. Peter did not.

The next round of gunfire ripped up the ground near our feet.

Ryan jerked at our numb hand.

We tore into the clump of trees.

I looked back only once.

It was enough to memorize the scene. Our van, doors flung open, luggage spilling out like a disgorged monster. The police van pulled up at a safe distance. An officer hurrying toward Jaime.

Peter staring up at us, but seeing nothing.

SIX

Ryan and I ran until our lungs burned. Until our legs deadened. Even then, we might have kept going—*I* might have kept going—except Addie screamed at me *<Stop! Eva—stop!>*

I didn't want to. As long as I was running, I didn't have to think about anything but putting one foot in front of the other, the wind lashing against our face.

But I stopped.

As soon as I did, Ryan slowed down, too. Circled back to us. We'd passed the grove of trees. We were at the rear of a neighborhood now. A row of squat houses lined the bottom of the hill.

We ducked into the shadow of some high shrubbery. The branches scratched at our arms, even through our jacket.

"You saw her, right?" Ryan spoke in an out-of-breath whisper. "Hally. Ahead of me."

I opened our mouth, then shut it again.

<Addie?> I said helplessly.

<I don't know> she said. Our heart thundered *boom boom boom boom* through our body. *<I—I don't remember seeing anything.>*

"I saw her ahead of us," Ryan said. I wan't sure who he was more desperate to convince, Addie and me, or himself.

What could I do but nod?

"They shot at us." Ryan had been the one to drag us away from the van, to pull us along until our own self-preservation kicked in. But he was faltering now. He wasn't looking at us, though his fingers locked around our wrist. Like he needed the physical reassurance that I was there. "Peter—"

He fumbled over his words. My own thoughts fumbled. Each sentence started only to be interrupted by the sight of Peter's body on the ground. His eyes. The unnatural stillness of his limbs. The suddenness of it all.

I hadn't seen blood. Such violent death was supposed to be accompanied by blood, and screams, and thrashing. Not abrupt silence.

Death. Was Peter dead?

Put next to his name, the word lost all meaning. Addie and I had skirted around death our entire lives. I'd been destined to die years ago. They didn't call it *dying* when a recessive soul faded away, but that was what it was. Death hidden under semantics.

Then Lyle had fallen sick, and death had slept under his bed for weeks. It still lingered about the house, held off by his dialysis sessions and medications.

But I had lived. Lyle had lived. Addie and I had brushed against death at Nornand, and at Powatt, and both times death had passed us by. Perhaps we'd grown arrogant. We'd come to think death would always let us alone, and those we cared about.

Peter was dead.

I didn't know what that meant.

I thought about that little piece of metal ricocheting around Peter's insides, tearing up the soft tissue of his lungs, his heart, denting and breaking his ribs—

I bent over. Coughed and held our breath against a rising nausea that squeezed tears from our eyes, shoved us forward and backward like the earth tilting. Like a top spinning. Whirling.

When I opened our eyes again, Ryan had crouched down next to us.

"We have to keep moving," he said softly. "We have to find the others."

I nodded. Closed our eyes again. Forced our lungs to *inhale, exhale*. Forced myself to stand on shaky legs. "There's a meet-up location," I said through lips too numb to move.

Peter always set one up when we traveled, in case anything went wrong. He'd made sure we all memorized this one before leaving the farmhouse.

"That's miles away," Ryan murmured. "It'll take hours to get there."

He didn't add, *What will we do if we show up and no one else does?*

He didn't need to.

All around us, the woods were silent. Even the houses were still, not a single person puttering around the backyard.

"We can't go back." Our voice was quiet, hoarse. "The police will be all over the van."

I could see them now, shuffling through our meager belongings, searching for answers in the folds of our clothes. And Jaime. They had Jaime.

I grabbed at our purse. The zipper was closed, but I opened it just to make sure Henri's phone was still inside. A business card fell out. I snatched it before it could hit the ground.

<Marion> Addie said, and didn't need to say more. We'd lighted on the same idea.

"We have to find everyone," I said to Ryan. "But we can't do it alone. We don't have a car, don't have a place to stay. Nothing."

"We have an emergency number—"

"Our nearest contact is in the next state," I said. "It would take hours for her to get here."

"Then who?" Ryan asked.

I held up the card with Marion's number.

"No." Ryan's eyes were dark. I'd told him what Marion wanted from Addie and me. "How coincidental is it that the day she shows up is the day Emalia gets in trouble, and the day we get stopped by the police? How can we trust her?"

<Jackson said we could> Addie said softly. *<When he asked me to remember sailing.>*

There was something painful in her words, a wound I couldn't help heal. I wasn't sure if telling Ryan that Jackson had deemed Marion trustworthy would help. They hadn't exactly parted friends.

So I didn't bring him up. Instead, I looked at Ryan and said, "Trust *me*. You don't have to trust anyone else. But trust me."

I'd never used Henri's satellite phone before. It was smaller than most phones I'd seen, barely bigger than our hand. The screen took up almost half of it.

The screen that I now realized had cracked. I tried to turn it on. It wouldn't.

Just hours ago, we'd been back at the safe house, joking with Henri about taking the phone apart and putting it back together. We hadn't taken it apart, but it was broken all the same. Something must have smashed against it during the car crash.

"Can you fix it?" I asked Ryan desperately.

"I don't know," he said. "But right now, we're going to have to find a pay phone. Do you have money?"

I did. Addie and I had made sure to carry some—not much, but enough coins for a few calls, and enough cash for a couple meals, if we were careful.

I put the satphone back into our purse as gingerly as I could. We walked until we reached the outskirts of the nearest town. I slipped into the first phone booth we found and dialed Marion's number with clumsy fingers.

Marion picked up. She was somewhere quiet. A hotel room? I thought about phone taps and bugged lines and was almost too afraid to open our mouth. But she said *Hello? Hello?* and with Addie's strength pushing mine, I answered her.

I didn't give details. She could probably hear the suppressed panic in our voice. She didn't ask unnecessary questions. Just where she should meet us. If she should bring anything.

I told her the nearest intersection. Then hung up and went to sit with Ryan in the shade of a large tree. I hadn't realized how cold it was until then, as we sat huddled up against each other, heads bent in the wind.

Marion came within the hour. I recognized her car, nondescript and silver, as she reached the intersection. She looked around, but didn't see us hidden in the shadows, and pulled into a coffee-shop parking lot to wait.

Ryan looked at me. "You're sure about this, Eva?"

I nodded and stood. He rose slower. Cold sunlight dappled through the tree branches, glistening off the few remaining leaves. He took our hand, and we walked to Marion's car.

I hadn't told her it was just us and Ryan. She hesitated, but didn't ask about the others, just unlocked the doors and let us climb in. Ryan kept one hand on the door handle. I saw him test it, making sure he could still open it from the inside.

Marion had come, she said, from her hotel room near the farmhouse. She'd put up her hair, her eyes hidden behind large sunglasses. I suddenly wished I had the same option. Our face—our entire body—felt naked. We'd been in hiding so long, buffered by Peter, and Dr. Lyanne, and the others. There had been the feeling of safety in numbers.

Now it was just me and Addie, Ryan and Devon.

"Where to?" Marion said.

"Do you have a map?" I asked. Marion pulled one from the glove compartment, and I unfolded it over our lap.

"The hotel is on Steind." Marion pushed up her sunglasses and pointed. "Right after it intersects Mallers."

The reunion point was in the opposite direction. It was too far to walk—not unless we wanted to spend the better part of the day doing it, and risk getting seen.

I looked up. Looked right at this woman with her now-bared eyes, and the slight frown on her forehead, and the way she was pursing her mouth. I tried to read the way she'd let the nude-colored polish chip off her nails, the fact that she didn't avert her gaze, even when my staring had gone on too long to be polite.

"What do you really want?" I said quietly, and caught the tremor in her throat when she swallowed.

"I want to help," she said.

Then, finally, I looked away. I nodded.

"Here." I jabbed at a spot on the map maybe a mile from the meet-up point. "Take us here."

Marion studied the map, then started the car. But she couldn't help asking, as she pulled out of the parking lot, "What's happened, Eva? I'm completely in the dark here."

"Please," I said. "Just drive."

<You believe her?> Addie asked. It wasn't a challenge. *<That she wants to help?>*

<I believe> I said softly *<that she wants* our *help. And she'll do what she has to in order to get it.>*

SEVEN

The meet-up location was in a clean, touristy-looking town. Trees lined the avenues, and despite the chilly air, plastic flowers hung in baskets from the signposts, trying to fool people into thinking it was spring.

Ryan and I walked so close our shoulder kept bumping into his arm. We'd left Marion a few blocks away, at a shopping center. She'd protested, but only halfheartedly, asking how long she was supposed to wait.

"We'll be back before nightfall," Ryan had said.

He'd sounded assured at the time, and I'd made sure we looked the same. But the facade had dropped by the time we were out of sight.

Addie and I huddled in our jacket. Glanced at each vehicle that passed, watching out for police, or someone who stared too long. Being recognized was a risk Peter had drilled into us upon our arrival in Anchoit, and our faces hadn't been public knowledge then, the way they were now.

Peter had chosen for us to meet at 137 Danwill Street,

which turned out to be an old-fashioned arcade. We heard music blasting inside, even from the sidewalk.

I hadn't realized how much I relied on Peter's plans, his connections, his safety nets, until they were gone. Until he was gone.

Dead.

The word hit me harder this time. Like it had gained substance again during the drive here. We were following plans made by a dead man. Walking in the shadow of Peter's ghost.

Ryan looked in the window. When he came back, he said quietly, "There are a couple guys in there. College-aged, maybe. One older man." The look on his face was enough to tell us that he hadn't seen his sisters. Dr. Lyanne. Kitty.

I understood now, as I'd never truly understood before, how easy it could be for a person to simply disappear off the face of the earth. To be here one day, tangible and laughing and real, then gone like blown smoke the next.

"We should go in to wait," Ryan said, noticing us shiver.

Inside, the place smelled faintly like cigarette smoke, even though there was a lopsided *No Smoking* placard on the wall. It was low-lit. Two of the arcade machines bore *Out of Order* signs that had been there long enough to be covered in angry graffiti.

Ryan and I ordered a small tray of fries and two grilled-cheese sandwiches, keeping a cautious eye on the other patrons. They didn't pay us any mind. Neither did the owner, even though it was a school day, and Addie and I, at least, were obviously high-school aged.

The blasting music, hot, salty food, and frenzied noise of the arcade games helped drown out some of my fear. But an hour passed, and no one else came through the door.

<*What do we do if they don't show up?*> Addie said quietly. It was a question I hadn't wanted to ask.

<*We could call one of Peter's contacts to come get us. Or . . . we stay with Marion.*>

We didn't know Peter's contact. But she would be Peter-vetted, and we trusted that. Marion . . . Marion had her own agenda, apart from us. But then, didn't everyone? At least we knew what she wanted—her news story.

<*If the others don't come*> I said <*then that means they might have been captured. And if they're captured . . .*>

<*We're going to need some kind of leverage.*> Addie understood.

<*If we help Marion, then she'll give us Jackson, at least. Maybe find out about the others for us. And if we get that footage . . .*>

It could truly make a difference.

<*But this is only if we can really trust her, Addie.*> I spoke gently. <*I trust you, if you trust Jackson, but . . .*>

I fiddled with one of the remaining fries.

Addie's feelings flickered next to me, flashes of confused,

conflicted emotion. *<Back in Anchoit, Jackson took me sailing once.>*

I knew she was remembering it now, and I tried so hard to remember it with her. But I could only imagine it. The blue of the water. The rock of the boat. The wind and the smell of the ocean.

I didn't ask when it had happened. There were plenty of days in Anchoit that I had spent asleep while Addie lived. It would have been easy to snatch a few hours for sailing, to be out and back from the docks before I knew.

<When he was explaining how to steer . . .> Her voice softened. *<He said that even when you make a really big turn, you just need to move the tiller the tiniest amount. It might not seem like it's enough, but it is. You have to just hold on and have faith in it.>* She hesitated. *<I remember that was exactly what he said. That I had to have faith it was enough.>*

<You want to do this. Be a part of Marion's plan.>

<Who knows if we'll get another chance to save Jackson> she whispered. *<I—I know it's an insane risk, but . . .>*

I was cast back to nearly half a year ago—a Sunday morning in our bathroom at home, our bare feet curling against the chilly tiles, our damp, lukewarm washcloth pressed against our face. The Friday before, we'd gone to the Mullans' home, and Hally had become Lissa in the privacy of her bedroom. She'd told us what sort of life I *could* be living. Offered me a chance, one that Addie and I could take at great risk to both of us—but with the possibility of even greater reward.

Once upon a time, I'd asked Addie to take an insane risk for my sake, and now she was asking me for the same.

<*Okay*> I said. Because if there was any way to alleviate Addie's pain, I would give it a try. <*Okay, let's do it.*>

Before Addie could reply, the door to the arcade opened, and Hally walked inside. Her long, dark hair was down around her face, a curtain of curls that half shielded her expression. She took each step like the floor might crack beneath her feet. Then she saw us, and her expression bloomed into relief.

She glanced behind her, toward the door. Hope was a stubborn, buoyant thing in our chest. Why would she look behind her unless she'd left people outside? Unless there were others waiting for her?

Hally caught the attention of the college men like Ryan and I hadn't. Their gazes followed her across the arcade.

"Oh, God," Hally said breathlessly as she sank into the chair next to ours. There was something broken in her eyes. The jagged edges of it struck deep into our chest, made our heart hurt.

"Are you all right?" Ryan managed to keep his voice low and calm.

She nodded tightly. Her hands were shaking. I grabbed one. It was ice-cold.

"We can't talk in here." She looked toward the door again, and this time, she noticed the men staring. "We have to go."

Outside, the wind tore through our jacket. Hally wasn't even wearing one, and Ryan wrapped his around her shoulders as we hurried away from the arcade.

"Where are the others?" he said. He must have caught her glances toward the door, too.

We rounded the corner before Hally could answer. Kitty and Dr. Lyanne stared at us, pale-faced.

"Where are Jaime and Peter?" Dr. Lyanne demanded. And grew even paler when neither Ryan nor I replied. The looks in our eyes were answer enough.

The sun went down early, with November encroaching. By the time Marion pulled up to her hotel, it was dusk. The different buildings were separate, and stood alone, so at least we didn't have to pass a front desk.

To Marion's credit, she hadn't batted an eye when Ryan and I showed up again, hours after we'd left, with three new people tagging behind.

Wendy ran up as soon as Marion opened the hotel-room door.

"Can you find some food for everyone?" Marion said, and the girl nodded. I was about to follow the others inside when I realized Dr. Lyanne had lagged behind, one slim hand pressed against the side of a dark red truck like she needed it there to prop herself up.

I motioned for Ryan to go on in. He nodded, closing the door after him.

Dr. Lyanne glanced up when Addie and I were a few feet away. Her eyes, which could usually skewer with a look, were unfocused.

<What do we say?> I asked Addie. *<What could we possibly say to make anything better?>*

<There's nothing> she replied. And it was the truth.

"Go inside, Eva," Dr. Lyanne said, watching us approach. "The last thing we need is for you to get sick."

"I'm sorry," I said. Paltry words. But all I had. "About Peter."

I realized, suddenly, all the things I didn't know about Peter. About Warren, his other soul, who we'd never even addressed by name. What had they wanted to do with their lives, if there wasn't the resistance to be thinking about? What would they have done when all this was over?

Were they scared, when they died? Did they regret the choices they'd made, that had led them to that spot, at that moment?

Had Peter and Warren had any room in their minds, during those last seconds, for anything but a blaze of pain?

Had they realized they were dying?

Had they had time to make peace with it?

Had they had time to tell each other good-bye?

"If I do what Marion wants," I said softly, "then we might be able to bargain for Jaime's—"

"No, Eva," Dr. Lyanne said. Her voice was stony.

"We might be able to bargain for his return," I said over her. "Or kick up such a fuss that they won't be able to hurt him—"

"Eva," she snapped. Her eyes strayed heavenward. Her voice wavered. "Give me a moment before you start on another one of your harebrained ideas."

"Please," I said. "I want to help."

Dr. Lyanne looked back at us. The momentary vulnerability in her eyes had disappeared. "Peter had other plans." She laughed at the look on our face. "You think he didn't have contingency plans for if something happened to him?"

"I—I thought we were supposed to just call the closest contact."

Dr. Lyanne rubbed her fingers over her forehead. Lowered them over her eyes. "Not with the way things are headed. Things are getting worse here, Eva. If anything happened to Peter . . ." She took a sharp breath. Sighed. "He wanted us all on the next flight out."

"Out?" I echoed.

"Overseas."

Addie's shock jolted through me, as well. Combined forces with my own. I stumbled over my thoughts. "All of us?"

"You, Jaime, the Mullans, Kitty, Emalia . . . me. Henri would use his contacts."

"Henri's—"

"He left you his phone, didn't he?" Dr. Lyanne said.

Automatically, our hands went to our purse. Held it protectively. We'd told her how it had broken in the crash. "Although, God knows if he's okay himself right now. We'll have to wait until we get the thing fixed, then call and hope."

<Overseas> I said softly. The word echoed in my mind, bringing with it the memories of Henri's stories. The promise of peace. Of safety.

<This is a good thing, Eva> Addie said. *<This means the others will be safe. While we're gone.>*

Dr. Lyanne pushed away from the truck. She'd gathered herself, a regality seeping back into the set of her shoulders. "I know this sitting around, this hiding, is driving you crazy, Eva. But—"

I interrupted her. "Back at your house . . . back in Anchoit. You told me to clean up my mess. Those were your exact words. I can't leave before I do that."

We stared at each other a long, long time.

"Let Addie and me do this," I whispered. "We'd never be able to live with ourself otherwise. You know that."

We—*I*—had to make amends. By taking Darcie Grey's place in an institution, we would free Jackson and Vince. We might aid in Emalia and Sophie's rescue as well. Might help Jaime.

And Addie—Addie wanted to do this.

Dr. Lyanne sighed. "You're too trusting, Eva Tamsyn. It'll hurt you one day."

I hesitated. I didn't know how to reply to that.

The horizon gulped up the last dredges of sunlight, leaving us in darkness. Dr. Lyanne shook her head. "My God, Eva. The things you get yourself into."

EIGHT

The others were eating sandwiches and apples on the motel-room beds when Dr. Lyanne opened the door. Ryan set aside his food, grabbed his jacket, and joined me outside without my needing to say a word.

We drifted toward the edge of the motel property, then stopped at the side of a grassy embankment. Other than the sound of far-off traffic, the world was silent and lonely.

I knew what Ryan wanted, but I wasn't sure if he would ask. In the end, he didn't have to. Addie knew him—and us—well enough now.

<I'm going to go> she said. *<I need a little time away, anyhow.>*

She meant going under. That was what we'd come to call the act of temporarily disappearing from our body. It was a way of losing consciousness, like sleeping. But a sleep filled with intense, dreamlike memories. Or sometimes intense, memory-like dreams.

Whether they were memories or dreams, happy or sad,

they held a strange sort of peace. And they robbed you of reality. Sometimes it was a price. Sometimes, a gift.

<You're sure?>

<I'm sure> Addie said and disappeared.

"She's gone," I said, to Ryan and to the night.

He drew me down with him. We lay on our backs, staring at the thick, dark-underbellied clouds. "You're thinking about going along with Marion's plan," he said.

I didn't ask how he knew. Maybe I was an easy read. Maybe he just knew me well enough now to be able to guess where my mind wandered.

Ryan rolled over to face me. Waited until I turned to look at him. There was a bit of grass stuck in his dark hair. "You're not going to help anyone by getting caught yourself. This isn't even *maybe I might get caught*. This is walking into prison and praying for a prison break."

"It might help," I said. "Not just directly, with Jackson. What Marion is saying about the footage. It could really make a difference."

"That doesn't mean it's the right thing to do."

"The bombing of Powatt was different," I whispered. "This wouldn't hurt anyone."

"Except you," Ryan said. "And Addie."

I sat up. "That's our risk to take. They've taken Jaime. They've . . . they've killed Peter. God knows where Henri and Emalia are—"

"Exactly." Ryan sat up, too, his voice rising. "We've already lost so many people. We can't lose you."

My voice softened. "I'll be fine."

"You don't know that."

"I'll be fine," I repeated. Then again. "I'll be fine. I'm going to fix this."

"It's not your job to fix this," Ryan said, and there was a roughness in his voice born of frustration. Or maybe fear.

But it was. Deep down, I knew it was. I'd been the one who first fell into Sabine's plans. Who never told Peter, and convinced Hally and Lissa to keep quiet. I was the one who insisted on going back to the attic after Lankster Square. The chaos at Lankster Square should have been a warning. I hadn't listened.

Once upon a time, I'd been nothing more than a ghost. No will of my own. No responsibility. No actions, and so no consequences. I'd thought I'd known who I was: the one who reminded Addie not to forget things, the one who noticed things she missed, the one who took care of things when she was too flustered to do so. But then I'd regained the ability to make my own decisions, not just influence hers. And that had changed me.

Little by little, bit by bit. I'd become someone who could be tricked into murder.

And that realization had left me cold.

I could not be that person.

I reached into my purse. I was looking for Henri's phone, but when I drew it out, the photograph of Darcie Grey came with it. Ryan picked it up before I could. Glanced at the photo, too, then at my face. "She doesn't even look that much like you." His voice was edged. Bitter.

"She does," I said gently. "Look, we have the same—"

The sudden, urgent force of his kiss blew out every other sensation, like a photograph taken under too much light. He pulled me to him. The picture crumpled in his hand. The edges of it pressed against my flushed skin.

I sank into the warmth of his body. The drift of his lips to the hollow just under my jaw, where my heartbeat fluttered.

"Don't do it, Eva," Ryan said. And I didn't want to, but I pulled away. The moonlight caught those ridiculous, long eyelashes of his. "Don't go in there alone."

Alone.

Ryan had always followed me. He'd followed me back up the stairs our last night at Nornand, when I'd insisted on checking on the other kids. He'd followed me to our first meeting with Sabine and the others in their attic, had followed me back when we returned after the fireworks at Lankster Square. He'd followed me to Powatt, despite my best efforts. Now I was going somewhere he couldn't follow, no matter how stubborn he was about it. So he was asking me to stay. To not take that step.

But I couldn't.

"I have to, Ryan," I said.

Ryan and I stayed outside a little longer after that, but there was a new coldness between us that had nothing to do with the night air. Finally, he stood. Said, "Come on. You look like you're going to freeze."

Once we were back in the motel room, he joined his sister in the corner of the room. I headed for Marion. She stood by the trash can, paring an apple in one long, continuous peel.

"How will you get me out?" I said. "After we have the footage?"

Marion gave no indication of surprise, answering as easily as if we'd been talking about her plans the entire time. "I've been a reporter for a long while now. I have government credentials, and contacts in all the right places. I can't promise it'll be the world's neatest rescue, but if you have the right kind of ID, know the right people, it makes it easier to go where you want to go." She set down her pocketknife. "I've already figured out a way for you to send a signal. The security breach the institution suffered last summer means they're strict about the caretakers they hire, but they're a lot more lax about people who don't have contact with the patients: their manual laborers and—"

I went cold. "Wait. The institution—it isn't—"

"Hahns," Marion said.

Hahns was an institution in the mountains, far up in the north. The one Peter had tried to break into with the help of a woman named Diane, who'd been seeded as a caretaker. Things had fallen apart. The rescue attempt had failed, costing the woman, along with two children, their lives.

The breakout had been planned for summer due to the

harsh conditions around the institution when it grew colder. And now, Addie and I were scheduled to go in right as winter approached.

Marion must have seen the look on my face. "As soon as you get enough footage, I'll get you out of there," she promised. "It won't be more than a few weeks."

Addie and I had only been in Nornand for a single week. It had been long enough.

"You'll make sure Jackson's freed," I said.

"I will. And once we have the footage—"

"We might be able to use it as a bargaining chip for Jaime," I said. "I know."

"Jaime's thirteen years old," Marion said. "And he's their proof of the possibility of a cure. They won't mistreat him."

My laughter was a stark, dry thing. Like a thunderclap. "You and I have very different ideas of what it means to mistreat someone."

She looked away, back to the half-peeled apple in her hands. The peel spiraled down, a red coil.

"I'll do it," I said quietly.

NINE

Ryan didn't kiss me when we said good-bye the next morning. He didn't kiss me because he knew Addie was there, and I wanted her there. He didn't kiss me because his sister was in the room, and so was Dr. Lyanne, and Wendy, and Marion, and Kitty, all watching.

He didn't kiss me, maybe, because he was still angry about the choice I'd made.

But he didn't ask again for me to stay. Just stared at us, jaw tight and unhappy. Last night, he'd written down the number for Henri's satphone for us to memorize. Had made me swear I wouldn't forget it, no matter what, so I could call if I ever needed to. If ever I was lost, or alone. He, in turn, promised he'd fix the phone as quickly as he could.

I'd memorized the number to make him happy, and because it made sense to have whatever backup plans we could. But however much I trusted in Ryan and Devon's skills, I knew the phone was technology beyond anything they'd ever seen. It wouldn't be as simple to fix as Kitty's old camcorder.

I repeated the digits in my mind now. A string of comfort. I couldn't take our chip with us—the one that flashed red when its partner was near, that had given me comfort at Nornand, and afterward. There was too much chance of it being discovered. So the numbers were all I had.

Hally threw her arms around us. I thought she might cry and prayed she wouldn't and then felt horribly selfish. She didn't cry. Just said, "Stay safe, okay?" and squeezed us so tight I could barely manage a response.

"I'm going to come back," I told Nina, and she nodded like she believed me. Or maybe just wanted to.

Then Marion and I and Addie left, and that was that.

It was a bit shocking, how quickly it happened.

<We shouldn't be surprised by things like this anymore> I said as we zipped along the highway. Wendy had stayed behind at the motel. *<How many times have our lives changed utterly in a day?>*

"To be completely honest," Marion said after we'd sat in silence for too many miles, "I'm a little surprised you managed to convince Rebecca to let you go." She pulled a conspiring smile. "She's a bit frightening, don't you think?"

"That's why I like her," I said.

Marion gave a small, breathless laugh and tucked a strand of hair behind her ear. It was a nervous habit Addie and I had picked up on. "I can't believe you're fifteen."

A few weeks ago, I might have been irritated. Now the words hardly touched me. "What do you mean?"

Marion shrugged. "You seem older. That's all."

I turned away, staring out the window. "I always thought it was the opposite. I've always felt too young."

"Well," Marion said. "Maybe you've changed."

Marion filled the hours on the road explaining everything Addie and I needed to know. She slipped a ring onto our finger, a tiny camera and microphone hidden inside the plastic gemstone. Pressing the gemstone set it deeper into the band and started the camera recording. Pressing it again shut everything off. When the light on the underside of the band glowed red, it meant the memory was full.

Once, we would have laughed at the idea that this kind of technology existed. But Henri had shown us otherwise, and it didn't seem impossible that Marion, with her government connections, might be able to get her hands on something like this.

"The children are organized into wards," Marion said. "They call them *classes*. And every few weeks, they rotate them around." She hesitated. "It's to keep the girls from getting too close to one another, I think. But for you, it'll be a good way to mark the time. One rotation should be enough for you to gather sufficient footage."

One rotation. A few weeks. That was all the time we needed to remain within Hahns's walls.

Marion told us how we could signal for rescue. She gave us Hahns's blueprint, which Addie and I spread over the car's dashboard and memorized. She taught us, too, about Darcie herself, this girl we were supposed to become. She was an only child. She'd been born with a heart defect—one that had never been successfully fixed, but had nonetheless failed to prevent her from starting soccer at a young age. I wondered if she would still play after this. Wherever they were sending her.

We'd have to lighten our hair to match hers. Darcie tended to wear her hair shorter, too—above her shoulders. Darker, longer hair could be explained away by less time outdoors and fewer visits to the hairdresser. But if bleaching and cutting our hair made it easier to swallow the lie that Addie and I were Darcie, then it would be done.

"Probably, the officials won't even be suspicious," Marion assured us. "They won't be expecting something like this at all."

<Because it's crazy> I said. We were hiding under the ridiculousness of it all—one hybrid girl taking the place of another. And not just any hybrid. Addie and me. A girl the government coveted right now more than any other.

We'd hide right under their noses, with another girl's name. The last place they'd look.

We never actually met Darcie Grey. She was gone by the time we arrived, whisked away under the cover of darkness. Addie and I slipped into the empty space she left behind, like the understudy in some horrific play.

I wondered now, as we stood before Darcie's mother and

father, how much they knew about Marion's plans. How much they cared. Their daughter was escaping institutionalization.

Perhaps everything else was inconsequential.

"Are you sure they won't be able to tell?" Mr. Grey stood by his kitchen counter, a thin man with thinner salt-and-pepper hair. He seemed too old to be the father of a girl our age. He hadn't said a word directly to us since we'd arrived, speaking only to Marion or his wife.

"They won't be able to tell," Marion promised. She glanced around the kitchen. "You've gotten rid of all the recent pictures, though, like I asked?" There was a photograph stuck to the refrigerator, but the girl in it was only six or seven. She could have been us. Perhaps.

"We have," Mrs. Grey hurried to assure her. Her eyes wandered over to us. When they found us already looking at her, they darted away again. "And I can bleach and cut her hair."

"Good," Marion said. She asked for a moment alone with Addie and me. Darcie's parents obliged all too willingly, hurrying from the kitchen like they couldn't wait to have us out of their sight.

Marion's smile was fabulously fake, but she tried. I found my thoughts wandering back to Ryan and the others. Marion had paid for several more nights at the motel. What were they doing now? Were they thinking of us, too?

Marion reached out and awkwardly patted us on the shoulder. "You're going to be fine."

Addie took pity on her and didn't move away. I hoped

Marion wouldn't try any more platitudes. She looked like she was considering it.

"You remember everything I told you?" she asked instead. Addie nodded. For a long moment, neither of them spoke. The kitchen clock *tick-tick-tick*ed above the refrigerator. "Well—"

"Keep your promises." Our voice was low. Grim. Addie pinned Marion under the force of our eyes. "You're in this now. You can't back out."

After Marion left, Mrs. Grey and a sharp pair of scissors quickly took about six inches off our hair. She swept the wisps of curls off the laminate floor as Addie fingered the cut's newly blunt ends.

The bleaching took longer, Addie and I sitting at the edge of the bathtub, trying not to flinch under Mrs. Grey's touch. Finally, it was done.

"It looks nice," Mrs. Grey said faintly once she'd stripped off her gloves and put everything away.

The real question, of course, was *Do we look like her?* But Addie didn't ask it.

Mr. Grey had disappeared upstairs. I was relieved to avoid his stone-faced discomfort.

"Do you want to . . . watch a movie or something?" Mrs. Grey said.

To my surprise, I discovered that part of me did. Part of me wanted to sit down with this woman, who I didn't know at all, and playact a family.

But it would only be pantomiming a reality long lost. And Mrs. Grey didn't really want to sit with us. The smile on her face was a sad, kind lie, but a lie nonetheless. Probably, she wanted nothing more than to join her husband wherever he'd hidden himself, and mourn. She'd just lost a daughter. Two daughters, if she'd known about Darcie's hybridity for long.

"No, that's all right." Addie pretended not to see the relief her words brought to the woman's face. "Can I—can I see Darcie's room?"

"Your room." The words were firm. Mrs. Grey was committed to this charade, no matter how much pain it caused her. Her daughter's life was on the line.

"My room," Addie echoed.

We followed Mrs. Grey up the stairs and down the hall. Darcie's favorite color, judging by her room, was blue. Her bedspread was dyed the shade of summer sky. Her pillows rested like twin clouds against the headboard. Her curtains were a gauzy aquamarine, so long they trailed against the carpet.

Mrs. Grey lingered at the threshold, but didn't step inside. Addie had to maneuver past her. We studied the posters on the walls. A few of soccer players. One of a band we'd never heard of. The rest were old movie posters, mostly comedies.

There was a small vanity table in the corner, the surface cleared but for a plastic jewelry box. We heard a sharp intake of breath as Addie reached out to touch it. Mrs. Grey looked away when Addie glanced over and we slowly retracted our hand. It wasn't ours. None of it was ours.

Awkwardly, Addie went to sit on the bed. The mattress sank heavily under our weight.

"It's a nice room," Addie said.

"We were planning on painting the walls soon." Mrs. Grey's voice was a whispery, papery thing. "Cream instead of white. You—you wanted them cream."

"Darcie wanted them cream," Addie said. Mrs. Grey made to speak, but Addie interrupted her gently. "I'm not Darcie. I don't have to be Darcie until tomorrow. Tonight, I—we're still Addie and Eva."

The woman hesitated, framed by the door of her daughter's bedroom. Then, slowly, she came and joined us on the bed. Her fingers were cold but soft on our temple, against our cheek. She tucked a strand of hair behind our ear, and suddenly, we were fighting a battle against our tears. We won. Just barely, but we won.

"Lovely names," she said and kissed us on the forehead as if we were hers.

A woman came the next day. She had dark red hair, and deep brown eyes, and a soothing voice. She had documents explaining why the government thought it best that Darcie Grey be taken away from her family and institutionalized. Her black car rumbled beneath us as it carried us away. Addie and I watched Darcie's house, Darcie's parents, get smaller and smaller in the rear window. They didn't wave.

We were driven, then flown, then driven again. It all took

less than a day. Addie and I spoke little, which seemed to suit the woman fine.

All too soon, we were emerging from a car in front of the Hahns institution. The mountain air was bitterly cold. When we'd arrived at Nornand, we'd clutched a red duffel bag and the chip Ryan had slipped into our pocket. Two things to remind us of the outside world. Now we stood in front of Hahns, staring and shivering, with nothing but Marion's ring.

The first thing that struck me about the institution was how *old* it seemed. Nornand—even Powatt—had looked like a hospital. Cold and stark, yes, but beautiful in their own ways: Nornand with its enormous windows and bright steel; Powatt with its clean, white lines.

Hahns was like a crumbling stone prison. If I'd dared speak, I would have asked how long ago the institution had been built. Fifty years? Sixty? Longer? The earliest institutions had been constructed during the years after the start of the Great Wars, only a couple decades after the turn of the twentieth century. The invasions on American soil had been more than enough to incite hybrid hatred to new heights. Thousands had died or disappeared, either officially accused of treason, or simply vanishing at the hands of angry, fearful neighbors. Sometimes, angry, fearful family.

After the initial fervor, the institutions had gone up as safety boxes for hybrids. A means of protecting everybody. A shield.

Hahns did not seem like it could shield anything. I

understood now why children died here in the cold. The wind whipped tears into our eyes, blinded us with our hair. I took as deep a breath as our rigid lungs would allow. Then adjusted the ring on our finger so the camera captured the institution's facade.

"Come along," the woman said, and led us inside.

The air stank of musk and the coppery, metallic scent of rust. A man slouched at the front desk, his face soft with weight. His eyes roamed over us without particular interest. "Name?"

"Darcie Grey," the woman said, and as she said it—as both man and woman turned to look at us—I felt a sudden earthquake of fear. Of terror so deep it threatened to split us open, leave our insides naked in the pale light.

For as long as we stayed at Hahns, Addie and I were Darcie Grey. We were fourteen years old. We played soccer, and loved blue, and had once wanted to paint our bedroom walls cream instead of white.

The man jabbed a button on his phone. Said in a voice that was more bored than anything else, "Could I get someone down here to take care of a new child?"

The woman didn't even wait to hand us off. Just peeled away from the front desk and disappeared down the hall. A few minutes later, another man appeared. A *caretaker*, judging by his tan uniform.

"Darcie, right?" he said as he led us to the elevator. He reminded us of a teacher we used to have, his voice a low grumble, his jaw darkly scruffed.

I nodded.

<*We're really doing this.*> Addie's words rode on a silent, disbelieving laugh. <*We wanted nothing more than to escape, and now we're going right back in. And Hahns . . .*>

Hahns was known for being brutal.

<*This time, we know we're getting out*> I said.

Addie laughed again. It sounded off, the pitch twisted. <*Funny, we thought the same thing when we left for Nornand.*>

<*This is different.*>

<*Is it?*>

<*Yes*> I said quietly <*Because we're different.*>

TEN

The ancient elevator took us up one floor.

Once upon a time, someone had painted the hallway two-toned: white on top, a thick swath of yellow on the bottom. Perhaps it had looked all right when it was first done. Now, the white had faded mostly to gray. The yellow had reduced to a sickly, muddy color. And everywhere, great flakes and gashes of paint had chipped off, revealing the bleakness underneath.

We passed several doors, each evenly spaced, before the caretaker stopped. The other wards, judging from the blueprint in our memory. The lock on the door was old-fashioned. No keypad, like the ones in Nornand's basement. The caretaker only carried a single key. I tried to notice everything. There was no knowing what might become useful later.

Then the door opened, and we got our first look at our new prison.

At Nornand, we'd shared a bedroom with Kitty and Nina. It hadn't been anything fancy—two beds, two nightstands, a few extra square feet of floor space. There had been a modicum of privacy.

There was no such thing as privacy here. The caretaker led Addie and me into a long, cold room. Dozens of cast-iron beds stood in almost-straight rows. The girls in, and near, and around the beds all looked up as we entered. They wore uniforms, as we'd worn uniforms. But theirs were eggshell colored, and they had no shoes—not real shoes. Instead, they wore strange, soft slippers, almost like ballet flats.

I took a deep breath. Fiddled with our ring.

<*Don't*> Addie said. <*You'll draw attention to it.*>

I let our hands drop to our sides.

"There are plenty of empty beds, Darcie." As the caretaker spoke, several of the girls moved surreptitiously closer to a bed, claiming it as their own. But the man was right. There were perhaps thirty or forty beds, but only about twenty-five girls. Almost all of them looked under thirteen.

After months of being the youngest running with Sabine's group, it was strange to suddenly be the oldest. Our eyes went from girl to girl, watching them watch us.

<*Eva*> Addie said suddenly—high and choked. A warning.

I saw her, too.

Recognized her, too.

And from the look on her face, she recognized us.

Bridget Conrade, from Nornand.

Bridget, who had ruined our rescue plans. Prevented us from saving the other patients as we'd intended.

Bridget, who knew we were not Darcie Grey.

<Oh, God> Addie said. Her fear choked us. *<Eva, what if she tells?>*

Bridget had never liked us. Had no reason to keep our secret. What were the chances that we'd come all this way, after all this time, and find her waiting beyond Hahns's doors?

Bridget's eyes locked on to ours. Her hair, which had always been braided back at Nornand, was pale gold around her shoulders. Had she lost her ribbons?

"I'll find some clothes for you," the caretaker said, and then he was gone. Left us in this room with these girls who didn't know us, and the one girl who did.

As long as Addie and I didn't try to take their bed, most of the girls seemed more than happy to pretend we didn't exist. Even Bridget had turned away.

<We should talk to her> I said.

<And say what?> Addie battled her terror and forced it to retreat, but she trembled with the effort of it. I was too busy wrangling with my own fear to help with hers.

<I don't know. But we have to say something.>

I made our way through the rows of beds. Some were scooted into little clusters, others lonely by themselves. It made a strange sort of chaos. The girls in their wrinkled uniforms added to the entropy.

A group of them sat in the corner, their heads bent together in hushed conversation. Most were by themselves. Some picked at the walls, stripping wallpaper and paint. Little piles of both littered the ground. No one had bothered to sweep the floor in weeks, at least. Someone lay buried in blankets in the far corner, coughing.

A single girl, hair clipped short to the nape of her neck, drifted around the perimeter of the room, her fingers brushing against the wall, her lips moving like she was speaking, or perhaps singing, to herself. Her eyes met ours at random, then skittered away again. Other than us and Bridget, she was probably the eldest in the room. There was something missing in her eyes.

Bridget knew we were approaching her. I could tell by the way she started to angle away from us, then caught herself and stubbornly, awkwardly, stayed exactly where she was. She stood by the foot of one of the beds, her hand planted on the metal railing.

Back in Anchoit, Addie and I had thought endlessly about the other kids at Nornand. The ones we'd meant to save. Would have saved. Should have saved. Addie and I had gone down to the basement because we insisted on freeing Hally and Jaime. Dr. Lyanne had been the one responsible for getting the other children out.

Whose fault was it that they'd never made it?

Ours, for breaking away from the group?

Dr. Lyanne's, for not making it to the door, and Peter's waiting vans?

Or Bridget's?

Bridget, who told the nurse that something suspicious was

going on, blowing Dr. Lyanne's cover as she led the remaining children through the hall.

Bridget, who'd wanted so badly to be saved. Just not by Peter.

I drew up beside her. She was a little shorter than we were, her hair straighter, and even blonder than our newly bleached color. During our time at Nornand, I'd never seen her bite her nails, but they were ragged now, destroyed almost to the quick.

She fisted her hands when she caught me looking. "Darcie, huh?"

She looked around. Some of the other girls were watching us now. Curious, in a dull sort of way.

"Well, Darcie." Bridget put the slightest bit of overemphasis on our fake name. "Like the man said. There are plenty of beds. Don't feel obliged to choose one, you know, around here."

There was something ridiculous about the way she spoke. Like she was drawing reference from half-forgotten movies or books on how to be haughty. She was a caricature of disdain, and suddenly, I couldn't understand how Addie and I had ever seen her as more than just a thirteen-, fourteen-year-old girl utterly lost in a world that wanted her dead.

It didn't alter what she had done. But it softened my anger, and my fear.

"I've done nothing to you," I said.

She gave a bitter, huffing laugh. "You change things. You come, you mess around and—and things change for the worse. So please—" Her voice caught. She wrestled with it. Won. "Please pick a bed far over there and try not to ever talk with me again."

<*Friendly*> Addie said dryly, and I almost left it at that. I almost nodded and walked away. But there was the flicker of something in Bridget's expression. Or maybe it was the way her hand still gripped the rusted iron bed railing. I couldn't put it in words. But it made me stop.

"Do they listen?" I whispered.

Bridget frowned and looked around at the other girls. Then realization dawned over her face. Her gaze darted up to the ceiling. A security camera perched up there, its tiny light blinking red.

"No," she said. "They watch, but they don't listen."

I nodded. "Thanks."

Her arms crossed over her body. "For what? I answered a question, that's all."

I shrugged and offered her a small smile. Turned to go.

I hadn't taken two steps when she said, "They're going to take everything. They're very strict on security here, especially after what happened in July."

The breakout attempt that had ended in death and disaster.

<*Bridget was here for that*> Addie said quietly. I understood her sudden guilt. Bridget had been here, while Addie and I were safely tucked away in Anchoit.

Slowly, I turned.

Bridget pulled something from her pocket. Two little

lengths of white string, I realized. They looked like they could have been unraveled from someone's shirt. "Anyway, like I said. They take everything away here. So if you want to keep that ring, you better find some way to hide it."

I fisted our hand, the way she had when she caught us looking at her nails.

"Did that boy give it to you?" she said. "That foreign-looking boy. Ryan, or—"

"*Shh,*" I hissed before I could help it. Bridget's head whipped up, her eyes narrowed, her shoulders tensing.

<*Eva*> Addie said. A low warning and a comfort at the same time.

"Please don't talk about him." I couldn't help the note of panic in our voice. Bridget's words were hardly dangerous, and she wasn't speaking loudly enough for anyone to pay attention. But this went beyond needing to keep our cover. I didn't want Ryan's name spoken in this place. As if saying it aloud would cast some sort of spell to bring him. I couldn't have him here, in this prison of the desolate.

I thought, for a moment, that Bridget would talk about him anyway. Her eyes bored into ours, gray as frosted slate. Then, so quick I nearly missed it, she gave a short nod.

"It's pretty," she said. She looked about to turn away, but at the last moment, reached out and touched it. Her fingertips brushed against the band and against our knuckle, before darting back to her side.

* * *

The caretaker who brought lunch also handed Addie and me a uniform and directed us to the bathroom at the ward's far end. Standing in a stall, I suddenly couldn't force myself to unlace our shoes. They'd been part of our school uniform, scuffed brown oxfords that were the only things we retained of home.

Addie and I stood there for a long time, braced against the stall door, taking deep, ragged breaths and trying to calm down. The tiny size of the stalls didn't help. Addie and I usually used the handicap stalls of public bathrooms, when we could. There was none here, just little stalls designed for children younger than we were.

I took off our shoes. Set them side by side on the toilet seat. Stepped into the white slippers the other girls wore, the elastic snapping into place around our ankles. We could feel the ground through the thin sole.

After a moment, I dropped the ring inside the slipper. Hopefully, no one would think to check.

The rest of the uniform was similarly thin. As the cloth whispered against our skin, I heard in it the echo of Jackson's words about hybrid institutions.

Holding tanks. They hold us until we die, and they do everything short of putting a bullet through our heads to speed up the process.

I shivered. Said, as much for my benefit as Addie's, *<Only a few weeks. We're only staying until the next rotation.>*

When Addie and I returned to the main room, the caretaker had already distributed the lunch trays. Some kind of sandwich. A cup of water. Limp beans in a puddle of oil. The girls ate silently. Many were too thin to be healthy, but most picked at the food like it barely interested them. Someone coughed a deep, wet cough that made our own chest hurt.

"Here, I'll take that." The caretaker reached for our clothes, and I pressed the bundle against our chest. The man's smile flattened.

"I want to keep the jacket," I said. "It's cold."

He grabbed hold and tugged—so suddenly and harshly I didn't have the chance to fight back. "The cold's just temporary. A little glitch in the heating. It'll warm up soon. It's against policy for you to have anything but the standard uniform."

His smile returned. He handed us a lunch tray, and caught us looking in Bridget's direction.

"Do you know her?" he asked. I shook our head. Darcie Grey didn't know Bridget. "You look a bit alike, don't you?"

"I guess," I said. And then, to keep up the charade: "What's her name?"

He shrugged. That was all the excuse I needed to return to Bridget's bedside. She sat cross-legged on the scratchy gray blanket, her tray balanced on her knees.

When she didn't protest, I sat down next to her and whispered, "They don't know your names here?"

She shook her head. "We don't know theirs, either. It doesn't matter. They only work here a couple weeks." She wiped her fingers on the side of her mattress. "New system.

The higher-ups stay the same, I think. We don't really see them much anyway. But the caretakers come and go all the time."

<So there's less time for a mole to scope the place out and execute a plan> I said.

<So no one gets attached> Addie replied softly.

So they didn't end up with another Dr. Lyanne on their hands.

The caretaker lingered by the doorway. But he wasn't watching us, the way the nurses had at Nornand. He hardly seemed to care what we did.

The girls were subdued anyway. Glassy-eyed. A few spoke, but only in murmurs. The girl drifting around the perimeter of the room ignored her tray for too long, and another girl stole it. The man didn't notice. The girl in the corner who kept coughing sat up long enough to sip at her cup of water, then sank back against her pillow. No one touched her tray, even when it became obvious she wasn't going to eat it.

I turned back to Bridget. "What do you do all day?"

"Nothing." She poked at her food, then let her fork drop. "You know, after I got here, I realized why they gave us all those board games and piles of schoolwork at Nornand. It's a distraction. It keeps you focused, holds you together. Sitting here, day after day . . . it makes you go insane." She grinned wryly. "Not that we had much hope otherwise."

I thought of the pamphlets from our childhood, warning

about a hybrid's unstable mind, our propensity for insanity.

"Bridget," I said, "hybrids don't just go crazy. That's a lie."

She gave us a small, pitying smile. "Stick around here long enough, you'll start wondering."

ELEVEN

It was frightening, how quickly we fell into the rhythm of life at Hahns. It was easy, because the rhythm was so simple.

We did nothing.

The lights snapped on early, with a *clank* that worked as well as any alarm clock. Time dripped by until breakfast. Then lunch. Then dinner. Then lights out, with another *clank*.

Clank. Monotony. *Clank*.

There were no clocks, and only one tiny, high-up window in the bathroom. It made it almost impossible to tell the time. The days warped.

Addie and I recorded everything we could. The caretakers bringing in the trays of food. The girls eating. The way the bathrooms looked. The groups of children flocked together like spindly white birds, perched on their beds. The short-haired girl.

Her name was Viola, and she was actually fifteen, though she looked younger. Every day, she walked around the room. She never spoke to anyone except herself, her lips moving as if in prayer or just in conversation with some unseen ghost.

She was also the only one who ever went anywhere near Hannah, the sick girl. And then only because Hannah's bed hugged the wall, and Viola couldn't complete a pass around the room without drifting by Hannah's huddled form.

"How long has she been sick?" Addie asked Bridget, who shrugged.

"She was already kind of sick during the last rotation. But it got worse quickly."

Bridget had mentioned Hahns's rotation system earlier, then explained when Addie feigned confusion. We were in Class 6—the girls were always in the even-numbered classes, the boys in the odd-numbered ones. Bridget figured there were about twenty total, though it depended on how many kids were here.

Every few weeks, caretakers came to each ward to randomly assign new class numbers. The endless surprise rotations kept everyone tilted. A new friend might disappear the next rotation, not to be seen again for months—if ever. Girls disappeared all the time. A few during rotation, siphoned off as the rest were sorted into new classes. Others in the weeks following, to illness or God knew what else.

We stared at Hannah, sick and suffering alone.

"Doesn't anyone care?" Addie said. Hannah barely ate. Never spoke. Crawled out of bed to the bathroom, and crawled back. No one helped her.

"What good does caring do?" Bridget fiddled with her

blanket. Many girls unraveled bits of the spare ones, so they could use the string to braid bracelets, or make something to hold back their hair. It kept the hands busy. Kept the mind focused on something other than tedium. “She’s just the first. When winter really comes, it gets even colder than it is now. Most of these girls have terrible immune systems. The caretakers—they carry germs in, and . . .” She trailed off. Shrugged matter-of-factly.

“How do you know?” Addie said. “You—”

You’ve only been here since last summer.

But Addie didn’t finish the sentence. We tried not to mention Nornand much. Talking about Nornand was admitting that we weren’t who we claimed we were, and part of the unspoken truce between us and Bridget included looking the other way about our supposed identity.

Perhaps she assumed we’d successfully broken out of Nornand and then been recaptured. Or maybe she preferred to think we hadn’t been successful—had been carted elsewhere like the other patients at Nornand, and found our way to Hahns through a transfer. Intense curiosity had never been something we associated with Bridget. Even at Nornand, she’d liked to believe what she wanted to believe, and never deviate.

Bridget’s eyes flickered to Viola, who was making her usual rounds about the perimeter of the room. “When I first got here, Viola and I were in Class 14 together. She spoke then. We got separated during the next rotation. Next time I saw her . . .” She hesitated. “Stay here long enough, you lose your mind. It's just a matter of time."

"And then?" Addie said. "What'll happen to her?"

"Who knows?" Bridget said, and wouldn't talk more about it. We caught her eyeing Viola often, though. All the girls did, and we filmed their expressions, trying to decipher them.

<*Fear*> I told Addie, but she shook our head.

<*It's a bit like how everyone looked at Eli and Cal at Nornand.*>

<*That was fear.*>

<*No*> she said. <*It was more than that.*>

She was right. It was something like dread, and sorrow, and pity, all tangled together.

Hannah didn't stop coughing for days and days. For hours, it would be the only sound in the entire ward. The other girls rarely spoke above a whisper, when they spoke at all.

I dreamed about Ryan. About talking with him, seeing him. About the feel of his skin, his mouth, his hands. One night, I woke up screaming—not from nightmares, but because I'd dreamed I was with him in the photography-store attic, surrounded by those fairy lights.

And it hadn't been true.

The pain of missing him, the frustration of *this room, this room, this sameness*, seared through me so sharply I couldn't stand it.

Sometimes, I found myself just lying in bed, silently repeating the digits of Henri's satphone number like a mantra.

A prayer. A rope of numerals that could one day pull us out of here.

Maybe Viola had the right idea. Walking circles around the room was better than doing nothing at all. We started unraveling bits of the extra blankets, the way the other girls did, pulling loose long strands of the rough fibers and braiding them into a rope. Some of the beds were decorated by loops of braided string, the rusted bars wrapped with different kinds of braids. A mark of territory. An attempt at owning something, someplace, however temporarily. In the ward, a girl's bed was her castle.

We were passing Hannah's bed one day during lunch when the girl shifted to grab her cup and knocked it off balance. Our hand shot out to right it—but too late. The water spilled, soaking into our shirtsleeve. Addie jerked away.

For the first time, we looked directly at Hannah's face. She couldn't have been any older than Bridget—thirteen or fourteen. Her skin was so pale she hardly looked alive when her eyes were closed. But they were open now—open and brown like coffee grounds.

"Sorry," she said hoarsely.

We'd walked past this sick girl for days and said nothing, heard nothing but the sound of her coughing. The sudden connection was startling.

"D-do you want mine?" Addie stuttered. "My water, I mean."

The caretakers only gave us water at meal times. The rest

of the day, the girls drank from the sink if they got thirsty. There was no certainty that the water in the plastic cups was any cleaner, but at least it tasted better.

Hannah hesitated, then nodded. Addie darted back to our tray and retrieved our cup for her.

"Darcie, right?" The words escaped Hannah's lips in little breathless pants. She must have heard Bridget say the name. What else did she hear, lying here nearly motionless every day?

Addie nodded. Hannah continued watching us. But there was no expectancy in her eyes. We could have easily said goodbye, or made some excuse about getting back to our lunch.

But instead, Addie said quietly, "Mind if I sit?"

Hannah's surprise was obvious, but she shook her head. Addie sat, careful not to disturb Hannah's tray, which the caretaker had left balanced on the mattress. The food—little circles of carrots mixed with cubed meat—sat untouched.

"Don't you want any?" Addie asked.

Hannah shrugged. She seemed to rarely eat. Didn't appear to care what effect that might have on her health. Addie shifted awkwardly. The bed creaked. We didn't look away, but I had the feeling everyone else in the ward was sneaking glances in our direction. Were we going to be the ward's new pariah?

Addie of a few months ago would have asked me what to say. Would have grown too flustered to figure out anything herself. I felt the ragged edges of her agitation, but she didn't demand my help.

"Do you need anything?" she said instead to Hannah, who

stared as if the idea that she might be allowed to need something, and then be given it, was a novelty. She shook her head. "Well," Addie said hesitantly. "If you do, just call for me, all right?"

That night, after lights-out, Addie turned to Bridget in the bed next to ours. I thought at first that Bridget might shift farther away. She looked, for a moment, like she might. But she didn't.

"We should say something to the caregiver," Addie whispered. "Hannah's burning up. And they must have medicine."

Bridget burrowed under the covers, searching uselessly for warmth. "Maybe. But why would they bother giving it to her?"

"It wouldn't hurt to ask."

Bridget went still. "Maybe it would. Viola said they take the sick away, when they become too sick."

"And?"

Even in the darkness, I didn't miss Bridget's *Are You Stupid?* look. "And that's it," she said. "They're gone."

TWELVE

Hannah got steadily worse. We tried to get her to eat, but she wasted ever thinner, like a pale, waning moon. Every hacking cough sounded like it threatened to snap her ribs.

We looked at Hannah and our own chest ached. I felt equal parts shame and disgust at how I recognized Marion could use footage of her. This sick, sick girl could strike pity into hearts that had never pitied hybrid children before.

<It feels wrong to film her> Addie said when I pressed the little gemstone that turned the video camera on, making sure it was hidden from the ward's security camera. *<Like we're using her.>*

<We're not using her.> I wasn't sure if I was telling the truth or not, but I said it anyway, and then I redoubled my efforts to keep Hannah as comfortable as possible.

When she was sleeping, we distracted ourselves by picking the lock on the bathroom window. Marion's instructions on what to do if the ring ran out of memory, or broke, had been simple: get it outside the building, and wait for a replacement.

Each ward only had one window—and there were only about twenty wards. Someone sent to look for the ring wouldn't have too many places to search.

The window was about three feet wide and one foot tall, set into the wall perpendicular to the toilet stalls. It was also about six feet off the ground and tinted, so we couldn't see true sunlight even here standing beneath it. But it could open. The lock, if nothing else, proved it.

Addie and I had spent the last few days sneaking pieces of plastic silverware whenever we could. We'd shatter them in the bathroom, hoping to get splinters thin enough to use as lockpicks. Devon had taught his sisters and us the skill during our safe-house stays.

But Devon had paper clips and screwdrivers. Addie and I had shards of plastic utensils. And before we could even attempt to pick the lock, we had to reach it.

We were waiting until the next rotation to signal for rescue, but it didn't hurt to practice.

<*Try climbing on the sink*> Addie said.

I glanced over our shoulder. There was no bathroom door, but no one was looking our way. I carefully moved to the edge of the sink, the porcelain cold through our thin pants. The window was still a good two or three feet away, but I caught the shadow of clouds, dark behind the tinted glass.

"What the hell are you doing?" Bridget said.

I almost toppled off the sink. Caught ourself at the last moment and threw her a dirty look. "Nothing."

"That's not even trying to lie." Bridget came closer, but thankfully kept her voice low. Her hair was in its usual neat braids. "The window's locked."

"I know."

"You're not thinking of breaking it, the way you broke that window at Nornand?"

I didn't want to remember that day. We'd been trying to escape with Hally and Lissa, and thinking of them made me think of Ryan, and Devon, and all the others we'd left behind. Made me miss them with a force that was almost blinding.

You could be with them right now, whispered the weakest part of my mind. *They never wanted you to go. Ryan asked you to stay. He practically begged you to stay. But you were stubborn. And now look where you are.*

"I'm not breaking the window," I snapped. My irritation made Bridget's mouth tighten.

<Eva> Addie said, in the way I used to say her name when I was trying to calm her down. To soothe her when I felt her start to panic, or grow too flustered to think straight.

<I'm fine> I said. I wasn't. But her voice helped. The reminder that she was there, would always be there. Addie, at least, I would never leave behind. And she would never leave me behind. Some people would think that a curse. Right now, it was my best gift.

When I spoke again, I made sure our voice was calmer. "They don't have an alarm system on this window, do they?"

I knew they didn't. Marion had told us. But it didn't hurt to check with Bridget, and asking her was my way of apologizing.

She snorted. "Alarm system? Why? No one could fit out that window."

I hesitated, then unclenched our hand to reveal the makeshift lockpicks we'd made. Bridget's eyes flashed over them, then met ours again.

"It would be nice to get some fresh air," I said quietly. "Don't you think?"

Bridget sat on the cold bathroom floor, arms around her knees, and watched me try each sliver of plastic in the lock.

"They don't actually watch us very closely here, do they?" I said.

She shrugged. "It's an old building. I think they went through enough trouble just setting up the security feeds out there. And honestly, they don't care what we do. We could probably start a fight, and they'd let us."

I tapped at the lockpick the way Devon had taught us, trying to get the pins into place. I prayed the plastic picks wouldn't snap when I tried to turn them.

"Will you teach me?" Bridget said suddenly. The request surprised me so much I stopped and looked down at her. Her jaw was set stubbornly, as if prepared for my incredulity and already defensive about it.

<Is this her way of asking to be friends?>

<I don't know> I admitted, but aloud, I just said, "Sure. It's not like we have much else to do."

The last pin slid into place with a barely audible *click*. I grinned at Bridget. And to my surprise, she grinned back.

"Ready?" I whispered.

She nodded, standing. I let ourself fall forward—*thunk*—against the glass with our full weight. It groaned open an inch, and only an inch.

I rested against the glass, panting. Waiting.

The window didn't open any farther. No one shouted out. Even if they had, I wouldn't have been able to turn. We were entirely off balance, our knees still on the sink, our weight against the windowpane.

The sunlight smelled crisp. Cold. I sucked in the fresh air. I hadn't realized how stale the air in our ward was, how artificial the light. I pulled ourself higher so we could see out. The vertigo was dizzying, especially after so long of seeing nothing but the ward.

The grounds were deserted. White with snow. Only tufts of grass poked through around the edge of the building.

"Bridget," I whispered. "You have to come see this."

Bridget didn't answer.

I turned to look at her.

And found the entire population of Hahns institution's Class 6 staring back at us.

THIRTEEN

Bridget took charge.

"Go," she said to the other girls, flinging out her arms, herding them like geese. "Back to your beds. *Now.*"

To my surprise, they obeyed. I jerked the window shut again. Bridget whirled to Addie and me. "They'll have caught the girls gathering on the cameras. They'll be in here in a second. You better come up with an excuse."

I jumped off the sink, our shins jarring as our feet hit the tiled floor. The slippers offered no cushion at all. I winced, stumbling to regain balance.

"I fell," I hissed at Bridget, spitting out the first excuse that came to mind. There wasn't even time to collaborate with Addie. "Say I fell. That's all. I fell, and there was a noise."

Bridget shouted out the door, "She fell, all right? That's what you say if anyone asks." Her voice carried the same sharpness it had at Nornand, the same quality of *Listen or Else.* If any of the other girls protested, we didn't hear it.

What we did hear was the door open. Then a woman's

voice, rough with irritated concern. "What's going on?"

Bridget and I looked at each other. I held our breath. For a long time, no one said anything. Footsteps approached—the clack of real shoes against the tile.

Addie and I grasped each other, silent.

Then a small voice we didn't recognize said, "Someone fell."

A woman appeared in the bathroom doorway. She didn't wear the caretaker uniform of tan shirt and dark pants. She had a nice blouse instead, deep plum purple. Our eyes drank it in—this new color that wasn't rust, or paint-chipped walls, or off-white uniforms.

"Who fell?" She was trying to look stern, sharp, confident. I could feel it. But all I could think was, *You're not nearly as good at it as Dr. Lyanne.*

"I slipped," I said. And then, because it seemed like something this woman might want to hear, I added, "I'm sorry."

I tried to look contrite. I tried to look nervous, and small, and unassuming. Plum-blouse Lady glanced around the bathroom, at the window, the stalls. Everything seemed in order.

"You're all right?" she said brusquely.

I nodded. Suddenly, the woman's eyes narrowed. She frowned. Looked at us a little closer and *our heart—our heart—our heart stopped.*

<She knows> Addie whispered. *<She recognizes us.>*

<She doesn't. She doesn't.>

I stayed absolutely still, willing myself to betray nothing.

"What's your name?" the woman said.

"Darcie," I replied softly. "Darcie Grey."

She stared at us a moment longer. Then nodded and left.

I leaned against the wall, just under the window. Drenched in a cold sweat.

Addie and I sat on our bed, stiff with terror and fighting not to show it. We had to playact for the security cameras. Hide the fact that with every passing second, we feared Plum-blouse Lady might come back, jab her finger at us, and tell us to go with her.

Bridget came up to us, her face solemn.

"A—" she started to whisper, then caught herself. "Darcie. Are you going to tell me what's going on this time? Before things start going crazy? You weren't just opening that window for fresh air. You didn't just learn how to lockpick with plastic slivers for fun. And you're terrified of that woman for a reason."

Our eyes met.

Addie's agitation fluttered, though I could feel her straining to stamp it down. *<We should have been more careful. We never should have—>*

<Bridget always suspected there was something going on> I said. *<How could she not?>*

"Is there a plan?" Bridget leaned toward us hesitantly, like she feared we might jerk away. "Is there going to be another rescue? Is that why you're here?"

She said *rescue* like it was a jewel of a word. Something so precious she could barely let it past her lips. Her eyes, gray like winter storm clouds, caught ours and refused to look away.

"I didn't think you wanted to be rescued," I said, and regretted it as soon as I did. Bridget's gaze hardened. I couldn't stand the pain lurking behind her shuttered expression, but I didn't know what to say.

I was still running through possibilities, each one sounding worse in my mind than the last, when Bridget sank back onto our bed.

"I want to go home," she said quietly. "It's the same thing I've always wanted."

That, I believed.

"It's just that before, I hoped I could be fixed first. At Nornand, they said they could help us. Here, they're not even trying. So if I can choose between going insane here, or going insane at home, then I'd rather be home."

"Bridget," I said. "You're not going to go insane."

Viola passed a few feet from our bed, and we both quieted as her slippered feet whispered against the ground, her fingers tapping slowly against the wall. Her lips mouthed words we couldn't hear. Viola and who? Who did this girl speak to? Where was she, in her head?

Somewhere better, I hoped, than here.

Bridget stared at her retreating back. "When I first met Viola, she was a little distant. Like the others. Quiet, sometimes. She'd look at you like you weren't really there. But she'd get over it. She'd be normal again—or as normal as we get, anyway. Then she got worse. She stopped talking to us. She started drifting around. I asked her what she was doing, and she told me she was trying to keep track—of what, I don't know." Bridget picked at our blanket, unraveling a frayed edge. "For a while, she used to wake up from time to time. Be completely lucid, you know? Just for a little while. And she'd look so terrified. She'd lie there, making noises like she was dying. Saying she couldn't think straight anymore. Couldn't function anymore. They cut her hair short because she got it so tangled up, pulling at it all the time."

Viola was all the way across the room now. Two younger girls shifted out of her path.

"I'm the oldest one here now," Bridget said. "Before you came, anyway. It's always the older ones. That's what Viola told me. The older ones lose their minds. And then they're taken away." She paused. "So. If there's any chance I might get out of here before that happens to me, I'd like to know."

<Can we trust her?> I asked Addie.

She hesitated. *<We shouldn't, Eva. We already had a close call today—if that woman's suspicious now, the last thing we need is to start spreading our secret.>*

She was right.

<Besides> she said softly *<Marion isn't going to rescue her.>*

<We don't have to tell her about Marion or her plan. We could just tell her about Henri. About the

Underground. The life we had before we got . . . recaptured.>

About how we weren't alone, and we weren't crazy, and we didn't deserve to be locked away like this.

Addie sighed. <*I don't know, Eva. We don't need to. We don't have to. And we—we don't owe it to her.*>

Not when she was the one who'd ruined our last escape plan. If Bridget hadn't screwed that up, maybe she would have ended up in Anchoit, like Addie and me. Maybe Eli and Cal and all those other children at Nornand would have escaped along with us in Peter's vans.

But that was useless to think about. And it wasn't as if Bridget didn't regret it.

<*She made a mistake*> I said. <*We've made mistakes.*>

I took a deep breath. Heard the echo of Dr. Lyanne's voice in our mind: *You are too trusting, Eva Tamsyn. It'll hurt you one day.*

But maybe not today. Not now, with this girl waiting for our reply, her life and her hopes in the balance.

I scooted closer to her on the bed, and she leaned toward us like she was expecting a secret. I didn't think she was breathing.

"After Nornand," I said softly, the way Addie and I had shared stories in the quiet of the safe houses, "I met a man who'd come from overseas. And he told me that so much of what we know of the rest of the world isn't true."

* * *

The Plum-blouse Lady hadn't recognized us, it seemed. She didn't come back, and our days at Hahns sank back into their old routine.

But not exactly. Because now, Addie and I gave Bridget our stories. We told her of Henri's world across an ocean, where so much was the same, and so much was different. Where in many places, it was common knowledge that people had been to the moon. That the Great Wars we'd heard so much about had been devastating, but not annihilating. That hybrids were not destined to go mad.

We didn't tell her the specifics of why we were here. Didn't tell her the truth about the ring.

I hoped we were doing the right thing. *Keep hope*, Jackson had told us, and hope was good. Hope helped us survive. But hope could be painful, too. Hope could be dangerous, if it grew too large and then shattered.

One day, I looked up while telling Bridget about cloning—how across the ocean, they'd come up with the ability to duplicate animal bodies, and it might be applicable to humans one day—and realized the girl I'd thought was lingering by our bed wasn't just lingering. She was listening. Her eyes caught ours, then darted away again.

For a moment, I was terrified. <*What if she tells?*> But the look on her face hadn't been suspicion. It had been curiosity. Hunger.

So I pretended like I didn't notice her eavesdropping.

And when the next girl came, I did the same. Until the group gathered around our bed was too obvious, and we had to say something before whoever was watching the security tapes got suspicious.

The storytelling moved to after lights-out. The bulb set above the bathroom doorway and the one above the main ward door never went out. Probably more for the benefit of the security camera than for ours. But when the main lights clanged off, most of the ward was dark, and the corner of the room near our bed was darkest of all.

Girls drifted here and sat for hours, eager in a way Addie and I hadn't seen since we arrived.

I finally started learning the other girls' names. During the day, I matched voices to faces. There was Janice, tall and bird-limbed at thirteen, with milk-white skin and thin lips and thick, dark slashes of eyebrows. Ruth, eleven, had freckles and eyes that reminded us of Jackson, palest blue. There was Jeanie and Lauren and Alexandra and Brooke and more.

Some latched on to us after breaking that initial barrier. Others fluttered at the edges, never speaking more than a few words, but showing up night after night to listen. And some, as the days passed and nothing happened to Addie and me, started telling stories, too.

We heard about mothers and fathers and family dogs. About siblings who weren't hybrid, and ones who were, but had been sent elsewhere, never to be seen again. About friends who'd stopped being friends as they got older, and it became obvious one of them wasn't settling, wasn't normal.

We didn't record anything, at first. We didn't even think to do it, especially since it was too dark for a camera to catch anything. But by the time the nights were more than half-filled with stories that weren't ours, Addie and I taped everything. It wasn't even for Marion. It was for us, and for the storytellers themselves, even if they didn't know it. I wanted to capture this little piece of them. Save these whispered fragments of their lives.

<Is this dangerous?> I said to Addie one night. *<If Marion uses this . . .>*

<That was the point, wasn't it?> Addie said. *<Besides, we're the one who the government would target, and we'll be gone by then. The blame would fall on us, not them. What will they have done wrong? Told stories?>*

<Who knows?>

We spent our nights spinning tales. During the days, we kept our promise to teach Bridget how to lockpick. She was a fast learner, easily frustrated with herself, but diligent with a narrow-minded sense of purpose.

When Addie and I weren't with her, we spent as much time as possible with Hannah—or Millie, as her other soul was named. They couldn't make it near our bed at night, so we whispered to them during the day. But they continued fading. They no longer coughed. They didn't seem to have the strength.

<We have to get them help> I said desperately. *<Medicine.* Something.>

<*There's nothing we can do.*> Addie's voice was as tense as mine. <*Bridget said—*>

<*Bridget said they might be taken away, if we say something. But if we don't?*> I stared at the pallor of Hannah's skin. The pink of her eyelids. The blue tinge of her lips. Her bed stank, and the smell permeated the rest of the ward. Some of the other girls had started falling sick, too, their coughing and sneezing making up for Hannah and Millie's silence. But thank God, none of them seemed to have anything worse than a cold. <*They're going to die, Addie.*>

I hadn't let myself believe that. Not truly. Not until this moment, when I let the word slip from my mind to Addie's, crossing the at once infinitesimal and infinite space between her and me.

So Addie didn't protest when, at dinnertime, I stopped the caretaker as he handed us our tray. "Hannah needs help," I said.

Every girl in the ward stopped what she was doing and stared at us. Every girl, that is, except Hannah and Viola. The former was utterly still. The latter hadn't stopped moving, her mind someplace beyond the reach of my words.

"Sorry?" The caretaker seemed more confused than anything.

"Hannah." I pointed to the corner where her bed remained all alone. "She's been sick for . . ." I realized I didn't know how long we'd been at Hahns. "For weeks. And she's gotten worse. I don't think she's going to recover without medicine."

The room was silent.

"I'll see what I can do," the caretaker said finally. He even smiled, just a little. Like he meant it to be a comfort.

We ate. He left. The lights went out.

Everyone gathered, as usual, for the storytelling. But Addie and I didn't share. We could think of nothing but the girl in the bed in the corner, and how we couldn't hear her breathe.

We were one of the first to wake up the next morning. The other girls lay huddled in their beds, cocooned inside layers of blankets. Bridget's eyes fluttered open, then shut again.

Blearily, I sat up.

And saw.

Hannah's bed had been stripped clean. No pillow. No blanket. Not even the mattress remained. Only the cold metal frame. A skeleton.

Hannah and Millie were gone.

FOURTEEN

One missing girl shouldn't have made the ward seem so different, especially one who'd barely spoken, hardly ever moved. But Hannah's absence ripped a hole in the fabric of the room. The other girls were quieter than normal, and they gave the bed in the corner an even wider berth, like it was haunted or cursed.

When the ward's main door clanged open, I didn't even bother looking over. It was getting to be breakfast time, and I was too focused on the carcass of Hannah's stripped bed. But Addie said <*Eva*—> and that was enough for me to notice Bridget stiffen. Our eyes went to the door. The caretaker standing in the threshold had no cart of food.

"What's going on?" I said.

Bridget didn't look at me. Just stared down at her blanket and finished braiding her hair. Her voice was tight. "We're being rotated."

Our chest squeezed.

Rotation. This was what we'd been waiting for since the

day we arrived. We’d promised ourselves to stay this long before signaling for rescue, and now our sentence was up.

But the rest of these girls—the ones Addie and I had just started getting to know—they had no such promise of freedom.

The caretaker called everyone out of bed. We gathered in a clump in the middle of the ward—all except Viola, who continued in her circling. No one went to grab her.

“Bridget,” I whispered, drawing up next to her. “If we get separated, I just wanted to say—”

She was suddenly impatient, shoving us away and warning us to keep our distance with a sharp look. I ended up next to Jeanie and Caitlin instead—until they hurried away from us, too.

<What’re they doing?> Addie’s confusion mirrored mine.

<Maybe it’s about Hannah and Millie> I said. *<They know we spoke up, and then . . .>*

“Stand still,” the caretaker barked, and started counting us off, pulling each girl aside as she assigned her a number—two, four, six, eight, ten, twelve . . .—and snapped a plastic bracelet around her wrist. Hospital bracelets, impossible to get out of without scissors or a knife.

The caretaker didn’t go in any particular order, but two girls standing next to each other never got the same number.

<They were trying to stay with us> I said slowly. *<That’s why they didn’t want to stand next to us.>*

It was a foreign concept. Addie and I had never been the

one other people sought out. If anything, we'd been the one nobody wanted.

"Twelve," the caretaker said when she got to Addie and me, and snapped the corresponding bracelet around our wrist. We went to stand with Ruth, the only other twelve so far.

I could practically see Bridget's mind whirring. Trying to figure out where she should stand to get the same number, and if she could move without the caretaker noticing. The remaining group wasn't large.

"Fourteen," the caretaker said to the girl who'd stood next to me. Mayree. Then, "Sixteen" to the girl next to her. Claire. Then back to "Two . . . four . . . six . . . eight . . . ten . . ."

"Twelve," she said to Bridget.

Bridget betrayed no emotion at all as she came to join us.

Viola was last to be sorted, labeled a number four. But there were still two girls remaining: Coreena and Iris. They did not get numbers. Or bracelets.

I remembered, suddenly, what Bridget had said about girls disappearing during rotation. Marion hadn't told us about the possibility of being siphoned off—to where? For what purpose?

Coreena and Iris stared wide-eyed after us as the caretaker ushered them away from the group.

For the first time in weeks, we emerged beyond the confines of the ward into the hallways. We noticed everything. The pattern of cracks along the molding. The scuff marks and little indentations on the ground.

The caretakers weren't releasing all the classes at once. There weren't enough girls in the hall for that. But there were at least two other classes out here, being separated into new wards. The girls in our class stared at them. Some of them stared back, but most seemed too deadened to care. Their hands hung limply at their sides, the weak overhead light glinting off plastic bracelets.

The ring was hidden in our hand, though I let the gem peek through. I filmed as much as I could of this quiet, solemn migration of children. There were only ten doors on this floor. Were the boys' wards mixed in with ours? It seemed more likely they were on the third floor, or the fourth.

"*Oh—*"

It was the only warning we got—Bridget's startled cry—before Viola fell.

I reached out and grabbed her just before she hit the ground.

It was the first time we'd ever touched her, and her shoulders were frail in our hands. She didn't make eye contact.

I'd dropped our ring.

Panic shot ice under our skin, blasted frost in our lungs. I let go of Viola, who'd wavered back onto her feet, and spun around.

<Do you see it?> I cried.

Addie's silent delirium was answer enough. A burst of heat replaced the first flush of cold, ravaging our thoughts. Our eyes raked the floor. It couldn't have gone far. But there were so many pairs of feet—

The caretaker behind us had noticed the holdup. She approached—

Bridget darted from our side. Snatched something bright off the floor.

"Keep moving, girls," the caretaker said. "You're clogging up the hallway."

We kept moving. Even Viola, with her clouded eyes.

"Here," Bridget whispered when she'd caught up with us. Her hand bumped against ours, transferring the ring from her fingers to ours with a touch.

I gave our *thank-you* with a glance. I didn't dare open our hand until we were shepherded into our new ward. There were fewer girls this time. Only about fifteen. Just a trick of the numbering system? Or had Hahns really lost that many girls in the weeks since the last rotation? How many other girls had been stolen in the night like Hannah? Or taken away today?

This ward looked almost identical to the last. The only differences lay in the unique wear and tear of the walls—the murals of bleak destruction, boredom, and the erosion of time. A caretaker stood with a pair of heavy scissors, snapping the hospital bracelets from wrists. Some of the girls were already headed toward beds, studying the chains of braided string wrapped around the metal bars. Laying claim.

Ruth hesitated, then left our side to do the same. Only Bridget remained. But she didn't follow us when we hurried to the bathroom. There, hidden inside a stall, I finally opened our hand.

The ring looked normal. At first.

Then I noticed the crack along the side of the gemstone. When I gingerly pressed down on it, it didn't click into place the way it had before. Instead, it ground against the band in a way that frightened me so much I didn't try it again—what if the stone popped off entirely?

<*Someone must have stepped on it.*> There was a hollowness to Addie's voice.

I didn't reply.

There was nothing to say.

FIFTEEN

We couldn't be positive the camera embedded in the ring was broken. No more than we could know if everything we'd filmed over the past few weeks had been erased.

If it was all gone . . .

This rotation was supposed to grant us our freedom. Instead, it might become the reason for an extended sentence.

<*We put the ring out the window and wait*> I said. <*There's nothing else we can do.*>

Addie took the better part of the morning to braid together a rope that would reach the ground, then jimmied the window lock open. The blast of frigid air made us shiver. She knotted the end of our string around the ring, our fingers growing numb in the chill.

We peered out onto the grounds below us. The snow was so thick that even the bushes growing snug against the institution walls were half-buried under a white coat.

We'll send someone, Marion had said. *Get the ring out the window, and someone will come pick it up.*

Hahns had increased background checks on all their caretakers after Peter's last breakout attempt. They were less strict, though, with the people who trimmed the lawns. Picked up the trash. Shoveled the snow.

Addie set the ring on the sill and pushed it over the edge. It hung against the side of the building, a glimmering thing in the morning light.

<*Quickly*> I said. <*Before someone sees.*>

Addie unraveled the string from around our wrist. Lowered the ring, bit by bit, until it disappeared into the bushes. She tied our end of the string to one of the nails screwing the window frame in place. Thin and gray, it was all but invisible.

She shut the window and shivered again, squeezing our fingers to warm them up.

<*Now we wait*> I said.

That night, after lights out, Addie and I were just about to close our eyes when a shadowy figure appeared by our bed. It was Ruth. Her hands wrung at each other. Bridget, in the bed next to ours, sat up.

"Aren't you going to do it?" The softness of Ruth's voice reminded me of Kitty and Nina—how much we missed them.

"Do what?" Addie said wearily. We wanted to do nothing but sleep away the hours until someone collected the broken ring. Until we knew our fate.

Ruth bit her lip. "I thought you might gather everyone up again. For the stories."

Bridget waited, too, for our response. But the last thing Addie and I wanted tonight was to talk.

"I don't know if I can think of anything," Addie said. "I—"

"It doesn't have to be anything new," Ruth said earnestly. "None of them have heard any of your stories. They wouldn't know if you told an old one."

"I don't feel well," Addie said. "Maybe tomorrow, okay?"

Ruth was quiet. So was Bridget. We couldn't stand their silent disappointment; we slipped out of bed and fled to the bathroom. There, Addie shoved open the window and put our forehead to the cold glass, closing our eyes. The night wind whipped in from outside. We looked down at the string around the nail. The string connected to the ring that no one had come to collect.

<What if we demand to go home, lost footage or no?> Addie whispered.

<How can we demand anything? Marion controls our escape.>

It was a harsh truth I hadn't let myself dwell on before. Our life was in Marion Prytt's hands. I'd put it there, against all warning, against Ryan's anger, and Hally's frustration, and my own misgivings.

<I'm sorry, Eva> Addie said. *<We did this because of me—because I wanted to help Jackson—>*

<*We wanted to help Jackson.*> I hesitated. <*And it was always more than that.*>

We'd also come into Hahns because I wanted to make up for past wrongs.

Addie ran our finger along the window glass. The light shining outside the bathroom doorway just barely illuminated the cramped space. The darkness beyond the window was complete. A new moon, maybe.

I repeated Henri's satphone number in my mind, a mantra of comfort.

"Addie," Bridget said, and Addie turned. Then we both realized what had happened, and Bridget quickly corrected herself. "Darcie." She stood in the bathroom doorway, without even a blanket wrapped around her shoulders. "I think you should come see this."

The first thing we noticed was that the beds nearer the bathroom were vacant. They'd been filled before. Addie turned to Bridget, alarmed. But Bridget motioned for her to stay quiet. She pointed to the other end of the ward. We squinted, but it was too dark and too far to see anything clearly.

Then we heard a girl's voice. It wasn't until we'd almost reached her, moving carefully among the beds in the darkness, that I realized who the speaker was. And where the missing girls had gone.

Ruth Tarvie, eleven years old, sat on her bed in the darkest corner of the ward, telling the story of the time she won division championship in horseback riding. We'd heard the story before, back when we were both part of Class 6. Ruth was a good storyteller—knew how to spin a story so it looped around her listeners and entangled them, drew them closer to her with every word.

Girls crowded by her bed, some sharing the mattresses closest by, others sitting on the floor.

Ruth glanced up when she noticed us approaching. She faltered, and the other girls faltered with her. Even in the almost pitch-darkness, we felt the strength of their eyes. Bridget had already sat down, taking the edge of another girl's bed. The girl didn't say anything. In fact, she shifted so Bridget would have more room.

Addie folded ourself up on the ground, our legs crossed.

"Go on," she said quietly. "What happened then?"

Ruth cleared her throat and told us.

And so it started up again. Each night, more girls joined in. Each day, it got colder. We woke some mornings and saw our breath under the fluorescent lights. It usually warmed up a bit by lunchtime, but not much. I found myself relieved for only fifteen girls and more than thirty beds—it meant we could double up on blankets. Everyone spent both waking and sleeping hours huddled under them.

But more and more girls fell ill, too. So far, none seemed as bad off as Hannah had been in the beginning. But Addie and I shared the ward with girls flushed with fever, and girls pale with cold, and we could do so little to help.

<*Is it doing more harm than good?*> I asked Addie one night as we sat next to a girl whose breaths wheezed from her lungs. <*Them all gathering like this . . . they had a system before, and now . . .*>

They'd had a way, however imperfect, of keeping themselves as safe as possible. We'd broken that. We'd thought we were doing something good, and back in Class 6, when fewer of the girls were sick, it hadn't seemed to come at any cost. But our actions had grown beyond us. The other girls not only gathered after lights-out, they started flocking together in smaller groups during the day.

One morning, someone laughed, and it was like lightning jolted every soul in the ward. The room silenced. Heads turned.

It was Lilac Helms, and she pressed her fingers to her lips like she'd just said something wrong. For a moment, I thought she might apologize. Instead, she just looked away. After a moment, everyone else did, too.

But the echoes of her laughter remained.

Addie and I checked the string as often as we could. Each time, we felt a jolt of excitement as the glimmer of gold lifted from the ground. And each time, the anticipation flattened into disappointment. A week passed. No one came to collect the ring or leave us any kind of message—any sign that we had friends on the outside, ready to help if something went wrong.

Perhaps Marion had been caught. Perhaps she had made a wrong move, gotten someone suspicious, and now had to lie low. Perhaps she'd decided this whole thing was too dangerous, and given up.

She could do that, after all. It wasn't really her fight.

You are too trusting, Eva Tamsyn. It'll hurt you one day.

Fear and despair were vultures, whirling and waiting for us to give up. But I refused to let myself fall again. If *I* doubted, how could I expect anyone else in this ward to keep their hopes alive?

One morning, the ring still hanging untouched outside the window, I walked out of the bathroom to find Bridget sitting with her back against the wall. Her eyes were stony, her mouth an unhappy slash.

<Go talk to her, Eva> Addie said. Despite her earlier hesitance at calling Bridget our friend, she'd softened toward her.

I joined Bridget on the ground. We sat right in the path where Viola used to make her rounds in the old ward. Her constant circling had been like white noise in the flow of our days, comforting, in a way, because of its regularity. We'd counted on it.

From here, we had a view of the lower half of the room: the maze of metal bed legs, the blankets dragging on the floor, the legs and slippered feet of the other girls.

I glanced at Bridget, then at our hands. Our finger still felt naked without the ring. "Is something wrong?"

She gave us a look. "Besides the obvious things?"

I'd learned the art of dry smiles. "Yes."

She glanced away. Shrugged one shoulder. "I was just thinking about Viola. If she's . . . if she's still in Class Four, or—"

If she'd been taken away. Like Hannah and Millie.

What happened to Viola is not going to happen to you, I wanted to say, but didn't.

By all accounts, what happened to Viola shouldn't have happened to Viola.

"Do you know what her other name was?" I asked. "Viola, I mean. The other soul."

Bridget looked down at the ground. "What does it matter?"

"It matters," I said. "When I tell other people about her—about them—I want to use their names."

"Tell who?" Bridget demanded.

I looked at her fiercely. "We're going to get out of here. You have to believe that, Bridget."

She seemed to fight her emotions under control. "What does it matter what I believe?"

"It does," I insisted. The girl in the closest bed glanced over, then away again. For a long moment, neither Bridget nor I said anything.

"It was Viola and Karen Fairlow." She finally met our eyes, and there was something naked there, in that look.

There was something different.

"You're not Bridget," I whispered.

She tensed. Turned her face away again.

Said, so quietly I almost didn't hear: "Grace. You can call me Grace, if you'd like."

SIXTEEN

The snow fell even thicker now. Each day, a new layer covered the last, making the world anew. There were never any footprints. Addie and I tried to convince each other that there might not be, even if someone came to replace the ring. The snow swallowed everything.

There was always only the smallest resistance as we reeled the string in, the gold band glinting. The string was always damp with melted snow. The ring, when it finally fell into our hand, was always bitterly cold.

Then, one morning, it wasn't the same ring.

For a moment, I thought our eyes were playing tricks on us. That wanting had morphed into reality. But no, the crack in the gemstone had disappeared. When I pressed the stone, it sank into the band just the way it was supposed to.

Relief made us forget the cold. I untied the string and pulled the window shut, sitting heavily on the edge of the sink. *<Oh, thank God>* I said, and felt more than heard Addie echo the sentiment.

We weren't abandoned.

It wasn't until I slipped the ring on our finger that I realized the inside of the band wasn't perfectly smooth, like it had been before. Instead, something scratched against our skin.

I slid the ring off again and held it up to the light, tilting it so we could see the inside of the band. There, engraved into the metal, were the rough makings of a tiny bird. Wings spread. Head high.

And two words, followed by a pair of initials.

We're coming.

R. M.

Ryan Mullan.

"Where did you hide the ring?" Bridget asked a few days later. Automatically, Addie pressed our hand into our lap.

"What do you mean?"

Bridget shrugged. "You stopped wearing it for a while. That's all."

Now it was Addie's turn to shrug. She started to turn away, but Bridget halted us with a blurted, "Does it mean you really think we're going to get out of here again?" She pressed her lips together. When she spoke again, the words came more calmly, but with an uncomfortable rigidness. "When you stopped wearing it . . . well, you kept it because it reminded you of the outside, right? And if you'd really given up hope of ever getting out of here, maybe you wouldn't wear it, because it would just make everything worse. Being reminded. But for the last few days, you've been wearing it again."

Addie glanced down at the ring. <*I don't know what to say*> she admitted.

So I said <*Here, let me*> and she did, sliding aside so I could take control.

Before I could think too much about it, I removed the ring and dropped it in Bridget's hands. She startled. And as her eyes searched ours, I wondered if she knew about the switch. If she could tell between Addie and me. I'd known her for weeks, and right now I couldn't say for sure if the girl sitting in front of me was Bridget or Grace.

"It reminds me," I said quietly, "of Ryan."

His name caught a little in our throat. I hadn't wanted to talk about him before. Not here, as if speaking his name among the peeling walls and dirty floor might tarnish it.

But I'd learned that the opposite was true. Bringing happy memories into an awful place didn't make the memories any dimmer. The memories made the surroundings brighter.

Bridget's head was bowed, her fingers clutching the ring gingerly. "Lucky," she said. "You've always been lucky. I—"

Then she froze. Looked up at us.

"It's engraved." Her eyes had gone wide. "It's engraved. It wasn't before."

The ward door banged open.

I almost jumped up. Bridget stuffed the ring under her pillow.

The woman who stepped inside wasn't a caretaker, but we

recognized her. The Plum-blouse Lady. She'd come the first time Addie and I opened the window in the other ward, when we'd pretended we'd fallen. She'd asked me my name.

Now she stared at us, and everyone stared back.

I fought a shiver as the woman's gaze landed on us. But it passed, and we breathed again. A caretaker joined the woman.

<What's going on?> Addie said.

I never got the chance to reply. The Plum-blouse Lady said, "Her," and pointed.

At Bridget.

Bridget's voice broke free of her lips, tiny and confused. "What?"

She dodged the caretaker when he grabbed for her. I clutched her hands as the man latched on to her shoulders. The other girls sat or stood frozen in place, eyes wide open, mouths sealed shut.

"No!" I yelled as the man tore Bridget from our grasp.

Bridget's cry reverberated through the ward. It tore at our ears, stole the breath from our lungs. She clawed at him. He grabbed her wrists as she tried to pound a fist into his chest. Her shirt bunched up, tangling her limbs. She kept screaming, screaming, *screaming*.

And her screaming focused. Took on a word in the madness. Took on a name.

"*Addie!*"

I faltered. Bridget froze. The man took advantage of the

moment and grabbed her more securely around the middle. Hauled her to the door.

It all happened so fast.

She was there. She was gone.

The door shut.

Silence.

Then, from behind, the clack of shoes. Footsteps approaching. A hand closed, viselike, around our arm.

The Plum-blouse Lady swam into view. Our mind was blurry, but her face was somehow crystal clear. We saw everything. The faint lines on her forehead. The wisps of dark hair escaping from her bobby pins. The pasty look of the foundation right under her eyes. Her mouth sat in a grim, unhappy line.

"Well," she said. "You'd better come along, too."

SEVENTEEN

Unlike Bridget, Addie and I didn't struggle. Two caretakers waited at the door by the time we reached it, and neither looked like they could be taken by a fifteen-year-old girl.

So we went quietly. But our mind did not.

<Remember the blueprints> I said. I battled panic—not just mine, but Addie's where it beat against me, frenzied like a limed bird struggling for flight.

<I am.> Addie's voice was strained, but clear.

If we knew where they were taking us, we had a better chance of escape. At least I told myself we did.

The elevator came. They did not take us down, as I'd expected, but up to the fourth floor.

Our breathing came rougher now. We couldn't help it. I tried to focus on our surroundings—tried to memorize where we were going and block out everything else. *<Addie, Addie, Addie>* ran through my mind. I didn't know what I wanted by it. I just needed to say it. Needed the reassurance that she was here with me.

That we would be all right.

The caretakers shoved us into a room. A cell. Four white walls, maybe eighty square feet. A toilet in the corner. A bed pushed against the far wall.

Then we were alone.

<Check for cameras.> Going step-by-step helped keep me calm. I had to keep the panic at bay, dammed up so it couldn't sweep us off our feet.

There was nothing obvious, at first. Then I caught something tiny mounted in the far corner, opposite the door. It might have been a camera.

We sat, back against the wall.

What next?

<The ring> Addie said. *<Someone might find it.>*

<If anyone finds it, it would be one of the girls.> I forced a shaky optimism I didn't feel. *<And they'd want to keep it for themselves. They wouldn't hand it over. Even—even if they did, they wouldn't think it was anything but a normal ring. They wouldn't know it was ours—>*

<This is a government-run institution> Addie said. *<They might know all about that kind of technology. And if they see the engraving . . .>*

My mind buzzed, a frenzy of half-completed thoughts. About the ring. About Bridget and what would happen to her. To us. I kept having to shut them down. I focused on breathing. On keeping calm.

<Don't worry> I told Addie. *<It's going to be fine. We're going to be fine. We've survived worse.>* I tried to laugh and failed. *<We fell off a roof at Nornand, were betrayed and tied up by our own friends in Anchoit, dug out of the rubble at Powatt. We're going to survive this, too.>*

We had to, didn't we? How could we get past everything else and get caught like this? End like this? We'd learned so much, come so far. It wouldn't be fair. The world couldn't allow it.

But the world had allowed Viola and Karen to lose their sanity. Had killed Wendy's sister, and Peter. Had cut a soul from Jaime Cortae's body and eradicated it from the earth.

It was stupid to expect anything like fairness.

We waited hours before the door opened again. We jumped from the bed. Backed up so we had room to maneuver—to run, or fight back.

"You can sit back down," the Plum-blouse Lady said. She shut the door behind her.

I didn't sit. The woman did, though, right on the bed like it was hers. Addie and I shivered from the cold. This room wasn't heated any better than the ward.

"Here." The woman shrugged out of her jacket. It was fitted, mauve. I didn't take it. After a moment, she retracted her hand. "What's your name?" she asked.

"Darcie Grey."

"That's not what Bridget called you."

"Where is she?" I said. "What did you do to her?"

"You're shaking," the woman said. "Are you sure you don't want my jacket?"

"Where's Bridget?" I repeated, louder.

"You care about her an awful lot."

I gave a strangled laugh. "I've been in the same room with her for—for—weeks."

The woman carefully pulled her jacket back on and studied the buttons at the cuffs. "More than a month now. But you've known her longer than that, haven't you? I looked into Bridget's files. Before she came here, she was at Nornand Clinic. So was a girl named Addie Tamsyn."

I stayed silent.

She looked up. "*The* Addie Tamsyn, who helped bomb the Powatt institution. They say Mark Jenson had a particular interest in her, but now that he has Jaime Cortae back, he isn't nearly as concerned anymore."

Jaime. I struggled to quash the flash of pain across our face. Judging from the way the woman watched us, I wasn't entirely successful.

"Jenson has the boy, and all his plans for a cure." The woman spoke slowly now, half to herself. "But I have you."

"I'm not Addie," I said quietly. It was truer than this woman knew.

She just smiled. Addie and I had heard somewhere that you could judge a true smile from a fake one by looking at a person's eyes. Her mouth stretched, and her eyes crinkled, but it was still the fakest smile we'd ever seen.

"Who sent you here?" she said. "How're they getting the footage?"

"The footage?" Our voice didn't reflect the havoc the words wreaked on our insides. They shredded our lungs. Mashed our stomach. Our heart ran limping marathons, barreling and halting in our chest, our blood roaring in response.

"For the broadcast hijacking," the woman said. When I just stared at her, unable to respond, her smile faded. "You really don't know."

It didn't take long for them to wheel in a small television. The woman popped in the first tape. Pressed *play*.

An image of the president of the Americas appeared. And beside him, Jenson. The volume was too low, at first, to hear what he was saying. The woman bent to turn it up. Then we made out the words.

He talked about the *hybrid danger*, and about uprisings on the eastern coast that were being dealt with. About the cure. He mentioned Jaime—

The image cut out. Reduced to snow and static for a second.

Then there, on the screen, was Wendy Howard. Little Wendy Howard, who'd joined up with Marion for the sake of her dead sister.

Marion hadn't even tried to hide her face. We saw every uneasy twitch of her eyebrows and tremble of her lip as she talked about Anna. About what it had been like to have a sibling torn away, and never know her fate.

She cried in the middle of it, with that camera trained right on her face. Then we did look away, because the rawness was too much to stand.

In those few seconds, the footage of Wendy disappeared. But we didn't return to the president and Jenson. We returned, instead, to that night in the dark streets of Anchoit, when Jackson Montgomery was arrested, and Kitty captured the footage with shaking hands.

We'd never seen the film before. We'd never developed it—had left it behind in that hotel room along with the rest of our purse's contents. Someone must have given it to Marion. Or she'd stolen it.

<That was private> Addie whispered. *<We never gave her permission to use that.>*

The screen could only show us a sliver of what had happened. My memory filled in the rest. The arc of the policemen's flashlights. The way the officers had tackled Jackson to the ground.

The sick fear.

Addie was an earthquake of anger. I held on to her. Tried to steady her. But I was shaking, too.

Jackson disappeared into a police car.

The screen jumped back to static.

The Plum-blouse Lady pressed *pause*. Then *eject*. "That was broadcasted two weeks ago."

She put in another tape. This time, it was only Jenson speaking before the feed cut out, replaced by a blurry, but oddly familiar recording. We squinted.

Realized why the image looked familiar.

We'd recorded it.

"This," the woman said, her eyes hard, "was shown yesterday."

We could only stare. Here was Class 6 again, broadcasted in snippets. The peeling walls. The metal beds. Hannah's coughing. Viola's blank-eyed wandering.

Then darkness, and the whispered stories of the girls.

Marion knew we were still in Hahns, and she'd released the footage anyway.

We couldn't think about what that meant. Not now. Not with this woman watching us so closely. We had to keep calm. Play innocent.

Betray nothing.

We had no other choice. Not until we'd had time to figure things out.

"I thought it might be Bridget, at first, since she was connected to Nornand," the woman said. "But now that I know who you really are, it does make a lot more sense."

We swallowed. "I don't know what you're talking about."

That was the last thing we said aloud.

The woman stayed another twenty or thirty minutes, getting more and more frustrated. Her voice sharpened. Her eyes flashed. She vacillated between whispering and shouting, threatening and cajoling.

We stayed silent.

Finally, she left.

<We'll fight them when they next open the door> I said. *<We'll run. Fast as we can.>*

They tried to feed us. We flung the tray at the man who brought it, and tried to barrel past him. He threw us back inside.

When we tried the same thing hours later, the next caretaker they sent came bearing a needle.

Now we really fought. Now we screamed, and spat, and hit, and kicked.

We felt a stab of pride that it took three people to hold us still.

Then the needle went in, the pain blossomed as they injected the drugs, and the world went black.

EIGHTEEN

Time spiraled into itself.

I woke to Ryan standing at my bedside. So perfectly real. So perfectly there. But when I reached out our fingers went right through him.

Ryan, I said. *Ryan, I—*

Shhh. He put a finger to his lips. Started flashing red like the disks we used to share. Flashing meant they were close. Meant—

He melted. Collapsed into ash that spread like a living thing across the floor, setting the ground on fire. I screamed. The flames crackled. The ceiling rained soot into our eyes. I rubbed at them and rubbed at them, but it wouldn't come out.

Somebody grabbed at our hands. Pulled them from our face. Someone screamed something, and I screamed back—I couldn't stop *screaming*—

Pyxis, our father said
Pointing at the sky, the wide
Dark blue of it
His arm circled around us
Blocking us from the wind

There are ghosts in our clothes, I told them.

A needle glinted.

No, I moaned. I shoved. I shouted. *No, no, please*—

Pain. Pain and pressure. Our heart. Hot.

It had been so cold, and now it was *so hot*—

Pyxis, named after a mariner's compass
Three faint stars in the southern sky
Tell me the story, I said
Four years old, and sleepy
And falling asleep.

Addie?

Addie. Addie. Addie. Addie—

Too much, they said.

Stupid, they whispered.

Why do you walk? I asked Viola. Viola by our bedside with her finger on our cheek. *What did you see?*

You have to count the days, she said.

1

2

3

Then she burned, and I burned with her.

There is no story for Pyxis.

Lyle tapped Morse-code messages through the walls.

I tapped them back. The world was black with smoke, and in the darkness lurked things with moist, sucking breaths, and I could no longer see, but my little brother was tapping messages to me through our bedroom wall, and he wouldn't go to sleep until I tapped something back. He had to go to sleep.

Sleep.

S

L

E

E

—

NINETEEN

I am not a ghost.

I woke as if through water. Through smoke and haze and fog. My thoughts pressed through cotton, trying to surface. Things got lost on their way from our eyes to our brain, from our brain to our mouth. I spoke and heard nothing. Heard nothing and something all at once—

I saw Ryan again. He didn't look at us. He was focused on something in his hands, his brow furrowed the way it did when he was concentrating on a problem, on a bit of machinery that wasn't going the way he wanted it to.

He wasn't really there, but I watched him, anyway.

There was something buried in the skin on the back of our hand. A thin, clear tube that snaked up, up, up, until it connected to a small, clear bag. There was fluid in the bag. Fluid that, I supposed, was going into us.

Some mornings, I still burned. I made incoherent sounds, and no one came, and then someone did. A woman with a low, gravelly voice who spoke softly.

"You had a bad reaction," she said and ran her finger over our cheek, where the skin was damp.

"They gave you too much," she said. She reminded me of the nurses back at Nornand. "They aren't used to being careful."

She pressed our eyelids closed.

"They don't usually have to worry about the subjects surviving."

TWENTY

I ripped the tube out.

And almost screamed.

It *hurt*. Blood beaded at the wound, dripped down our wrist. The end of the tube was dripping, too—clear liquid that sank into our covers.

The door banged open. A man rushed in. Grabbed our hand. I tried to struggle, but our limbs felt like noodles.

"Don't," I cried. "I don't want it."

He hesitated, but relented, pasting a bandage on our hand to staunch the bleeding. He collected the dripping tube and the rest of the IV apparatus. Then he was gone again.

I could barely sit up. Our skin felt raw. Our eyes. Our throat.

<Addie?> I whispered.

A sudden wave of nausea made me close our eyes. When I opened them again, the room was clearer. The lights less blinding. Our eyes focused. I breathed through our mouth.

My mind was still cottony. I reached for her, trying to grasp her and drag her up, with me, to clarity.

I found nothing.

There wasn't the hole there usually was when Addie went under, whether through the use of Refcon or through her own means. There was no gaping chasm, no utter nothingness.

There was just the fog. And that was slowly disappearing, too. My head, my thoughts grew clearer.

And Addie simply wasn't there.

I gulped down panic. Our hands fisted on the blanket. I reached out again, in my mind, but there was nowhere to reach. There was no space. No extra room. No connection.

Just me.

The door opened. The Plum-blouse Lady was back, though she wore a red blouse today, with a loose turtleneck. She came toward us. Me.

<Addie?> I cried. Her name echoed in the singular chamber of my mind. My thoughts—my emotions—the space in our head—it felt so *closed*. Like I'd spent my entire life living in a house, and now half the rooms had disappeared, leaving me scrambling at walls that used to be doors.

"If you don't want the IV," the woman said, "you're going to have to be agreeable and eat."

I stared at her uncomprehendingly.

"Addie." She leaned toward us. I would have shrunk away, if I could. But I was already huddled against the wall. "Are you lucid?"

I hoped I wasn't. That this was just another nightmare.

Our voice was cracked. Our throat still hurt. But I spoke. "If I weren't lucid, would I know it?"

Her lips pursed. "Addie—"

"I'm not Addie," I whispered.

Now it was the woman's turn to laugh. "Bit late to say that. Especially after all the things you've been shouting in your dreams."

Our mouth snapped shut.

"The drug was supposed to do that," the woman said. "Help you tell the truth. Loosen inhibitions. Things like that. It's had better trials. Some of the other girls, they tell us everything."

I could only stare at her. She was lying. She had to be.

"You had a bad reaction to it, though," the woman said. "Hybrid brains . . . they're all a little different, I've found, depending on the division of strength between the two minds. It's tricky finding something that will have predictable results. But I suppose the difficulty will work in my favor once I succeed."

"Refcon," I whispered. "Did you give me Refcon?"

Her eyebrows raised. "Why would I do that?"

I swallowed. "To try and cure us."

She smiled pityingly. "You're thinking of Nornand, Addie, and Powatt. Here at Hahns, we don't bother with curing."

I waited for Addie to come back. I counted seconds in my mind. Seconds that turned into minutes that turned into hours. They brought in food. A bowl of something like porridge. Breakfast? Lunch? Dinner?

The longest I've ever heard of anyone being out is half a day, Emalia told me once. Had Addie still been with me during the delirium? I couldn't know for sure. If she'd already disappeared then . . .

But I couldn't think like that.

I refused to eat, at first. I felt too sick. But they brought the IV back in, and threatened me with it, so I choked down what I could. It was ashes and sandpaper in our throat, motor oil in our stomach.

I didn't dare tell them Addie was gone. No one mentioned it. Was it on purpose? Had they tried to make Addie go away, thinking the recessive soul was easier to control? Easier to manipulate? Or was this just an unforeseen side effect of their experimental drugs? Of the *unreliable reactions* of our hybrid mind?

Was this where the chosen girls went? To be used as lab rats? It couldn't be legal, but what did that mean up here in the middle of nowhere, with children already lost to the world?

They cleared away the tray. Left me in my solitude and the ticking time.

I receded into myself. Clawed at the walls of my own mind. Left fingernail gashes in my thoughts.

<Addie?>

Half a day, Emalia had said. But that was only what she'd

heard about, right? There was a whole world out there she'd never seen before. Mankind had reached space. Henri's sat-phone could transport information in seconds across the vastness of an ocean.

Perhaps Emalia had been wrong.

What frightened me most was how I couldn't feel the space where Addie should have been. Parts of me had shut down. Disappeared.

A caretaker brought in more food.

"They just fed me," I told him.

"That was hours ago," he said.

I threw up in the toilet, acid burning all the way up our throat. He grabbed our shoulders. Asked me what was wrong. I hadn't thought he'd care. But the Plum-blouse Lady wasn't finished with me, so I guess they needed me alive.

Everything was wrong. How couldn't he see that?

Addie was gone, and that meant—

I tried to speak, but I couldn't pull enough air into our lungs. Our chest burned.

The man was yelling something. The food tray flipped over, splashing porridge all over the ground.

More people came. It was so loud.

So loud. And crowded, and—

Still so silent in my mind.

I can't breathe, I tried to tell them.

I can't breathe.

I can't breathe alone.

TWENTY-ONE

Once, when Addie and I were four years old, we saw the stars together on a grassy hill and tried to count them, one by one.

Once, when Addie and I were seven years old, a boy tricked us into climbing into a trunk, then locked us inside. We lay curled in the sweltering darkness for hours, and Addie repeated <*They're going to find us. They're going to let us out*> until I started believing it.

Once, when Addie and I were ten years old, I lost control of our legs in the middle of the elementary-school hallway, and she dove into control, saving us before we crumpled to the ground. Saving me from the embarrassment of my own terrified, frustrated tears.

Once, when Addie and I were twelve years old, Addie whispered <*I'm sorry*> as we stood by our bedroom window, and I felt the last of my strength drain away.

Once, when Addie and I were fifteen years old, she risked everything—everything—so I could have a chance at being free.

* * *

I decided it could not be permanent.

It was impossible.

Addie was gone now, but she would be back.

It didn't matter how many hours it had been. How many days.

The Plum-blouse Lady returned every day, asking the same questions: who had sent us here; how many people were involved; where were they now. How had I kept in contact with them.

I answered nothing. Sometimes, I laughed at her. I told her I looked forward to seeing her, and it was true. When she was there, I had something to focus on. Something to listen to, even if it was just questions I couldn't allow myself to answer.

When she was gone, the silence crushed me like I was a hundred thousand miles under the ocean.

I started talking to Addie, even though she wasn't there.

<*Do you think she'll ever give up?*> I asked.

<*This is going to be one hell of a story someday*> I said.

<*You're lucky you're not here for this*> I whispered.

A splotchy bruise covered the back of our hand, where the IV had been. I pressed on it sometimes, just to feel the pain. A reminder that I was still there.

The door opened. The Plum-blouse Lady walked inside.

I still hadn't learned her name, and I supposed it didn't matter. I'd figured out enough to know that she was at the head of Hahns, the way Mr. Conivent had run the hybrid wing of Nornand.

"Your shirt matches my bruise," I told her. It did, too.

The woman ignored the comment. She situated a chair across from my bed and sat down, crossing her legs. I had a feeling she'd only managed to keep her temper in check these past days because she thought I was still half-delirious. Maybe I was.

"I like your shoes." I wriggled our own feet at her. The longer she thought me crazy, the longer I could stall. "They took away my slippers, even. Do you still have my original shoes? My oxfords. I liked them."

"There was another broadcast today." She sounded tired. I could read it in her eyes, in the slope of her back. She'd passed frustration, passed anger, even. Now she was just weary.

"Oh?" I said. It came out sounding almost casual. I felt anything but casual.

The woman must have thought it sounded casual, too, because the weariness vanished, flooded by a rush of anger.

"I could report you," she said. "However much Jenson is preoccupied with his own little plans right now, I'm sure he'd make time for the girl who supplied the footage that's been causing so much trouble."

Had it been causing trouble? I felt a stab of pride, and tried not to let it show.

<*Why doesn't she report us?*> I asked Addie, and waited, as if she would reply. As if we could bounce ideas off each other, the way we always had. We'd figured out things twice as quickly when we were together.

But Addie wasn't here, and I had to figure things out myself.

<*Maybe she wants the credit*> I said. <*Figuring out the source of the broadcasts . . . that would go a long way. If she turned us over to Jenson, she could only get credit for finding us—and even then, she might get in trouble for not noticing who we were in the first place.*>

I looked up, studying this woman. There were traces of desperation on her face, bleeding through the cracks in her mask. Had she been in charge back in July? Probably. So the summer fiasco—the escaped and dead children—had happened under her watch. She wouldn't want another mistake on her record. Especially with the experimental drugs she was testing on the hybrid children thrust under her care. Surely, that wasn't government approved.

Though I supposed it wouldn't matter in the end, if she truly made a breakthrough. The government would only be all too happy with another weapon to use against hybrids.

"I don't want to involve Jenson," the Plum-blouse Lady said quietly. "And I don't think you do, either." She smiled a safe, unassuming smile. "I could ask for your parents. Your mother, for example? I could get her. It wasn't hard to find her number. I could fly her up here, if you wanted to see her."

I opened our mouth, but our throat squeezed too tight for words.

I'd suddenly had a sickening thought.

If she could bribe me with my family, then she could also threaten me with them. Hadn't Mr. Conivent done as much? No one would think anything of it if Lyle had a complication. If he ended up back in the hospital.

If he didn't make it.

She knew what she was doing. I saw it in her face. In the satisfaction in her eyes.

"Tell me who's behind the broadcasts, and I could have your family up here tomorrow," she said.

Tell me who's behind the broadcasts, or something could happen to your family tomorrow, and it'll be entirely your fault.

"Jenson will be keeping tabs on my family. He'd know if anything happened."

"What do you know about Jenson?" the woman said.

I didn't tell her about the explosion at Powatt. The way we'd sat among the rubble, him and Addie and me. We were both alive because of each other. He'd borne us toward the door when we couldn't walk. Maybe Addie and I would have escaped Powatt without Jenson's help. Maybe he would have survived the bomb without our warning. But we'd never know.

"Addie—" the woman said.

"I'm *not* Addie," I said with such fierceness that she silenced.

And finally, she understood.

"Eva," she said, and I shuddered. She repeated my name, quieter. "Eva, tell me. You don't have any other choice. Who sent you in here?"

It took everything in me to refuse to speak when my family was on the line. But nothing was sure. Last time, when I'd screwed up, I'd allowed devastation into not only my life, but that of so many people I cared about, who were innocent.

That couldn't happen again.

If I didn't speak, my parents and Lyle were in danger. If I did, everyone else was in danger—Ryan and Hally and Kitty and Dr. Lyanne. Not to mention Marion and Wendy. Probably even Jackson and Emalia and Henri, since their rescue might depend on the consequences of our plans.

Of course, they were all in danger anyway.

Eventually, the woman left. But she hadn't given up. If anything, she'd brightened. And why not? It didn't matter if I didn't tell her today. She'd be back tomorrow. And she knew I couldn't hold out forever.

I pulled the blanket tighter around us. I still hadn't completely recovered from our days of delirium; I tired easily. Couldn't always think clearly. *<We're—I'm going to have to start making things up. It'll distract them awhile. Buy us a little time.>*

I closed our eyes.

Of course, buying time was only good if I could do something with it.

<Addie> I whispered as I drifted to sleep. *<If you can hear me at all . . . I need you. You have to come back.>*

Sometime, possibly much later, I woke when the door creaked open. The lights had already dimmed. It must have been late.

"Finally," someone huffed. "You'd think picking this lock would be easier than the window."

A girl's voice.

Bridget.

TWENTY-TWO

I tumbled out of bed, tangled in the sheets. Bridget ran to help me up again. Hissed in my ear, "Come on. We don't have a lot of time."

I didn't ask questions. I took her hand and let her hustle me from the room. At the last minute, she darted back and grabbed my blanket to take with us.

We ran down the dimmed hall. I heard distant shouting. Not the keening of fear, or pain, but *shouting*—like people at a rally, children on a playground. And above it, the noise of adults fighting to restore order.

"What's going on?" My words were more air than sound, but somehow, Bridget understood.

"What does it look like?" she demanded. "We're breaking you out."

"They came?" Our voice went high at the end, twisted to a point. Marion? Ryan?

Bridget frowned at me over her shoulder. "Nobody came,

Addie." Her name stabbed pain in my side. "*We* did it. Us. The girls. The patients."

I stared at her. She jerked on our hand. Our lungs were on fire.

"Class Twelve?" I whispered.

She gave me a grim smile. "Class Twelve isn't Class Twelve anymore. After they let me go, they put me back into the same ward, but they rotated everyone again the day after. Didn't want me spreading stories, I guess. Only I already had. I told every girl in that ward all about you. How stupid you are, how utterly idealistic and naive."

We were almost to the stairwell. Bridget hesitated. "By the time they rotated us, every single girl in that class thought you were a freaking martyr. I made sure of it. And I made sure they knew to tell their new classes the same thing. That today, we were going to rescue you." The exit sign glowed green. Bridget pressed her ear against the door, then jerked it open and shoved me toward the stairs. "So come on."

Bridget explained as we hurtled down the steps. They'd come up with a plan. During the next rotation, the first few classes allowed out of their wards would scatter, causing as much chaos as possible. The classes still locked inside would join in the commotion. They shoved beds against the door like battering rams. Swarmed the caretakers who dared crack the door open, unsure what to do. I guess their training—if there was training—didn't involve anything like this.

"Don't underestimate a mob of preteen girls," Bridget told me wryly.

In the chaos, Bridget managed to slip away. She figured they'd keep me on the same floor they'd kept her.

"I didn't think the next rotation would happen so soon—it's barely been more than a week. But I guess they wanted to keep everyone off-balance. And it worked out in your favor." She smiled hesitantly. Said, softly, "You're still a little lucky."

"It . . . seems so simple," I said.

Bridget shrugged. "No one expected it. None of those girls are getting out of here tonight. They know it, and the caretakers know it. So they can't understand why they'd all band together to do it anyway."

She wavered when we reached the ground floor, and I realized she didn't remember the way out. How could she, when it had been months since she first walked through the front door?

But I had memorized Hahns's layout, and now Bridget followed me as we crept through the hallways, our footfalls hidden by the buzz of the generators, the hum of the air-conditioning.

There were only two ways into this institution: the front door, and a back door near the stairwell. I took us past it, but chances were, it was locked. There was a camera trained on it, so I didn't dare check. We'd only have one chance at this. Better to check out the situation at the front door before making any decisions.

We could hear the shouting even on the first floor, coming muffled through the ceiling.

The lobby was only slightly better lit than the hallways. A single guard remained at his station, staring at a panel of monitors. On them, we saw the chaos upstairs. The masses of girls. Some had grabbed their pillows, using them to beat at the caretakers like it was all some sort of macabre pillow fight.

The security guard's station was only a few yards from the door. Easy to catch anyone making a run for it. I tugged Bridget back down the hall until we were out of earshot, then whispered, "What's going to happen here? When we're gone?"

"Oh, don't think so highly of yourself," Bridget said. "We survived before. We'll survive after."

Not everyone survived, I thought. Then realized. "We? You said *we*."

Bridget gave me the look only she could give. The one that said, so plainly, *Are you insane?* "What?"

I grabbed her hand. "You said, *We survived before. We'll survive after.* We."

Her shoulders drooped a little. But she didn't look away.

"No," I said. "You're coming with me."

I wasn't leaving her behind again.

Bridget yanked her hand from ours. "Someone has to stay. To watch out for the girls still here. They're mostly rather stupid. They agreed to this plan, didn't they?" Her grin was cockeyed, then flickered. "Besides, someone has to distract that guard."

I couldn't manage words.

"You better not freeze." Bridget looked me up and down, and shoved my blanket at me—her slippers, too, after she tugged them from her feet. Automatically, I took them. "I'm going to be mad as hell if I hear you froze in the snow, after all this trouble."

"Bridget—"

"Oh, right," she said. She lifted her left hand; I hadn't been paying it any attention—not in the darkness, not in the midst of everything else. There, around her finger, was our ring. She slipped it off and pressed it in our palm. "You can't forget this. One of the other girls took it after we'd gone. I got it back for you."

I clutched the ring in our hand. Bent to put on the thin slippers.

"Do what you do," Bridget said as she turned to go. "Make things change."

It took me a second to find the words. But I called them after her, as loudly as I dared.

"I will," I said. "I'm going to make the whole world change."

She turned. Nodded. Just once.

She ran out, toward the security guard.

Screamed. Shouted.

Distracted him, while I slipped out the door and into the snow.

* * *

I slammed into a white world, and my first thought was, *Oh, God, I've made such a mistake.*

Bridget was right. There were piles of snowdrifts.

There was also a blizzard.

There was no way I could survive out here. Not even with the blanket. The snow burned through our slippers, soaking them.

I kept running. Adrenaline was friend and enemy, angel and demon. It shoved me off the institution grounds. Into the woods, the copses of barren trees.

I ran, and it snowed. It snowed, and I ran.

I ran, ran, ran.

Until I collapsed.

I couldn't breathe. The cold air knifed up our lungs, tearing them to ribbons. They couldn't expand.

I struggled onto our knees, gasping.

<Keep going> I said, and pretended it was Addie who said it. *<Keep going, Eva.>*

I did.

Eventually, it stopped snowing. The wind stilled. The ground was clear in patches, here under the skeletal canopy of the trees. I tried to keep to the barer parts, hoping the snowfall earlier had buried our footprints.

It was so cold. Our palms and cheeks burned. Our feet went numb.

I pushed onward. Through the trees. Downhill. That was

the only direction I knew to go.

The moon was half-full, egg-yolk yellow in a dark sky.

I walked until our legs gave out. There was no way to know how far I was from civilization. If I was even headed in the right direction. Down was down, but population was sparse here around Hahns.

I remembered the story Peter had told us about the attempted rescue in July. Diane and the six children she'd tried to save had crashed off the side of the road. Only four kids had made it to the town below, and it had taken them what, ten hours? Ten hours, and it had been summer.

I collapsed underneath a tree. Our eyes were closed before I could think anything about it. I forced them open again. I knew enough about hypothermia to know falling asleep didn't help.

But I had to rest. At the very least, I had to wait until daylight. I'd been walking for hours already, moving on autopilot, which worked well enough when the only thing I had to do was *run, run away*. But now I needed to plot a course. I had to figure out which direction to go, where I could find the nearest town.

I needed sleep. But to sleep, I needed warmth. I couldn't risk lying down and never getting up again.

I gathered branches from the trees, as dry as I could find, then cleared a bit of the ground, digging until I hit dry dirt. I relied half on memories of Dad's hands on our camping trips, and half on more recent recollections of Lyle's novels, on his overeager explanations of fire building while Addie and I tried to do our homework.

Joy was seeing the first sparks fly off the end of the spindle. Feeding the fire until it crackled and flickered, until I could tug the damp slippers from our feet and lay them out to dry. Joy was slowly regaining feeling in our toes, seeing the color bleed back into them, and to our fingers. I thawed in the glow of the flames.

<When we see Lyle again> I said to Addie as I fell asleep, wrapped in our blanket *<we're going to have so many stories to tell him.>*

TWENTY-THREE

I found the main road in the morning, mostly through luck. That, and the almost unearthly silence that muffled the woods. It was so quiet that when the cars did start passing by, I heard them long before I saw them.

I needed to stay by the road. It was my best shot at finding civilization before night fell again. But staying close to the road meant a higher chance of being spotted.

I trekked on. Soon, our face was completely numb again, our legs itching with the cold. Our slippers, made for smooth institution floors, started to wear through. I walked with a limp, trying to avoid the growing hole near the heel of the left slipper. Our right ankle, the one we'd injured at Powatt, ached deep in the bone.

Each time I heard a car coming, I melted deeper into the woods until the vehicle passed. Most seemed to be headed downhill, but a few were going up, toward the institution. Had the woman finally alerted Jenson?

For the first time in a long time, I was hungry. Compared

to the cold and the exhaustion, it was the least of my worries. But as the hours wore on, the hunger manifested itself as a sharp pain right under our breastbone, as a weakness in our legs, a cloudiness in our head.

I walked until I heard the most beautiful sound in the world.

Traffic.

I recognized the town. We'd passed through it when we first drove to Hahns. Addie and I had wondered if this was the same place those four kids had shown up after the July breakout, bloody and wild-eyed.

I wasn't bloody, but I was freezing. And I had no money, no way to make so much as a phone call. I couldn't walk into a store and ask to borrow their phone. People here undoubtedly remembered what had happened in the summer. They might recognize Hahns's uniform.

The sun was low again, dyeing the snow a rich yellow as it sank over the rooftops. I lingered at the edge of the trees. Hesitant, despite everything, to leave the woods behind.

<I feel like a criminal> I muttered. Then laughed. *<We are criminals, Addie. I'd forgotten that.>*

The laughter disappeared as swiftly as it had come. I'd be even more a criminal by the time this was all over. I needed clothes, and food. That was just to start.

Luckily, it was too cold for most people to just be hanging around. I waited until there weren't any cars passing, then darted out from the trees and ducked behind a building. A restaurant. I breathed in the heady smell of food like it could actually fill our stomach.

The restaurant's back door creaked open.

I dove behind the trash bins. A steady stream of noise came from inside the restaurant: the low roar of voices, the clink of glasses. A television blared some kind of sports game.

Slowly, I peeked around the side of the bins. The girl in the doorway buttoned up her coat over her waitressing uniform and shivered, setting out across the parking lot.

I let our blanket fall to the ground. Caught the door just before it closed.

If I was going to steal food without being noticed, a darkened, noisy restaurant might be the best place to do it.

The place was large enough for no one to notice as I snuck in the back door. A large bar took up the front, and a crowd had gathered there to watch a football game. The dining area was emptier, with a few tables, and fewer booths. Despite the setting sun, it was still a little early for the dinner crowd.

A table near the back was deserted, but hadn't been cleared yet. A good quarter of a sandwich remained, oozing half-solidified cheese. I wrapped it up in the red-and-white checkered wax paper and held it by our side before swiping the quarters that had been left as a tip.

One of the teams scored a goal. The group gathered around the bar exploded in cheers. Emboldened by their lack of attention, I snuck a little farther from the back of the restaurant.

Someone had left their coat hanging on their chair. I looked around. Everyone who wasn't deep in conversation seemed fixated on the football game, or on their meal. I grabbed the coat, retreating quickly to the shadows.

It was far too large, but better than nothing. I'd rather look like a girl who'd borrowed her boyfriend's jacket than one escaped from a mental institution.

There was more leftover food on the tables, but I didn't want to risk it. The coat's owner might come back at any moment. I hurried for the back door, slipped through, and didn't stop moving until I'd left the restaurant far behind.

It didn't take long to find a pay phone, even in such a tiny town. It was near a main square, though, and I hesitated before approaching.

A man near the pay phone complained about snow getting into his boots. Two women chattered excitedly about a trail they'd skied earlier today. A little boy begged his mother for spending money. Christmas trimmings had already gone up, the storefronts festooned with loops of evergreen and bright red bows.

Sitting in the institution, I'd forgotten about things like Christmas decorations.

I wrapped the coat tighter around our shoulders and hurried into the phone booth. My stolen quarters clinked into the slot.

The digits to Henri's satphone had run through my mind so many times, it felt almost dreamlike to actually input them.

We're coming, Ryan had carved on the new ring. But he would think me still at Hahns. I couldn't stay anywhere near the institution—not when police could canvass this entire town in a matter of hours.

I had to contact him. But the phone blared an error noise that slashed apart all my hopes. The satphone wasn't connected, or wasn't working. Ryan still hadn't fixed it.

Doubt crept cold fingers up my insides. Maybe I'd gotten the number wrong. It had been so long, and it wasn't impossible that some night at Hahns, I'd switched a number around in my mind.

If Addie were here, I could ask her. Could double-check.

But she wasn't.

I started to hang up.

Heard the crunch of shoes against snow.

And whirled around, fingers tight around the phone, to face whoever had snuck up behind us.

TWENTY-FOUR

His pale eyes widened.

We stared at each other. I gripped the phone like a weapon.

I was dreaming. I was still freezing up in the woods, or back in the cell at Hahns, dreaming about the impossibility of this moment.

Then he grinned. A match strike in the snow. It lit me from the inside out. I dropped the phone and threw our arms around him.

Because I wasn't dreaming. And it was Jackson.

"Eva," he said quietly. It wasn't a question but an acknowledgment. He pulled back, held me at arm's length so he could study me. "Where's Marion? Did she get you out? I—"

I shook our head, filled to bursting with questions of my own. "The other girls at the institution helped me. It's a long story. But we can't stay here. The woman who runs Hahns—she's going to come looking for me." I glanced at the evening crowd outside the phone booth. "I have to leave town."

"Lucky you, then," Jackson said with a grin, "running into me."

I lingered near the phone booth while Jackson called someone named Ben. Their conversation was brief: "Yes, I found her—no, you need to come right now—we'll be by the ball field."

He hung up and turned back to me. His hair was even longer now. Almost to his shoulders, and darker than I remembered it. His skin, on the other hand, looked paler. There was a fatigue that hung about him, even when he was smiling.

"Who's Ben?" I asked.

"Also a long story. Come on. Let's go someplace more secluded."

I followed him to a chained-up baseball field at the edge of town. Someone—Jackson himself?—had smashed the padlock on the abandoned bathroom door.

Jackson hesitated as I walked in after him. "It's gross, I know."

I looked around. A ratty blanket covered most of the space between the stalls and the sink. A sleeping bag lay on top. "Actually, as far as public bathrooms go, this is pretty good."

"Yeah, the real five-star establishment of the toilet world." He grinned. "There's no heating, of course. But the walls and roof are nice."

The initial overwhelming relief at seeing Jackson had

faded enough to allow other emotions to bleed through. For me to remember how our lives had been the last time we'd seen each other.

During those early days in Anchoit, Jackson had been one of our few connections with the outside world. But that was all *before.* Now I couldn't disentangle Jackson from Addie's feelings for him, and Sabine's betrayal, and Powatt.

"Eva?"

Our head snapped up. I'd forgotten the intensity of his stare. The way he'd used to study us. Or Addie, I suppose. I fought not to look away.

"Who brought you here?" I asked.

"No one," he said. "Vince and I shook off Marion's friends about a week ago. They wouldn't come here. They said they were bringing me to her, and they wouldn't consider anything else."

"You knew I was at Hahns."

"Only because I overheard Marion's friends talking about it." Jackson made sure I was looking at him before continuing. His eyes were solemn. "When she told me she wanted to help me, she didn't say anything about a deal. I had no idea about her sending you into Hahns—about the whole deal with the footage—until I got out."

I fidgeted with the ring around our finger. Felt the scratch of the engraving underneath the band. In dealing with the aftermath, I hadn't had time to properly think about Marion's betrayal. Because that was what it was, wasn't it? She had to have realized what she was doing when she released that footage.

And Ryan? The others?

<No way they knew> I whispered to Addie.

My silence must have made Jackson uncomfortable. As always, when he was uncomfortable, he started talking. "I haven't been here long. They didn't even get me out until ten days ago—then I had to get *here*, and—"

I made myself smile. "What was your plan? Come barging into the institution by yourself and save me?"

When he smiled, too, I realized why my own had felt so familiar—it was the kind of smile Jackson and Vince wore so often. The unflinching smile that didn't care for propriety, or circumstance. The kind that said, *Given the choice to sink or swim, we chose to swim.*

"I'm sorry," he said, "are you making fun of my plans? You, the one who ran into a building you *knew* was going to blow up?"

God, it felt good to laugh. It felt strange to laugh. I almost pointed it out to Addie, and then I remembered, and my laughter turned rancid in our throat.

"There was no real plan," he admitted. "All I knew was I had to come find you and Addie." It was the first time he'd spoken her name. The syllables seemed to crackle in the cold air. He cleared his throat. "But it seems like you did fine all by yourself."

"Hardly," I said quietly. I told him about Bridget and the other girls. What they'd done, and what I'd done in leaving them behind. I told him about the Plum-blouse Lady who came to our room day after day to demand information. About the experiments she was running, and the threats she made.

I didn't tell him about the effects of our drug-induced delirium. Addie's absence.

I couldn't.

Jackson filled me in on the world outside Hahns's walls. He hadn't been free yet when Marion's first two broadcasts hit the waves, but he'd seen and heard enough since then to know the impact they'd made.

"The broadcast of my arrest . . ." he said with a wry smile. "Not how I expected to have my fifteen minutes of fame, you know?"

"Kitty filmed it by accident," I said. "And Marion was never supposed to get her hands on it—"

He nodded. "Well, broadcasting it served her purpose. And I guess it served ours."

Hybrids were already the topic of the day before—but now, no one talked about anything else.

"Things were just starting to calm down when the Hahns footage released," Jackson said. "Those girls? The sick one—"

"Hannah and Millie," I said softly, and his eyes dulled a bit. He nodded.

"Jenson's probably going mad trying to figure out who's responsible for it all."

I shrugged. How long until the Plum-blouse Lady caved and told Jenson the truth? Until Addie and I were once again centered in his crosshairs?

"It isn't all just talk, either," Jackson said. He told me how some people who'd lost kids to the institutionalization system had started looking for them—even ones they'd given up years ago. The government wasn't any help, so they banded together.

Sometimes, they had to travel great distances. Not everyone could afford places to stay, and people began opening their homes to these travelers—secretly, of course, but news traveled among hybrid sympathizers, until a network of sorts was set up.

"It's like a safe-house system," Jackson said. "That's how I got by after getting away from Marion's friends."

Safe house made me think of Peter.

Jackson didn't know about Peter.

I tried not to let our face betray my sudden pain.

"Sabine said it would happen," I said quietly. "She always believed hybrids just needed to know they weren't alone. You haven't . . . you don't know where she is, do you? Or Christoph and Cordelia?"

Jackson shook his head. "Not captured, as far as I know." He looked like he might say something more, but swallowed it.

"What?" I said.

He hesitated, then blurted out the words like he needed to speak them before he lost the nerve. "Your whole family—apparently they've disappeared. No one knows where they are.

That's what I've heard, anyway."

My family was missing. Had been missing.

"For how long?" I demanded.

"I don't know," he said. "At least—at least a month or two."

"A *month or two?*"

He rushed to explain: "I can't be sure—I've heard it all secondhand, and honestly, I think it's more like fifth- or sixth- or seventhhand. Everything's a tangle of rumors and hearsay right now—"

The Plum-blouse Lady must have known. Had she been lying when she said she could get my mother?

Or had she been telling the truth?

Could she get my mother, because they already had her locked up? A prisoner, along with my father. And Lyle. Lyle needed medical care—dialysis if he hadn't gotten the transplant, medication if he had, to keep his body from rejecting the new kidney. I knew all the facts—had long memorized our little brother's needs.

Suddenly all I could think about was Lyle—Lyle pounding up and down the stairs; Lyle tapping Morse code to us through the walls; Lyle reading; Lyle sick and Lyle healthy.

My guilt was old and familiar. It knew just where to press to hurt the most. How to cripple me without killing me. How to draw out the pain.

<Addie—Addie, what do we—>

"I—I need some fresh air." I stood. Jackson stood, too, but I warded him away, our head and heart pounding. "I'll just—I'll just go walk around the baseball field. I'll be fine."

He hesitated. "Eva, can I speak with Addie?"

Addie's gone, I could have said.

I don't know what's happened to her, I could have said.

I don't know when she's coming back.

I don't know if—

"She gone under right now," I said. "I—later, when she's back."

After a long moment, he nodded.

I turned and fled outside.

TWENTY-FIVE

I walked five slow circles around the edge of the baseball field. It was already fully dark, though it couldn't have been later than six. The sky was cloudy, the moon half-obscured. I trailed our fingers along the bleacher seats, the way Viola had along the walls of the ward room.

What had happened to the girls I'd left behind? Maybe the caretakers had drugged them all into a stupor. Maybe they'd decided it was too dangerous to keep any of them anymore, now that they'd had a taste of rebellion. Maybe they were all gone. Shipped off to be used as test subjects. Nobody would care. Anything could happen, because nobody was watching.

I should have come up with some way to save everyone. If I'd only given it more thought, or tried harder, or—

Now I was free again, and they were not.

<*Lucky*> I said bitterly. <*We're always so* lucky, *Addie.*>

But thinking about the girls we'd abandoned at Hahns paled compared to thinking about Mom, Dad, and Lyle. I could hardly go near the thought of their disappearance—could only circle around it. Try to shield myself from it.

By the time Jackson came to find me, I was standing by the chain-link fence, fingers digging into the rusted metal, fighting the urge to shake it until the whole thing came crashing down.

He didn't ask if I was all right. Ryan would have. Addie hated that. She thought it was a sign of his lack of confidence in us—a sign of our perceived weakness.

I liked knowing someone cared enough to ask.

I missed him so badly I couldn't think straight. Not just Ryan, but Devon. I missed his steadiness. The assured way he approached everything. The dry humor he pulled out from time to time. I missed the way Hally was always ready with a smile. Lissa's unwavering loyalty. Nina's chatter about nonessential things and the way Kitty sometimes hummed the songs her brother used to play on the guitar.

"I'm sure your family is all right," Jackson said quietly.

I nodded, staring out beyond the fence, watching the way the moonlight glinted off the snow.

"Are the others with Marion?" he asked. "Peter and them, I mean. You know, I can't believe Peter agreed to let you—"

"Peter's dead," I whispered. I was already keeping one huge secret from Jackson; I couldn't handle another. Then I turned to face him, and regretted I hadn't been more gentle with the news.

Devastation marred every line of Jackson's face. Froze his

limbs as the cold wind blew between us. Softly, I told him everything he'd missed after that night in Anchoit. The traveling and hiding we'd done with Peter and the others. Marion's arrival. Henri's leaving. The news of Emalia's disappearance. The car chase, then accident as we tried to run.

Peter's death. Jaime's capture.

By the time I finished, Jackson's eyes had gone blank. He'd clenched his hands into fists, and without thinking, I reached out and put my hand over his.

He didn't speak. Neither did I. But in that moment, we understood each other perfectly.

Ben arrived. A middle-aged man with a sun-leathered face, he had a mouth so intensely flattened I felt a little jolt of surprise every time he opened it to speak.

"You're sure about her?" he said to Jackson, as if I weren't right there.

Jackson nodded. "I'm sure."

Ben didn't relax. But he nodded and unlocked the doors of his beat-up old van, and I supposed that was about as much of a *get in* as we were going to receive.

The backseat was already piled with stuff. I shoved aside a pile of clothes—jackets, pants, wrinkled shirts—and tried to find room for our feet. Jackson unrolled a sleeve of cheese-flavored crackers as if it were his and offered it to me. I glanced at Ben, but he didn't say anything, so I accepted it.

Eating crackers, jostled in beside Jackson and what looked

to be the pieces of Ben's life, I started my journey back to the rest of the world.

Ben's van shuddered to a stop, pulling me from the lull of the road and the staticky music on the radio. The car's headlights revealed an old, colonial-style house with a yellow face. Snow patched a dark, sloped roof. I sat up blearily.

"We're here," Vince said.

I'd spent most of the drive staring out the window, but the last time I'd glanced over, it had still been Jackson sitting beside me. The switch startled me. Back at Hahns, many of the girls rarely switched control from one soul to the other. Most of them I didn't know well enough to distinguish between souls, anyway.

"The place used to be a bed-and-breakfast," Vince said as we approached the front door. He grabbed the brass knocker and pounded it twice.

A little boy, maybe nine or ten years old, answered. He grinned up at Vince, then at me. "Are you the one he went to rescue? Nobody thought he could do it."

"And I didn't." Vince's smile was fainter than it might have been, but he tried. I was cataloging all the ways he was different from Jackson: he walked faster; his smile was sharper; his eyes didn't linger on me. "You don't have to tell anyone, though."

The boy stepped aside, letting the three of us come in after stomping the snow from our shoes. "This guy from all the way on the other side of the country came," he said. "He heard his brother was at Hahns. Did you see Hahns?"

Vince nodded toward me. "I didn't. She did."

The little boy looked at me, intent and solemn. "Did you see a David Birnes?"

"I—I didn't," I said. "I didn't see any of the boys. Only the girls."

The boy's mouth twisted in disappointment, but his expression quickly cleared again. "I think there's a man and a woman on the second floor who're looking for a girl who might be at Hahns. I can't remember her name, but I can go ask—"

"Whoa there," Vince said. "You can do us a favor first, Aiden."

The younger boy brightened. Straightened.

Vince glanced at me, then back at Aiden. "Remember the people I described to you? Go see if the newcomers know anything about them."

The little boy nodded, flashed a grin at me, and ran off. He rounded the corner, then disappeared up a flight of stairs.

"Everyone who comes here," Vince said as he showed me down the hall, "is looking for someone."

It wasn't a large crowd at the bed-and-breakfast. Most introduced themselves by first name only. Some didn't bother introducing themselves at all, only naming the person or people they were looking for. An elderly couple from two states over was following a lead about a granddaughter who'd been taken three years ago. A woman around my mother's age was searching for a daughter who shared her same brilliantly orange hair.

There were a few on the other side of the search. The hybrids, like Vince and me. They didn't say if they'd escaped from institutions, or had been in hiding. They were quieter.

Some, I had a feeling, recognized me. Eyes trailed after me. Gazes lingered just a little too long. I had no idea if they'd continued showing our picture on the news.

Then again, after our time at Hahns, maybe Addie and I didn't even look that much like our picture anymore. Our hair had grown out a bit, the darker roots showing through. We'd always been pale, but never as pale as this—a sickly, sallow hue that made us look ghostlike. Our limbs looked funny, the muscles atrophied. There was a darkness around our eyes.

"Probably better if you don't drop your real name," Jackson whispered in our ear. It was Jackson again now, and I almost wished it weren't. I wasn't reminded of Addie's absence every time Vince looked at me. "What did you go by at Hahns?"

But I didn't want to use Darcie's name. Darcie was a real girl, with a real family, all of whom could be hurt. So I stole the first name of a girl Addie and I had been friends with in second grade, and the last name of a boy I'd had a crush on when I was eight. For the time being, I was Morgan Shelly.

I listened to the descriptions of these missing people and tried to describe my own. Marion. Ryan. Hally. Dr. Lyanne. Henri. Emalia. I didn't actually drop any of their names, though. I doubted they were using their real ones, either. And I didn't want to run the risk of someone recognizing a name from the news alerts.

These people were supposed to be on our side. But it didn't hurt to be safe.

In the end, no one had heard any news of them. It was disappointing, but unsurprising. I hadn't heard of any of their lost loved ones, either.

<Of course> I murmured to Addie. *<We've had the disadvantage of being locked up for the past month and a half.>*

There was nothing but silence for a reply.

Perhaps, whispered a part of me that refused to be shoved aside, *perhaps from now on, there will only be silence.*

I swallowed. Fought against the sudden buzz in my ears drowning out the rest of the world. Jackson and I were in the kitchen, along with what seemed to be the rest of the house. Dinners were communal here, and people accidentally jostled one another in their search for plates and forks, or for a helping of the barbecue chicken laid out on enormous ceramic plates. Mrs. Shay, the owner of the B and B, hustled everyone along.

"Be right back," I muttered to Jackson. Or hoped I did. The words blurred a little in my mouth.

I stumbled away from him, away from the heat—the overwhelming human shove—of the kitchen and into the family room. Collapsed on the couch and drew my legs against my stomach. Covered my face with my hands. Screamed as hard as I could into the darkness where Addie was gone.

Gone.

"Hey," Jackson said. "It's all right."

My head snapped up. He must have followed me from the kitchen. He shut the glass doors behind him, sealing away the dinnertime chatter, then hovered by the couch for a second before sitting down next to me.

"Sabine used to have panic attacks, did you know?" He didn't wait for a reply, and I was thankful for it. "Christoph told me, once. They started when she was still locked away, and they lasted for months and months after she got out. But she—"

"She's gone," I whispered.

He frowned. "Sabine?"

I shook my head. Closed my eyes, but that only made things worse. I stared at the fireplace instead. It was cold, the logs blackened and dead. I focused on the whirls and crevices in the wood, the scattering of the ash.

"Addie's gone."

"What're you saying?" His voice had gone flat. It was so unlike him it was frightening.

My first instinct was to match his coldness. To bind my own emotions. Turn my insides to concrete.

"Back at Hahns," I said, "they drugged us. I don't know what with. A cocktail of things. Addie and I . . . we reacted badly. I—I was hallucinating, and . . . when I became lucid again, she was gone." I took a deep breath. Let it out. "I thought she would come back, at first. I—I thought whatever effect the medications were having, they would wear off. But the days kept passing, and now I—I don't think—"

I turned to face Jackson. Stared him right in the eye like it was the only thing in the world that could keep me steady. Here, at least, was someone who could understand a fraction of my pain. My loss.

"I don't think she's coming back," I whispered.

TWENTY-SIX

My words froze the moment. Crystallized us.

It hadn't seemed real until I said it out loud. Until I admitted it to someone else. And to myself.

I could feel my throat closing again. The rapid thrum of our heart—*my* heart.

It was only my heart now.

I didn't realize I was crying until the room began to blur. Until Jackson snapped out of his daze. For a moment, he looked nothing but helpless.

That, that of all things, I understood the most.

"You don't know for sure," Jackson said quietly, but fiercely. "You can't know for sure."

I didn't tell him how it felt in my head. How it wasn't the same at all as when Addie went under by herself.

He was Jackson. He had to keep hoping. I couldn't take that away from him.

Someone opened the door to the kitchen. People drifted out, carrying plates and looking for places to sit. Jackson turned away. Stared at nothing. Was he speaking with Vince?

Vince would know the best things to say to him. Things no one else would know, because no one else knew him so well. No one else had spent a lifetime sharing his body, seeing through shared eyes.

Addie and I had shared a life. Now, like Jaime's second soul, she was gone.

The thought of it shattered through me.

I escaped upstairs to the room Mrs. Shay had allotted us. Crawled into bed and turned off the light and lay there in the darkness feeling more alone than I ever had in my life.

Was I still hybrid?

Was I still hybrid, with Addie gone like this?

Hunger woke me. Hunger and some wide-jawed nightmare that disintegrated into confused flashes as soon as I woke, but left me trembling.

The room was dark. My bedside clock read a little after midnight. I heard the quiet rasp of Jackson's breathing. Saw the shadow of his body in the bed next to mine.

I slipped from the room and down the stairs, moving slowly in the darkness. The kitchen light was already lit. I peeked around the doorway. I must not have been as quiet as I thought I'd been, because Ben was looking right back at me. He sat at the wraparound counter, picking at a plate of leftover barbecue chicken.

"You hungry, too?" he said. When I nodded, he motioned

toward the fridge. "I can't eat with all those people running around. All the fuss."

I managed something that was not quite a smile. "You must not like restaurants."

"Not really, no," he said. "I also hate hotels, so this is an all-around pain in the ass." He stabbed a bite of chicken and waved it at me in a vaguely beckoning manner. I drifted closer, climbing on the stool next to him.

In the flurry of last night, I hadn't thought to question Jackson about the man who'd driven, with such short notice, all the way up the mountain to pick up a boy he barely knew and a girl he didn't know at all. Was he hybrid himself? Did he have family who was?

"Go ahead and ask," he said. I looked at him in surprise, and he shifted in his chair. "It's a strange change of pace, isn't it? You get it ingrained into you—*Don't mention your missing son. Don't tell people what happened to him.* Then, all of a sudden, you're surrounded by people blathering on about their own lost children, or siblings, or what-have-you, and you're expected to just . . . *share.*" He snorted. "But I won't find what I need to know by keeping silent. So ask."

"You had a son," I said cautiously.

"I had a son," he echoed. He took another bite of chicken. Chewed ponderously for a moment. "I'm hoping I *have* a son, but I'm realizing it's more and more possible that yes, I had a son and don't anymore."

"I—I'm sorry," I said. "I didn't mean—What's his name?"

"William," he said around a mouthful of chicken. "He'd be eighteen now. I'd describe to you what he looks like, but I haven't seen him since he was eleven years old, so all I can say is that he has brown eyes and brown hair and a scar on his chin from when he fell while helping me out on the ranch."

I didn't tell him how the older children disappeared at Hahns. I wasn't sure if it was the case elsewhere, and besides, he probably already knew. Perhaps William had escaped years ago. Perhaps he was roaming the shadowy parts of the country, looking for lost family.

Perhaps they'd find each other again, someday.

"From what I've overheard"—Ben gestured at me with his fork—"you're looking for two foreign-looking siblings, about your age, and some doctor lady."

I nodded. I'd mentioned everyone, but Ryan, Hally, and Dr. Lyanne were the ones I'd best been able to describe.

"I noticed you never mentioned anything about parents. Unless your mother's the doctor lady."

I shook my head. He sobered. "Already know where they are? Or just not interested in finding them?"

I hesitated. "I guess . . . I've got other things I have to do first. Before I can think about going home."

Ben shook his head. "Things to do. I should laugh at a girl your age who says that so seriously. But things have been different these past couple months. Those people who blew up the Powatt institution were only kids, too."

I kept my expression neutral.

“Place I was staying before here,” Ben continued, “there was a little girl, barely older than that Aiden kid, running around by herself. Said she was trying to find her family. Find her brother.” He gave a low laugh. “How many of us do you think will actually find who we’re looking for? What will happen to that girl, if she doesn’t? Who will take her in? Even a pretty little fairy-looking child like her.”

I froze. “What was her name? The girl?”

Ben frowned. “You think you know her brother?”

“I—” I grabbed the counter to steady myself. “Just—what was her name?”

“I wouldn’t normally remember,” Ben said. “But it was easy enough—Kitty.”

TWENTY-SEVEN

I spent the rest of the night pestering Ben for everything he remembered about Kitty and Nina. He promised me she'd seemed fine. Quiet, mostly, but determined. She'd arrived shortly after he did, riding in with a woman she didn't seem to know. The woman had left again soon after, but Kitty stayed, asking for news of her brother. Ben got the impression that the man used to live nearby, but perhaps didn't anymore, prompting Kitty's search.

He had no idea why she was alone.

After Ben went to bed, I stayed in the kitchen a little longer, just thinking. I grabbed the phone off the counter and dialed Henri's satphone number again, echoing the *beep* of every digit with *Please, Please, Please.*

Please work.

It didn't.

You were supposed to fix it, Ryan, I thought desperately. *Why haven't you fixed it?*

I was back in our room when Jackson woke hours later,

rocketing up with a gasp and a shudder. He recovered quickly. Closed his eyes and fell back against his pillow.

It wasn't until he opened his eyes the second time that he noticed me sitting cross-legged on the other bed.

"Hey," I said.

"Hey," he replied, just as softly. "You were already asleep when I came up last night."

"I guess I was tired," I said, and he nodded. "I was talking to Ben, and he mentioned Kitty."

Jackson sat up. "He's seen her? He didn't say anything to me. Where were—"

"She was at the safe house in Grental Plains," I said. "And she was alone. But that was weeks ago. He doesn't know where the others could be—or why she isn't with them. I called the satphone again, but it's still not working."

"It's still a better lead than I've been able to come up with," Jackson said, just as I said, "*Everything's in pieces.*"

My voice shook, but I had to say it—had to tell someone, and there was no one else. "Sometimes, I wonder . . . if we hadn't done what we did at Lankster and Powatt. Then, well—things wouldn't be like they are now. We'd all still be in Anchoit. We'd all be together. Peter would still be—"

"Don't, Eva," Jackson said softly. "You can't go back and analyze everything. We couldn't have known any of it would lead to any of this." I tried to interrupt, but he continued over me in a rush. "Besides, if we hadn't done what we did, maybe none of the rest of it would have happened, either. All this change—all this talk about hybrids that was buried before. People are speaking out like they haven't in decades. That's good, isn't it? It might all be a mess right now, but at least when things are messy, it means they aren't sure. And that means they might change. I—I'm not saying it was *worth it*, or that it all balances out, or anything like that. Just . . ." I felt his agitation as keenly as if it were mine. "It's happened. There's no regretting it now."

I didn't bring up Addie, and neither did he. Maybe we both knew there was nothing more we could say about it.

It was enough that we both knew. And both understood.

He pushed aside his blankets. "Grental Plains is at least a six- or seven-hour drive. I don't think I have enough money to get us there on our own. Let's see if anyone's headed in that direction soon. There's that couple two doors down, and I think I heard them say—"

I took a deep breath, and he looked up, halting midramble. He grinned. It was shakier than it had been, before Powatt. Before everything. But that was understandable.

I loved it a little more, for the shakiness. For the crack in it that mirrored the cracks I could feel in every part of me. We were both holding ourselves together.

"We'll get her back," he said, and I nodded.

I didn't ask him which *her* he was talking about.

The couple Jackson had mentioned, Frank and Elizabeth, were in fact headed toward Grental Plains. They planned to leave the next day, which left me an entire twenty-four hours to worry and stress. I knew an extra day wouldn't make much of a difference, considering it had already been weeks since Ben left Grental Plains. But I couldn't shake the feeling that we couldn't afford to waste another minute, let alone another day.

I tried to keep myself busy. After the desolation of Hahns, the small bed-and-breakfast was a circus. Mrs. Shay was thankful for someone to help out. I wasn't much of a cook, but I liked to be with her in the kitchen. Liked to have her smile at me and tell me I made life a little easier.

It wasn't until noon, when I went into the pantry to get a can of beans and saw the calendar hanging on a hook, that I realized.

Vince was the one who found me standing there, frozen.

"What?" He peered over my shoulder. "Found a goblin hiding in here?" He grinned at me, but I didn't smile back.

"I'm sixteen," I said.

His eyes shifted to mine. "What?"

"It was my birthday," I said numbly. "Two days ago. December fourteenth. I didn't realize."

His grin widened. "Happy belated birthday."

But it wasn't.

My sixteenth birthday was the first one in my entire life I hadn't celebrated with Addie.

We left right after lunch the next day, when most of the house's occupants were still gathered in the kitchen, helping clean up. I waited in the foyer while Frank and Elizabeth packed their meager luggage into the trunk. Mrs. Shay wanted to send us off with extra food, and Vince had gone to help her with it.

The other tenants of the safe house had surprised me with a new set of clothes, culled from their own suitcases. Mrs. Shay gave me a proper pair of shoes—worn, but exactly the right size, and much better protection against the elements and the cold ground. Elizabeth handed me two shirts that were slightly too big, and a pair of pants I cinched with one of Ben's belts.

Ben found me standing alone. "Find the girl," he said.

"I will," I promised, and added, "Good luck. With finding William, I mean."

He nodded. Mrs. Shay and Vince returned with plastic bags full of leftovers, and what snacks she could spare. She pressed one bag into my hands, then kissed me on the cheek so gently tears sprung into my eyes.

I'd blinked them away by the time I climbed into the backseat next to Vince. Then I had to do it all over again when I shuffled through the bag of individually wrapped sandwiches and found a small white envelope containing a wrinkled ten-dollar bill.

Grental Plains reminded me of Lupside. The suburb we pulled into, after hours on the road, could have fit easily next to my old neighborhood, but for the style of the houses. They were all one-story and spread out, with wide roofs and boxy exteriors.

It was already dark. We navigated by streetlights and a yellow moon.

"Here?" My voice was hushed. "Are you sure? Where is everyone?"

The house we'd pulled up to was barely bigger than mine had been. The driveway was clear of cars.

"They're probably directing parking elsewhere," Elizabeth said over her shoulder. "It would be suspicious to have a mess of cars by their house all the time."

Vince slipped from the van to go ring the doorbell and ask. I watched as he spoke briefly with a man at the door, then came back to the car and told us to park at a shopping center down the road.

Elizabeth insisted I get out here, too, to save me the walk back. From the way she glanced at me, I guessed I still seemed sickly.

The man who owned the house was named Lucas, and he barely looked old enough to be out of college. He rented the house from his uncle, who he assured us lived across the state and would never show up unexpectedly to check on him. I could tell the setup still made Vince nervous. He kept glancing toward the door as Lucas explained that there weren't any more beds or couches, but plenty of floor space, and pillows, if we had sleeping bags.

"Actually," I said hesitantly as he offered to show us around, "we're looking for someone. A girl named Kitty? She's eleven. Short. She's got really long, dark hair—"

Lucas's face brightened. "Kitty. Yes—but she left about a week ago, headed for Brindt. She was looking for her brother, Ty. Guitar player. She heard from someone that he'd moved there a few months ago, was playing downtown at some of the bars . . ." His voice drifted off at my obvious disappointment; he added, quickly, "There's a bus that goes from here to Brindt. Won't take more than a few hours. But I don't think there'll be one running this late. You'll have to wait until tomorrow."

We'd missed Kitty by a week. So in the end, the extra day we'd stayed at the bed-and-breakfast hadn't made any difference—we'd have missed her no matter what.

But every second we delayed meant something. This time, we'd missed Kitty by a week, but next time? Next time, it might be an hour, or thirty minutes, or less.

It only took a minute for someone to get into a car. Ten minutes for her to be miles and miles away.

TWENTY-EIGHT

That night, I woke up, not because of my nightmares, but because of Jackson's. As soon as he climbed to his feet, my eyes fluttered open, too. The living room was completely dark. I had no idea what time it was. But I sat up and whispered, "Jackson?"

I could hear the rasp of his breathing, as if he'd been running and couldn't catch his breath.

"I just want to go outside a bit," he murmured.

"Can I come with you?" I asked, and he hesitated, then nodded.

We crept from the house, opening and closing the front door as quietly as we could, grabbing our jackets on the way out. The night was frigidly cold. It woke me up with a shudder of icy air.

Jackson shivered, too, but didn't say anything about going back in. If anything, he seemed to relish the alertness the chill brought with it. We moved away from the house, wandering through the neighborhood. I looked at all the darkened windows, imagining the families sleeping behind them, marveling at their peace.

Jackson glanced at me. The cold gave everything an urgency and clarity. The nearest streetlight was half a block away, but it seemed like it was the brightest thing I'd ever known.

Back at the B and B, I'd caught Jackson looking at me like this, sometimes. As if he was searching for some trace of Addie in the way I walked, or sliced an apple, or mopped a spill.

I'd watched him, too. I'd tried to see him the way Addie had seen him. I tried to see the *world* the way Addie would have seen it. To become her, for a little while. Just a moment. As if that would bring her back.

I understood, a little more, how Addie could have fallen in love with this boy. More than that, I understood *him*. When he stared off at nothing, I understood. When he startled at a touch on his shoulder, I understood. When he buried everything underneath a smile, I understood.

"What would you do if all this ended tomorrow?" he asked.

"What do you mean?" I wasn't sure if it was the cold, the fact that I'd been so abruptly woken, or a combination of both and other, unnameable things, but I felt at once like I was in a dream, and like I was the most awake I'd ever been.

"If tomorrow, there was suddenly nothing wrong with being hybrid. And everyone accepted it, and you could just be like everyone else, what would you do?" He spoke in a whisper. We didn't want to disturb anyone. But there was also no knowing who might be listening. Who might hear these words, so innocently spoken, and hunt us for them.

"I'd be like everyone else," I said.

His lips twitched. "Would that be enough?"

"I don't know," I said. "I've never done it. But it would be a start, and then I could go on from there." I looked away, back to surveying the darkness. "To be honest, I can barely think about it. It seems so distant. There's so much to do."

"But what's the point of doing it, if you aren't dreaming about the outcome?" He sounded so earnest.

"What if all the dreaming gets in the way of actually doing things? What if there isn't time for dreaming?"

"There's always time for dreaming," Jackson said. "If it makes you happy, then there's time."

"I guess." I smiled, just a little. "You're always full of little bits of wisdom, aren't you?"

"Except Powatt," he said, and I nodded.

"Except Powatt," I said solemnly. "Because God, that was stupid."

There was a beat of silence. Then Jackson started to laugh. He laughed until I was laughing, too, both of us half-hunched over, cracking up like madmen, gasping for air. Slowly, my laughter quieted to giggles, then a gasping sort of smile.

We looked at each other. The moonlight and the streetlight mixed and cast darting highlights in his hair, odd shadows on his face.

I wanted to kiss him.

I wanted to kiss him, and the wanting felt normal. Felt right. I was reaching up, on tiptoe, my lips a hairsbreadth from his before I even knew what was going on.

He froze.

I froze, too.

He wasn't breathing. If he'd been breathing, I would have felt him against my skin—I was that close.

I backed away. Pressed my fingers to my temples, trying to drive my thoughts into straight lines, press my emotions back into familiar territory. Iron them straight.

Addie, I thought. These were Addie's feelings—they had to be Addie's feelings. But when I cried out for her—shouted for her in the quiet of my mind—there was nothing but silence and echoes.

"Sorry," I said, and my voice wavered at the end. "I—I don't—"

I didn't look at him. He didn't say anything.

"We could pretend that didn't happen," I whispered, and forced my eyes to search for his. After a moment, I caught them.

He stared at me. At me. Through me.

His voice was hoarse. "Is she really gone, Eva?"

My throat tightened. "Why—why would I say she was, if she wasn't?"

He broke eye contact. Shook his head. "I don't know. I guess I just—when you—"

"It was a mistake," I said shakily. My heart tried to convince me it was more than that. That it had been a sign. Proof that Addie still existed somewhere inside this body, sleeping but living. But try as I might, I didn't feel the slightest hint of her.

Was it only my imagination?

I didn't want to believe Addie was gone.

My heart would do anything it could to convince me she wasn't.

A car zoomed by, music thudding. The bass shuddered all the way through my bones.

"Just a mistake," Jackson echoed.

I was so shaken that I didn't immediately notice the second car when it turned into the neighborhood. Didn't realize how it was cruising toward us without any lights on.

Then I did, and I yanked Jackson deeper into the shadows. "*Police.*"

My first instinct was to head back to the house—Jackson's was to run the other way. Our hands were still linked. We pulled each other to a stop.

"We have to warn them," I whispered.

He tried to tug me away. "Too late—by the time we wake them up, the police will have the place surrounded."

He was stronger than I was, but I kept resisting, and finally, he stopped pulling at me. I looked over my shoulder. A second police car had arrived, as quietly as the first. Who had tipped them off? A suspicious neighbor? Lucas's uncle?

It hardly mattered now. Not to the people sleeping

obliviously inside that house—who'd wake to someone breaking down the door.

Jackson was right. We were too far away, and we'd have to go back in by the front door—right in the view of the police cars. Most likely, we'd only succeed in waking up half the house before we were all arrested.

But that was only *most likely*. So much of me rebelled at the idea of running away when there was even the slightest chance of saving them. I was no stranger to small possibilities—my existence, my entire life, had been a series of small possibilities, of risks taken.

"Eva," Jackson whispered. "We can't."

The police car doors opened.

I could save them. I could maybe save them. Risk everything—the chance to find Kitty again, Ryan again—help Emalia and Jaime and Bridget.

"You're right," I whispered. I swallowed. Turned away from the house and tried to ignore the pain carving holes in my heart. "Let's go."

We focused on stealth at first, keeping to the shadows, trying to stay silent. Then the shouting started—the screaming and the banging—and we abandoned stealth and put everything into speed.

We ran as fast as we could. Out of the neighborhood. Along the silent, deserted suburban roads. We ran until we couldn't run anymore, and then we walked. Anything to get as far away from that no-longer-safe house, and the police, and my own guilt. First Peter and Jaime, then the other girls at Hahns, and now this. Somehow, I kept running away. I kept leaving people behind.

"There wasn't anything we could do," Jackson said, once the silence between us became stifling.

"I know," I said.

But was it a lie? A platitude I told myself, because I hadn't been brave enough to stay?

The sun came up slowly, a line of yellow on the horizon that seeped upward into the passing clouds. By daybreak, neither Jackson nor I had any idea where we were. We risked ducking into a gas station to grab a map of the area and find the bus station. Turned out, it was on the other side of town.

"I don't like this," Jackson muttered as we huddled in our jackets and hurried through the streets. "We stand out too much."

We did. It had been better in the darkness. Now, with the sun up, there were more cars on the road, but almost no one else out walking. Thank God neither of us owned pajamas, and had slept in our regular clothes. Mrs. Shay's ten-dollar bill was tucked safely into my pants pocket.

By the time we finally made it to the bus station, I was a bundle of frozen nerves. The sight of the old station, bearing the vestiges of blue-and-white paint, was like waking up from a bad dream. We hurried inside, where the blast of warmth made me shudder, made me rush to take a lungful of air that wouldn't stab its way through my lungs.

The woman working the counter barely looked up. She was too busy flipping through stations on her television, a squat little thing that kept fuzzing into static every other channel.

"I'll get the tickets," I said to Jackson. "I look less like myself than you do."

He looked like he was going to protest, but I was already headed for the counter. When I glanced at him over my shoulder, he was looking at me worriedly, but stayed where he was.

I had a sudden memory of the press of his mouth. His fingers tangled in my hair. It had been dark when I woke up that day in his room, back in Anchoit. But I remembered the blue of his eyes when the lights came on. That day, I'd found out about him and Addie, and I'd been furious about it then. I'd flinched away.

But last night—

<I wasn't myself last night> I whispered to Addie. It was the first time I'd spoken to her since admitting to Jackson that she was gone. *<I didn't want to be me. I wanted to be you.>*

There was, as there had been since Hahns, no reply.

"Where to?" the woman at the counter asked. She'd let the TV settle on the national news channel, one of the few that reached almost everywhere with good clarity. I tried not to look at it, terrified it might broadcast a report about me. Three days had passed since my escape from Hahns. Had Jenson been notified?

"Brindt," I said. "Two tickets, please. When's the earliest bus?"

She was just about to answer when the television plunged into static again. She sighed and slapped her palm against the side of it. The second slap snapped the picture back.

But it wasn't the news station anymore. Both the ticket woman and I stared at—

At Henri.

TWENTY-NINE

Henri was alive.

Henri was alive—and overseas. He'd made it back. He said as much. He stared out from the fuzzy television screen in this dingy bus station and explained how he'd come to the Americas in secret to see the inside of a country so long hidden from the rest of the world. How he'd discovered the lies that the people learned here—in schools, in newspapers, in stories.

"The world beyond your shores," he said in that now-familiar, lilting accent of his, "is not what you believe it is. Not what your government tells you it is."

He said he'd show us the truth.

But my eyes had been drawn to something else. In the very corner of the screen, nearly hidden from view under one of Henri's papers, was a quarter-sized chip. It flashed faintly red.

It looked like my chip. Or Ryan's. Not exactly, and it couldn't be, since ours were not with Henri. But someone had gone through some trouble to make a replica. To catch my attention.

The flashing was irregular. Like—

Like Morse code.

C

A

L

L

It flashed once, then again.

Call.

And then it flashed a different message—something long that I didn't recognize until it looped back again. A string of numbers.

A phone number.

The video changed. Cut to a young man who spoke a language we didn't understand. He was standing on a street corner, smiling at the camera. Waving our attention toward a city we'd never seen, full of enormous, shimmering billboards and unfamiliar lights. Then another video. Another person. Women. Men. Children. Cities and towns, schools and homes and dinner tables and birthday parties and strangers so eager to share their world with us. Some spoke English. Some didn't.

It cut off sharply. Back to static. Had someone at the station wrestled back control? Overridden something to cut off the video?

The ticket lady and I stared at the snowy screen like it might reveal more secrets. Then the woman leaned back against her chair, as if shaking herself from a dream.

"*Well*." She didn't seem to know what else to say. Her eyes found mine. "That was obviously fake, wasn't it?"

"What?" I breathed. I was repeating the string of numbers again and again in my mind, imprinting them into my memory. But I kept getting distracted by the footage that had followed Henri's appearance—visual proof of what seemed like another world.

"The footage, darling," she said, as if she thought me a bit slow. She frowned. "You all right?"

A hand closed on my shoulder. I jumped, whirling around—but it was only Jackson. He smiled at the woman. "I think the broadcast kind of threw her."

"Yes—" I said quickly, finding my voice. "I just—it was so weird. And all these broadcast hijackings. It makes me nervous. I just—I wonder what they're going to do next, you know? Who they are—"

"Foreigners, of course." Her eyebrows lifted into her hairline. "This has just gone and confirmed it, hasn't it? It's all foreign propaganda, trying to . . . well, God knows exactly what they're up to. It's got to do with hybrids, whatever it is." She eyed me. "But if you're worried about all that, you shouldn't be heading into Brindt. That's where the trouble is now."

I wondered if she'd ever know about the safe house only a few minutes' drive away. How close *trouble* had brushed to her own life.

"What's going on in Brindt?" Jackson said.

"Anarchy," she said. "Protestors and vandalism and people scared out of their wits. My sister lives there. Her son had to quit his basketball team because she doesn't want him out on the streets any more than he has to be." She looked back at me. "The next bus leaves in half an hour. Do you want your tickets or not?"

"We'll come back later," I said before Jackson could say *yes.*

Jackson hid his confusion well. He smiled again at the woman, then walked with me back to the station door. I waited until I was sure no one was listening. Then I told him about the message hidden in the broadcast.

I'd started grinning, and I couldn't stop. Henri was alive and well. Ryan and the others must have gotten in contact with him. I had a new number.

Jackson hurried with me to the nearest phone booth. Thankfully, he had a few coins. He propped the door open, leaning against it to keep it ajar, while I made the call.

We were both utterly still as the phone rang.

Then the ringing stopped. I heard the *clack* that signaled the line had connected.

No one spoke.

The silence stretched. Jackson mouthed *what?* and if I didn't speak now, I might get disconnected.

I said, in a rush of breath—"Hello?"

"Eva?"

He had to say it a second time before I managed to respond. And even then, all I could say was, "*Yes*—yes, it's me."

I took a sharp breath that was half laughter, half the beginning of ridiculously embarrassing tears.

"Eva, are you all right?" Ryan Mullan said, and it was like pieces of my world finally shifted back to their proper places. Like there had been something cramping up my lungs for weeks upon weeks, and I hadn't realized—hadn't truly noticed how bad it was until suddenly I could breathe freely again.

"I'm fine." I laughed and clapped my hand over my mouth, startled by the sound of it. I forced my hand down. "Are you? Is everyone?"

"Everyone's great," he said. I could hear the relief in his voice. And then I could hear someone else—a girl saying, *Ryan, is it her?*

"Is that Hally?" I couldn't remember the last time I'd felt so light.

"Where are they?" Jackson smiled, too, but it didn't completely cover up the anxiousness in his eyes.

Ryan asked me the exact same question.

"I'm in Grental Plains," I said. "Where are you? Is Kitty with you?"

"You heard about Kitty?" The tension in Ryan's voice was immediate. *Where?* Hally demanded in the background, but he shushed her. "From who? What did you hear?"

I told him about Ben, and the story he'd passed on to me.

He was quiet a moment. Long enough for me to say, "How did she get separated from you guys?" and then to regret it.

I couldn't see his face, but I heard the guilt clearly enough when Ryan said, "We're in Brindt now. Her brother's here somewhere. We'll find her."

"They're in Brindt," I whispered to Jackson.

"Who's with you?" Ryan asked.

I hesitated. "Jackson."

"Oh," Ryan said. There was a pause—Hally was talking again, or maybe it was her and someone else. He spoke over them. "Did he help you out of Hahns?"

I started to reply, but a clear sentence finally broke through the background mumbling, cutting me off: *Don't stay on too long. Tell her where to meet us.*

"Dr. Lyanne." I hadn't even meant to say it. I discovered I was starving for the sight of her. For the reassurance of her sharp features, her thin mouth. There was a shuffling sound, as if the phone had exchanged hands.

"How quickly can you get here?" Dr. Lyanne said, all business. If I hadn't known her like I did, I might have been hurt by her lack of sentiment. But I did know her, and right now, it helped. It made me shove my own emotions into order.

"A few hours," I said. "We're right near a bus station, and the next bus leaves in thirty minutes."

"We'll meet you at the station here," Dr. Lyanne said.

I nodded, was just about to say, *Yes, okay,* when she spoke again.

"It's good to hear from you, Eva."

Then she was gone again, Ryan back at the phone. "We can't keep the line open," he said, the words rushed.

"I'll get the bus tickets now," I said—I still had so much more to say. "I'll be at the station—"

"I'll be waiting," he said.

I gripped the phone and smiled like I'd never stop smiling again. Not for the rest of my life.

"See you soon, Eva," he said.

"See you soon," I said, and waited for him to hang up, because I wasn't about to. Even after he had, I listened to the beeping signaling the disconnected call.

My eyes darted up, to Jackson's face. To say I'd forgotten about his presence wouldn't be entirely true. More like I'd gotten lost. I'd disappeared for a few seconds, somewhere not only without Jackson, but without the phone booth, or the road we were standing on, or the entire city surrounding us.

Where there was nothing but the phone connecting me and the boy who'd once whispered stories as I lay immobile on his couch, fighting my way back from the life of a ghost. I remembered the grip of his hand anchoring me to the world. I remembered the first time I'd opened my eyes under my own control and seen him looking back.

<I miss him, Addie> I said, with a dizzy, giddy sort of feeling. *<God, I miss him.>*

And finally, I was going back to him.

THIRTY

The bus pulled up to the station an agonizing twelve minutes late, brakes screeching in a way I suspected meant there was something wrong with them. But at this point, I'd have climbed into a bus with three wheels, if it could still get me to Brindt.

Jackson and I found seats together, then waited another excruciating ten minutes for everyone else to board. My heart pounded out the seconds.

Finally, we were on our way. I stared out the streaked window, watching the suburbs tumble by before we hit the highway. I'd been on so many highways the last few months. So much traveling.

It was strange. I'd hardly ever traveled before. It wasn't until I had to go into hiding—until I was on the run—that I even started seeing my own country.

After the tiny tourist town I'd stumbled into outside of Hahns, the secluded bed-and-breakfast, and the quiet suburbia of Grental Plains, entering Brindt was a shock. Skyscrapers erupted around us, looming and gleaming silver. Billboards rose from the ground. People thronged the streets.

We passed store windows pasted with holiday ornaments, signs blaring sale prices and free in-store wrapping. I felt strangely removed from it all. My birthday. The holidays. They'd lost meaning in the face of everything else.

The bus squealed to a stop at the station. I stared out the window, but didn't see anyone I recognized.

"Maybe they're inside," Jackson said.

"Maybe," I said, but didn't really believe it. Ryan wouldn't want to wait inside, where he couldn't see our arrival.

Finally, it was our turn to disembark. We tumbled out into the street. I turned in all directions. Looking. Searching.

"I don't see them." Jackson kept close to me as the other passengers peeled away, some reuniting with friends or family, others heading down the street to hail taxis.

I didn't either.

Until I did.

Hally, first. Hally—or maybe it was Lissa—she was still too far away to tell. She'd bundled up her hair under a woolen, cream-colored hat. Jackson turned at my gasp. I tried to say something—could only grin. Arms wrapped around my shoulders from behind, pulling me into a hug that sent my heart lurching.

"Found you," Ryan said, a whisper in my ear.

And then I really couldn't speak at all.

* * *

Eventually, I found my voice again. By then, Hally had reached us, too. It was Hally by the bounce in her step and the glint in her eyes—by the way she pulled me from Ryan without apology and crushed me in a hug of her own.

"This isn't safe," I kept saying. "You shouldn't both be here. What if someone sees—"

Ryan smiled. "That's what everyone said. But then we all came anyway."

"Everyone?" Jackson said.

"Dr. Lyanne's a little ways down the street." Ryan didn't sound friendly, exactly, but he looked at Jackson when he spoke to him, which was an improvement over the last time they'd talked.

"She's with the car." Hally, at least, grinned at Jackson—though really, she was just grinning constantly. "We should head back, before she worries."

Ryan and Hally sandwiched me between them as we hurried from the station to a beat-up old car I didn't recognize. But I did recognize the woman sitting behind the wheel. She'd tied her long, brown hair back. She didn't smile. Just unlocked the doors and said, "Any trouble?" when Hally pulled the front one open.

"No," Hally said cheerfully.

Dr. Lyanne nodded. "Well, get in. Hurry up."

"Where's Marion?" Jackson said. He was the last one to enter the car, and he hesitated as if he feared Ryan wouldn't move over to let him in. Ryan did, of course, but Jackson's unease didn't fade. "Have you been with her this whole time?"

I didn't miss the way Dr. Lyanne's eyes briefly met Ryan's in the rearview mirror. "Not the whole time, but almost."

"We can talk about that later, can't we?" Hally said, twisting around in her seat to face us. Her expression was stubbornly happy. *What would she say,* I thought, *if she knew about Addie?* Would she be able to force a smile, even then? I swallowed hard.

"We won't have the chance to talk about it later." Ryan's fingers were entwined with mine. He hadn't released me since the bus station. "Marion's waiting at the hotel."

"What about Wendy?" I asked.

"Marion couldn't send her home. Not after the broadcast. But she didn't want to keep dragging her around, either. So she dropped her off someplace safe." He paused. "She claims so, anyway."

Hally was quiet. Everyone was quiet for a moment, until I broke the silence. "Do you know where Kitty is?"

"Here, we hope," Dr. Lyanne said as she pulled away from the curb.

"Her oldest brother's here, anyway," Hally said. "But it doesn't seem like the rest of her siblings are. Marion has a contact who says they split up a little while after . . . well, after Kitty was taken. All the younger kids live with an aunt or something. But Ty moved here."

I knew the rough edges of Kitty and Nina's past. Their parents had passed years before, leaving them in the care of an aunt. Ty, the oldest, had moved out as soon as he was able. More than anything else, Kitty had liked to talk about Ty's guitar playing. How he'd begun to teach her. How he'd promised to keep teaching her.

Ryan explained how Kitty and Nina had slipped away while the group was near Grental Plains. The guilt I'd heard on the phone was back, and his hand tightened around mine. She'd talked endlessly about how close they were to her old home, but no one had thought she'd actually run off. They'd feared she'd been taken, at first. But asking around the nearby safe house had revealed her intentions.

So they'd come to Brindt in hopes of finding Tyler Holynd—and by extension, Kitty and Nina. But it wasn't a simple matter. Ty wasn't listed in any phone book. Even Marion, with all her connections, hadn't been able to unearth an address.

"We think he's part of the resistance here," Hally said. We'd hit the main road, squeezing and weaving our way through traffic.

"It's hardly a resistance," Dr. Lyanne replied. "Just a bunch of kids tagging buildings with graffiti and pasting up posters. Scaring people and putting themselves in danger for nothing."

"Not for nothing," Ryan said calmly. Dr. Lyanne sighed, but didn't argue. "Point is, it won't be as easy, but we'll still find him."

"Marion's circling in on where the resistance might be

headquartered," Hally said. "So if Ty really is with them—"

"Marion cares about finding Kitty?" Jackson said.

"I think she just wants the story." Ryan sounded more bitter than I'd ever heard him. "You know: *Eleven-year-old Girl Reunites with Brave Protestor.* Better yet if someone gets shot."

The callousness of the words, even spoken in irony, surprised me. It seemed like something Devon might have said, only this wasn't Devon.

Ryan had changed, too, in the almost two months we'd been apart. I didn't know how I could have been self-absorbed enough to think I'd be the only one. That somehow, the people I'd left behind would be the same when we reunited.

I'd spent weeks and weeks cooped up in an institution. But Ryan had been out here, in the thick of things. Watching as the country changed.

"Has it gotten that bad?" I said quietly. "Have people gotten hurt?"

Hally nodded. She'd grown subdued as well.

"It'll be fine," Ryan said. He held up my hand to get a better look at the ring around my finger, then laughed. I'd missed hearing him laugh. "You didn't have to keep wearing it. Marion will want to extract the data, anyway."

"I'll give it to her," I said. "But then I want it back. I like it."

"You've certainly earned the right to it," Ryan said.

Hally rolled her eyes and leaned over to whisper in my ear. "I *told* him it's awfully presumptuous to engrave your own initials on a ring to give a girl. *Especially* when she can't possibly refuse it since it's doubling as a top secret spy camera."

I stifled laughter.

Ryan shot his sister a suspicious look. "What?"

"Nothing, brother dearest," she said primly. Then winked at me.

THIRTY-ONE

The hotel where they were staying was in a quieter sector of the city. The buildings here weren't quite as shining, the streets more meandering than bustling. Dr. Lyanne dropped us off, then went to find parking.

I glanced at Jackson as we walked into the lobby. He was subdued, fading into the background despite his height. Hally filled up the silence, chattering away as we headed for the rooms. They were on the first floor—Dr. Lyanne didn't want us trapped upstairs if anything went wrong.

Hally looped her arm around mine. "You'll stay with Ryan and me. Dr. Lyanne and Marion have been taking the other room."

"Does that leave me with them?" Jackson said it jokingly, but not quite jokingly enough.

"Of course not," she said, a little too quickly. "You can fit with us, too. There's an armchair and everything—not that you have to sleep there, I mean. I could. There're only two beds. We'd have to—"

"I can sleep anywhere," Jackson said, smile crooked. "It doesn't matter."

Ryan stopped us in front of a room before anyone could say anything else. He was just about to unlock it when the door swung open.

And there was Marion, looking just as I remembered with her pale brown hair and stark features. She tried to smile at me and nearly succeeded, the delicate lines of her face almost comical in their uneasy rearrangement. "I heard you all talking. Come in."

I'd expected to be furious when I came face-to-face with Marion again, but instead, I just felt sick. We filed inside, awkward and quiet. I missed the easy exuberance at the bus station.

"There was food," Marion said, looking everywhere now but me. Or Jackson, for that matter. "I can't remember where—"

"It's in our room," Ryan said. "I'll get it."

"I'll come with you," I said quickly, and thankfully, no one else offered to help as well.

We slipped out the door, Ryan leading the way down the hall until we found the second room. He shut the door behind us, and I was just about to joke that Hally and Lissa hadn't gotten any neater over the months, when he spun to face me.

"I didn't know she was going to do it, Eva." He spoke with such urgency I stopped in my tracks. "I had no idea. I wouldn't have let her—"

"I believe you," I said.

He fell quiet. The takeout bag was on the dresser, but neither of us reached for it. "Did they hurt you?"

Did they hurt me?

I tried to answer, but couldn't. It was like a rubber stopper had slammed into my throat.

Yes. Yes, they hurt me. They hurt me in the worst possible way. They stole the most precious thing I had.

Ryan was immediately concerned. "Eva? What is it—what did they do?"

"Do you remember what Emalia told us?" I whispered. We'd sat down on one of the beds. "About how hybrids could only go under for a few hours—half a day at most?"

He nodded, his confusion palpable.

The blankets rumpled in my fists. "Addie's been gone for more than a week."

I told him, haltingly, about the medication and the delirium and the loneliness that had greeted me upon waking. I had to force the words out—because the words led to memories, the memories to the aftershocks of pain and confused terror.

Ryan stood. Pushed his hand through his hair and paced to the dresser and back again and then just stared down at me like he didn't know what else to do.

"God, Eva," he said hoarsely.

"I didn't tell them what they'd done," I whispered. "They don't know. So they won't do it again to someone else."

"She'll come back—"

"It's been more than a *week*." I'd started to shake. "What if she's just gone? What if I'm alone for the rest of my life—"

He sat down next to me. Cupped my face. "I can't say for certain that Addie's going to come back. But I can tell you right now: you're not going to be alone."

When he kissed me, I believed it. I wanted to believe it. More than anything.

I closed my eyes. "I love you. You know that?"

At first I was afraid he wouldn't say it back. I was afraid, and I was afraid, and then he did. He said it with such clarity and such certainty that I didn't understand how I could ever have feared at all.

By the time Ryan and I rejoined the others, Dr. Lyanne had returned from parking the car. Her eyes lingered on me as the takeout boxes went around. It was the same way she'd studied Addie and me during the days after the explosion at Powatt, as the aftereffects of our injuries slowly made themselves known.

She wasn't the only one whose gaze I felt too strongly. Jackson looked away when I tried to meet his eyes. "Dr. Lyanne was just telling us about how Henri got them another phone," he said.

I looked to Ryan. We'd hurried back with the food before someone came to check on us, and now I had a feeling we were both acting suspiciously overcasual. "How did he contact you?"

"With much hassle," Ryan said wryly. He explained how Henri had panicked when he'd returned overseas and found he could no longer call them through the satphone. It had taken weeks, but eventually, he'd managed to track down their whereabouts through mutual connections and send another phone.

After that, it had been a matter of letting me know the new number. I imagined revealing our overseas connection to Marion had been a hard decision to make, but the woman seemed more thrilled and excited about it than anything else.

"We had to find some way to hide it in a broadcast," Marion said. "The others assured me you knew Morse code, so we snuck it into a video of Henri. The footage from overseas was a bit of a rush job." She sounded genuinely regretful about it, like it had been a piece of art that could, with more time, be refined and edited into a more powerful work. "But it did what it was meant to do."

She turned to me, and her smile faded a little. Her eyes, though, were unnervingly sincere. "It was your recordings from Hahns that helped Henri solicit footage. So in a way, you aided in your own rescue."

I stared at her in disbelief. "None of that had anything to do with my rescue."

She didn't even know the girls who'd made my escape possible. Who'd put themselves in danger for me. The room fell silent. We regarded each other, Marion and I.

"Henri's footage is already causing an uproar," Dr. Lyanne

said. “And it’s not going to get calmer anytime soon. If Ty’s connected to the group making trouble here in Brindt, he’s going to find himself in jail, if he isn’t careful.”

“We’ll find him before anything happens,” Hally said, but I could read the discomfort on her face. “Kitty, too.”

“It was bound to get complicated.” Marion broke our eye contact. “It’s revolution.”

Back in the attic above the photography shop, Addie and I had dreamed about revolution. It had always seemed like a frightening thing. Like a wave that picked up speed until it went utterly out of control, smashing everything in its way into bits. There was nothing but the fervent prayer that what rose from the rubble would be better than what stood there before.

It wasn’t, always. That much I knew for sure.

After all, once upon a time, the single-souled rebelled against the hybrid, and formed the Americas.

In the wake of Henri’s recent broadcast, the furor over hybrids took a sharp, foreign turn. The news filled with “proof” that Henri’s footage had been faked—everything from the fact that parts of the backdrops were *clearly* two-dimensional, to the idea that the video had actually been taken here, in the Americas. I wasn’t sure how anybody was supposed to believe that, since I’d seen technology in that footage that was far beyond anything I’d glimpsed in our homes or streets. But it was a big country, and most people lived relatively isolated, regional lives. I supposed they could be convinced.

Sometimes, I feared we'd just strengthened antiforeign sentiment. Or fear, anyway, when fear and hatred went so smoothly hand in hand. But we were trying to inject the truth into a country that had buried it for so long. I supposed there was bound to be an uncomfortable reaction, like a fever that had to burn out before recovery.

For now, though, it meant that keeping a low profile was paramount, and any attempt to reach out to Ty had to be done carefully. Another wave of vandalism cropped up. Stores had their windows smashed and their walls covered in graffiti. Now, in addition to railing against the government, the hybrid institutionalization, and the cure, the dripping, spray-painted words talked about Henri's footage, blaring:

WHY WERE WE KEPT FROM THE TRUTH?

WHAT ELSE DON'T WE KNOW?

Marion figured at least one member of the group was familiar with the area. They'd targeted stores without security cameras. Only they'd made a mistake about one, and it had caught blurry footage of a girl and boy, no more than twenty or twenty-one.

"Not enough to see their faces," Marion said, "but it's something. It's a lead."

I could feel Ryan's hostility toward her enthusiasm. He'd explained to me how Marion had hijacked the television channels by feeding the footage to a man she knew who worked at the station. But they couldn't keep it up forever; loopholes in the system were patched up as quickly as they could find them, and security grew ever tighter.

"She's obsessed with the idea of getting one last big story," he said bitterly, and I knew he was thinking of Kitty and Nina.

I wished I could assure him we wouldn't let Marion take advantage of them. But whatever Marion's motivations, neither Ryan nor I could argue against the fact that we benefited from her help in finding Ty.

Jackson and Vince were strangely absent from a lot of our meetings. If the others noticed, they didn't mention it. But finally, one afternoon, I slipped from Marion's room and went down the hall to ours.

Jackson looked up as I came in. He'd taken to sleeping on the armchair, after all, but he wasn't sitting there now. Instead, he was on the ground, back against the wall.

I sat down beside him, and he smiled faintly. "Where are the others?"

"In Marion's room. Deciding what to do next."

He nodded. "You should join them. They'll wonder where you are." I didn't imagine the meaning in his eyes. "Especially Ryan. Especially since he knows about Addie being gone."

"It's complicated," I said. "He knows that, too."

"Only logically." Jackson laughed. "Which barely counts for anything."

"You should join us, too," I said.

"Yeah. I will."

But he didn't get up, and neither did I.

"Addie told me about the sailing," I said finally. I wasn't

sure why I said it, except that I didn't want to leave him alone here. I realized I'd never known Jackson to be alone. Not really. When we'd first met him at Nornand, he'd been the one reaching out to us—extending the hand of Peter's underground. At Anchoit, he'd spent weeks telling us all about the others, then finally introduced us to Sabine and her group.

Jackson had always been the one inviting us into a circle of friends, and now he had none.

When Jackson replied, I heard in his voice the echoes of how Addie had sounded when she told me about the trip. "I miss the beach. I miss Anchoit. I hadn't thought I would so much."

"You miss the way things were," I said. "I understand that."

His grin was like a shrug. "I'm the one who keeps talking about change."

I looked away. "Well—"

Something inside me—part of me but not part of me—shuddered. Trembled.

I froze.

<*Addie?*> I whispered.

The edges of my mind quivered again. Like the walls that had been up since I woke still half-delirious and alone in Hahns had suddenly gone soft.

Then I heard her. A flutter of a sound. A whisper that seemed half imagination—and half insane hope.

She said <*Is this real?*>

THIRTY-TWO

Her voice reached me like an echo. Like words rippling through water. I breathed in sharply.

<*Yes*> I said. <*Yes, it is—*>

She cut me off: <*Bridget!*> Her confusion crashed into me. Her anxiety beat against the wall separating us. Knocked it down piece by piece. <*What happened to Bridget?*>

I felt the moment she realized what our eyes were seeing: the sparsely decorated hotel room; the paisley-printed wallpaper. Relief, first. A stab of it like light. Then her dread bloomed like a heavy flower.

<*How long have I been gone?*> she said softly.

I hesitated. <*More than a week. Almost two.*>

Her gasp didn't come from the lungs, or through the lips. It was shaped from pure emotion. And it knocked into me like a wrecking ball.

<*How is that possible?*>

I told her what the woman at Hahns had told me. About

the medication they'd used on us. How we'd reacted in unexpected ways.

She protested <*But Emalia said—*>

<*Emalia was wrong*> I whispered.

"Eva?"

Addie flinched at the sound of Jackson's voice. Not physically, of course—not when I was in control—but I felt it all the same. I realized that as far as Jackson could see, I'd fallen silent in the middle of a sentence. Slowly, I turned to face him. Addie was nameless, wordless emotion.

"What is it?" Jackson said, frowning.

<*Don't*> Addie said. <*No, Eva—please. Don't tell him. Not now. Not right now. I—I can't.*>

So I lied, because Addie asked me to. And in my heart, she'd always come first.

"I just remembered something," I said to Jackson. "I'm—I'm sorry. I have to go find Ryan."

I hurried from the room, trying not to focus on the way he watched me—*us*—go.

I didn't go find Ryan, of course. I ran to a quiet nook of the hotel and sank into the corner, anchoring Addie as her terror grew—until I could almost taste it, sour and acrid, on the back of our tongue.

<*I can't remember anything*> she said. <*I—*>

<*It's all right. It's all right, Addie. I promise.*>

I filled her in as gently as I could. She remembered being locked up in our cell. She remembered the pierce of the needle. The delirious dreams.

Only for her, the dreams had never ended. Not until now.

I told her about our escape. Bridget's help. The harrowing journey down the mountain. And, of course, how I'd met up again with Jackson.

Addie was still dazed. I could feel it. After so many days of being subjected only to my own emotions—my own presence—it was at once disconcerting and comforting to feel the edges of hers.

<*Two weeks. I never . . . I never realized so much could happen in two weeks.*> She paused. <*You thought I might not come back.*>

<*I was afraid. I—I was terrified.*> I hesitated. <*Jackson, though . . . he never doubted you would. He's been wanting to talk with you.*>

I had no way of knowing what Addie was thinking. What she'd had with Jackson had always been separate from the life she shared with me. She'd wanted to keep it that way, even after he'd been arrested.

I'd felt utterly betrayed that day in the photography-store attic, when Sabine and the others revealed they'd all known about the plan to murder the visiting officials at Powatt. When they—initiated by a rageful Christoph—knocked us to the ground and tied us up. But it had been worse for Addie.

They'd been my friends. Jackson had been more than that, to her. And even if he'd come back to help us save the officials in the end, he and Addie had never spoken since then.

<I could go, if you want to be alone.> It was the last thing I wanted right now, but I'd do it, if she needed me to.

<No> Addie said fiercely. *<Don't—you haven't noticed, have you?>*

I didn't know what she was talking about, and my silence was answer enough.

<I've been trying to take control. Just to see if I could. But I can't. I—I don't think I could talk with Jackson right now, Eva. I don't think I could talk with anyone but you.>

It was a dizzying concept. I'd been born the recessive soul—it was something unchangeable that I'd learned to accept, even if I refused to let it signal my death.

But for the first time in our lives, I was stronger than Addie.

<It's only temporary> I told her. *<You were gone for nearly two weeks. The medication did that. It's probably still working its way out of our system.>*

<You're right> she said. But she wasn't convinced, and I knew it.

"Eva?" Lissa approached hesitantly in the hotel hallway, her brow furrowed. "Are you all right? Did something happen?"

I managed a smile and a shake of our head. She seemed

like she was going to say something. But instead, she just threw her arms around us. The strength of it squeezed the air from our lungs.

"It's going to be all right, you know," she said quietly.

I'd told her about Addie's disappearance, but no one else. It was a carefully kept secret, shared only between her, Ryan, Jackson, and us. Not even Dr. Lyanne knew.

<*Can I tell her?*> I asked Addie, because it hurt to see Lissa hurt for me.

But Lissa spoke first, her face uneasy. "Jenson's found out about the Hahns footage. How it came from you."

The news report was almost over by the time Lissa and I reached the hotel room, but we saw enough. Our picture was up on the television screen again. It was the one Addie had taken for our driver's learning permit, only a few months before we went to Nornand. The woman at the office had told us not to smile, so the flash had caught us frozen in a serious look. It had washed us out, too, so we looked unnaturally pale.

We'd never liked that picture. Addie had reasoned we'd get a new one once we tested for our real license. But here we were, almost a year later. The idea of getting a driver's license was laughable. And that hated picture was being broadcasted to every corner of the Americas.

So was our name. Both our names. *Addie and Eva Tamsyn.*

All my life, I'd yearned for recognition. But not like this.

Sharing the screen with our picture, of course, was Jenson. Impeccably dressed, as usual. We'd never seen him in anything less than a suit jacket. He always carried with him an air of cold formality. And a will that crushed any that dared oppose it.

Addie and I were dangerous, he said. *Dangerous, violent, and disturbed.* During our escape from an institution, we'd brutally attacked a man. During our time in Anchoit, we'd caused chaos at Lankster Square, and suffering at Powatt—the destruction of tens of thousands of dollars in government property, not to mention the endangerment of lives. And now we were trying to tear the country apart with these illegal broadcasts. These lies and accusations.

He acknowledged that we were young.

That perhaps we were being manipulated.

He said, even, that part of him pitied us, struggling with the insanity and instability of two souls crammed into one body. But it didn't negate the fact that we were dangerous. And it was all proof of the necessity of the cure. The cure that would not only bring peace back to our country, but save other hybrid children from themselves.

<Save us from ourselves?> I said bitterly. I'd just survived two weeks alone in our body. I never wanted to do it again. There were downfalls to being hybrid—I couldn't deny that. But there were so many joys in it, too.

Jenson's cold eyes told me he didn't pity us for our

supposedly unstable hybrid brain. He pitied us for what he'd do to us, once he had us in custody.

He paused. And then, quietly—as if he knew that somewhere, Addie and I were listening—he said, "The Tamsyn family is under government protection and is fully cooperating with our efforts. They understand, as do all of us, that Addie and Eva need to be caught before they do any more harm."

The report ended. The image flickered back to the anchor, who went on about a phone number to call if anyone had information or leads.

<He's lying> I said. Our legs had weakened. *<He's lying. It isn't true.>*

<That he has our parents and Lyle?> Addie said softly. *<Or that they're cooperating?>*

"Why is *he* covering this?" Marion said. Her question was a sharp reminder that we weren't the only ones who'd watched the broadcast. I'd forgotten about the other people in the room. Dimly, I realized Devon and Lissa were both staring at us, the latter with a face full of open worry.

Vince frowned at Marion. "It's hybrid affairs, isn't it? And he's director. What does it matter?"

"Yes, but he's only director for Sector Two," Marion protested. "I thought it was strange he was the one to announce the heightened security this summer, and not the president himself. But it made sense because it was connected directly to the cure. Now . . . this seems like it should have grown beyond his jurisdiction—they're talking about security concerns."

"Hybrids have always been considered a security concern." Dr. Lyanne put the television on mute and turned to us. "What's important now is that we need to leave the city."

This wrenched me from my haze.

"What?" Marion said. For once, I agreed with her completely. "We can't leave just because—"

"What about Kitty?" I demanded.

"I'd only need a few more days." Marion was the picture of frustration. "I've a good idea where Tyler might be. I know the other addresses haven't worked out, but I'm so much more sure about this new one. When have my contacts not pulled through in the end, given enough time?"

I realized I'd never heard Marion raise her voice before—or Dr. Lyanne, either. Both seemed close to it now. I'd been so focused on Ryan's antagonism toward Marion, I'd overlooked the strength of Dr. Lyanne's.

"You can have your time," she said now. Her voice was modulated, her expression controlled. But I caught the tension in her jaw. "*You* can stay and keep looking for him. But Brindt is already on the edge of becoming another Anchoit, and I wouldn't be surprised if Jenson already has his eyes on this city. I want us somewhere more remote."

"How am I supposed to contact Tyler, if none of you are here?" Marion demanded. "The boy is deep in hiding. He won't trust me—"

Even if she could find them on her own, I didn't trust Marion enough to let her. She didn't care about Kitty and Nina like we did.

"You'll figure it out," Dr. Lyanne said. The look she gave Marion was pointed, sharp. "You managed to get us to trust you when you showed up at our door."

Addie's exhaustion bled into me, made it hard to think clearly. This was all too much for her. And why wouldn't it be? In her mind, we'd just been at Hahns. She'd gone from fighting to escape from an eighty-square-foot room to dealing with this. I struggled to keep myself calm, to shield my anxiety from her.

"We're leaving tomorrow," Dr. Lyanne said. "There's a safe house in Diale. We can stay there until we figure out where to go next."

<*Where to run next, she means*> I said wearily. I was tired, too. Tired of being on the run. Sick of being Jenson's prey.

And I was sick of losing people I loved. Of leaving people behind.

<*Ty has to be told that the police are closing in on him*> I said. <*I can't risk his capture. Not when Kitty and Nina might be with him.*>

<*So what do we do?*> Addie's trust was a balm on the day's wounds. I had Addie's confidence in me. It was enough.

I looked around the room, seeking Devon's eyes. I shoved

away my fear for our family, to be dealt with later. I couldn't afford to fall apart now.

<Marion has one last lead> I said. *<Tonight, we help her follow it.>*

THIRTY-THREE

My glance was enough for Devon to follow Addie and me into the hallway after the meeting dispersed. He became Ryan as they reached our side, the shift so smooth it happened in the middle of a breath.

"I'm sorry," he said softly. "About your family."

I could only nod. I didn't want to be comforted. I was almost shaking with the need to act. But I knew, too, that I had to think things through. Risks were unavoidable, but I had to make sure they were worth it.

Ryan touched our arm. "What're you planning, Eva? Because I know you're planning something."

I hesitated. "I know I can't save everyone. I know sometimes I try to, and I just make things worse. But this is Kitty and Nina. If anything happens to them, and I know I could have done something about it—" I cut off, unable to even find the words. "I can't let it go, Ryan. Especially since Dr. Lyanne wants us out of Brindt because of me."

“That’s not true,” Ryan said. But it was, and we all knew it. We were all in danger, but Addie and I were the ones Jenson had rejuvenated his manhunt for.

“I’m going to get the address from Marion,” I said. “And tonight, I’m going to see if Ty’s really there. If he’d trust anyone, it would be me. As far as public perception goes, I’m about as prohybrid and antigovernment as a person can get.”

Ryan studied our face. The set of our mouth.

“I’m going with you,” he said.

“You don’t have to. It—”

“Yes, I do,” he said. “Come on. Let’s go find Marion.”

I convinced Ryan that I wanted to talk with Marion alone. Honestly, I didn’t want him to be around while Marion and I hashed out the details. There was no telling what she might say to anger him, and I didn’t want his hostility to get in the way of our trip tonight.

So I slipped into Marion’s room later that evening, when I knew Dr. Lyanne was absent. Marion seemed to be in the middle of packing. The table was strewn with various pieces of camera equipment—a small tripod, two different lenses, what looked like a film canister.

Marion startled at the sight of us, but recovered quickly. “Does that woman really think Brindt is the only city in tumult right now?” Her face was flushed. “In Roarke yesterday, there was an honest-to-God riot.”

I stared at her, and she seemed gratified by my surprise. "It's because of Henri's footage. And yours, of course. People are reacting. I knew they would."

"There's been nothing on the news—"

"Of course not," she said. "They don't want to give people any ideas. They don't want people to know how this country is starting to come apart at the seams." She hesitated. The uneasiness crept back over her features. But she smoothed it away again, slapping on a look of sincerity. "Eva, you know why I had to release your Hahns footage early, don't you?"

I felt Addie flinch.

"That's not what I came to talk about," I said quietly.

She spoke as if she hadn't heard me. "I would have lost the timing. There was a presidential address—" She smiled slightly, just thinking about it. "The first broadcast came out right in the middle of it, and I couldn't let too much time pass before the second. I knew you'd do anything to help the cause, so I didn't think you would mind—"

"Mind that it could have killed us?" I snapped. I hadn't come to talk with Marion about this, but she'd brought up the topic, and with it, all my suppressed fury. It flared, burning so hot Addie shrank away.

<*Eva*> she said, and the sound of my name reeled me back. Doused my anger into something cold, instead of hot.

Marion's eyes were on the camera equipment again. "I didn't know for sure they'd figure out which institution it was.

Or that it was *you* who was filming—there were hundreds of girls in that building." She glanced at Addie and me. "There *were* people coming to rescue you. I'd already arranged things."

Hahns was past. There was no point in being furious about it now, when I needed a clear mind.

"I want the address where you think Ty is staying," I said quietly. "Tonight, after everyone else is asleep, Ryan and I are going to see if Ty is there."

I caught the brightening of Marion's eyes, the half twitch of her mouth. But she quashed her smile, keeping her expression solemn. "I could come with you—"

I shook our head. Marion would just be another unknown variable. "Ryan and I are enough. And I don't want any of the others to know about this."

The look on our face was enough to keep her from arguing. She gave us the address.

"There's one more thing," I said, just before we left. I pinned Marion with our gaze. "Use these contacts you claim to have everywhere. Find out what's going on at Hahns. How things are there. If anyone's been hurt."

Because of me. Because of aiding my escape.

But I didn't say that.

Marion nodded.

Back in Anchoit, I'd dreamed about roaming the streets after dark, going to see the bustling downtown, where the lights of the bars and storefronts flashed all night long.

Addie and I had never liked crowds. The idea of dancing in the darkness, crushed by the weight and energy and unbound inhibition of hundreds of other people, sounded terrifying. And yet. There was something about the music. About the exuberance of it all.

Now we and Ryan were headed downtown in a city almost as large, but for reasons that had nothing to do with dancing or sightseeing. According to the map Marion had given us, we weren't far now.

<We don't really know Ty, do we?> I kept a careful eye on the people thronging the streets—alert to anyone who might recognize us despite the baggy hoodie we'd borrowed from Ryan. But no one on this pulsing, lit-up avenue paid us any attention at all.

<We knew he hadn't wanted to let Kitty and Nina go> Addie said. *<And they love him enough to come looking for him.>*

Marion's address led us to the quieter part of the bar strip, where the crowds thinned to a few giggling packs of girls and some couples looking for a bit of privacy. "*Merry Christmas!*" someone shouted at us drunkenly, though it wouldn't be Christmas for another few days.

The bouncer standing at the door gave me a skeptical look. Neither Ryan nor I had any kind of identification, let alone something saying we were twenty-one.

"I'm just looking for someone." I tried to peek past him into the darkened bar. It was small, and not very full. A bartender cleared glasses at the counter, and a low, slow song played through the speakers. A waitress used the phone on the counter to gossip. A man sitting near the door met our eyes and frowned. I averted our eyes.

"Does he work here?" the bouncer said.

I hesitated. "I don't know. His name's Ty. Tyler?"

"There's nobody here named Tyler." The bouncer planted himself a little more firmly in the doorway. "And I'm sorry, but you can't come in unless you have ID."

The man who'd caught our attention before was still staring in our direction. He was stout, with a high color in his cheeks and thick, dark hair. There was the flicker of something like recognition in his eyes.

<If the bouncer's not going to let us in, we shouldn't linger> Addie said uneasily.

I smiled thinly at the bouncer and pulled Ryan away from the door.

"Marion didn't tell me it was a bar," I muttered once we were out of earshot. We'd gone around the corner, ending up in a narrow alleyway between the bar and the store next to it. "I figured it would be an apartment."

<Maybe she didn't know, either> Addie said. *<What now?>*

I bit our lip. The music coming through the speakers

paused, and in the change between songs, I heard it. Another song, but fainter. The strumming of a guitar, and a man's quiet voice.

At first, I couldn't tell where it came from. Then our eyes fell on a door in the side of the building, a little farther down the alley. In the darkness, we hadn't noticed it before.

<*Kitty used to sing that song*> I said.

THIRTY-FOUR

"Ty?" I called his name as loudly as I dared. Ryan hurried after me as I approached the door. "Ty, please—I know your sister."

The music stopped.

We waited, our heart pounding.

The door to the back room opened just wide enough for a young, dark-haired man to step outside. He held his guitar in one hand, half protectively, half like a potential weapon.

"You know Willa?" His voice was lower than I'd expected from someone so sparingly built.

I hesitated. "No, not Willa. You're Tyler Holynd, right?" Judging from the way his eyes moved over us, he'd guessed who we were, too. "I'm Eva. Eva Tamsyn."

I was ready to tell him everything—how Kitty and I had been roommates at Nornand. How we'd escaped together. How she'd run away and I *needed* to know she was safe.

Then, from inside the room, a girl's voice cried, *"Eva!"* and all my words became irrelevant.

She shoved through the doorway, squeezing past her brother as she flew toward us. Her arms wrapped around me—she was stronger than I'd expected—or maybe I was just having trouble breathing anyway.

"You're back!" She was babbling, her voice high and breathless, her face flushed, her long, dark hair flying everywhere. She let us go and threw her arms around Ryan, too. Finally, she turned to Ty. Gave him the biggest grin we'd ever seen on her face.

"I told you they'd find us," she said.

The back room had been set up as a makeshift bedroom. There were two sleeping bags. A radio. A couple bottles of spray paint thrown in the corner. A foldout chair. And Ty's guitar case, where he carefully laid the instrument before turning to face us again.

Kitty wanted me to tell her everything, and I would have, if Ty hadn't been there. As it was, I tried to appease her without saying anything too incriminating. But soon, it became apparent that there wasn't much Kitty hadn't already told her brother.

"Who're these people letting you stay here?" Ryan asked. "Who're tagging the walls and putting up messages?"

Ty glanced at the pile of spray-paint bottles in the corner. They'd stained the floor, a constellation of drips. "I met them a few months ago, after I first got into town. I didn't know where Kitty was. If she was all right. By then, it had been a year and a half since they took her."

Kitty had stopped smiling. She wore the slightly blank look I'd come to fear and hate—the one that meant she was struggling not to think about anything. To push away the things that hurt her, and spare herself the pain.

Ty must have noticed it, too, because he glossed over the subject. "None of them are actually hybrid—at least, I don't think so. They're just angry, mostly. Angry at the government. At a lot of things. I've been thinking of leaving ever since Kitty arrived. I'm just not sure where we'd go."

"You can't stay here," Ryan said. "Not with the police honing in. Come back with us, tonight."

A knock came at the door. It was a blond man around Ty's age, with a scruff around his narrow jaw. His eyes moved suspiciously to Addie and me. "I thought I heard a commotion back here. You guys all right?"

"It's my friends," Kitty said, suddenly grinning again. "I said they'd find us, Michael, didn't I?"

Michael's smile was more hesitant. "You did."

"We just need a moment," Ty told him. "Then I'll explain to everyone."

<I'm not sure he needs to explain to him> Addie said. She was right. Michael definitely knew exactly who we were. And why not, considering what had been broadcast earlier today?

But Michael just nodded and closed the door again.

"We could go get Willa and the others," Kitty said, sidling

up to her brother. "I want to see them." Her lips twitched. "Even Jem."

<*She's not going to stay with us*> I said softly. <*Even if we convince them to come now, they're going to break away eventually.*>

The realization hit me hard. It wasn't disappointment, exactly. Not sadness, either. Something not nameable—like the greatest sense of loss.

Addie's voice was gentle. <*We should have expected it.*>

Ty was family, in the end, and we were not. We'd only known Kitty and Nina for less than a year, when it came down to it. Even if it felt like we'd known them for so much longer.

"We'll see," Ty said, laughing faintly.

"Are you coming with us?" Ryan started to say—

The door burst open. This time, it wasn't Michael. It was the stout man who'd been eyeing Addie and me through the bar door. His face was flushed, his eyes bright.

"You all need to leave," he hissed. "Right now."

Ty jerked Kitty behind him. "Who are you?"

"Logan Newsome." The man thrust his hand in our direction. At first, I thought he wanted us to shake it.

Then I realized he was holding something. A white envelope.

"I've been looking for you," he said to us. "I have something from your mother and father."

Addie faltered. <*Our—*>

I grabbed the envelope and pried it open.

The card inside was plain white, a golden rose embossed at the center. I felt the sudden surge of Addie's emotions, the flurry of our heartbeat. Hope swelled so large in our throat we couldn't breathe.

We recognized this card. Addie had bought the set months before we left home, giving them to Mom for her birthday. Mom had always said they were too pretty to use.

Tucked inside the card was a photograph. It had been cut to fit, the edges trimmed. But I recognized it all the same. It had sat on the mantelpiece for years. In the picture, a little girl with wispy blond hair squatted by a dark green tent. The sun was in her eyes. She squinted. She wasn't looking at the camera. All her attention was for the single blade of grass tucked between her thumbs.

We'd been trying to whistle through it, the way our parents could.

On the back were two lines of script in our mother's handwriting.

One was faded: *Addie & Eva, 5 years old.*

The other, tucked along the bottom edge of the photograph, was new, the ink bold and black.

Happy sweet sixteen, it said.

"The police are on their way here right now," Logan said. Only words like those could have pulled my attention away from the card in our hands. He looked to Ty. "You have a mole in your group. And he's just called for backup."

"That's not possible," Ty said. "I know all those—"

"You never thought it was strange it took the police this long to find you?" Logan demanded. "You really think you're that well hidden? They found you ages ago. They've been waiting."

He looked at Addie and me.

And I understood. <*The police were waiting for us to arrive.*>

Now we had.

"My car's parked just outside," Logan said.

<*Eva?*>

<*I don't know*> I whispered.

I don't know if this is real. I don't know if we can trust this man. I don't know. I don't know.

There were stories in Logan's eyes that I couldn't begin to understand. Did we go with this stranger who came bearing my mother's handwriting?

The decision, it seemed, lay with Addie and me.

<*We go*> I said softly.

<*We go*> Addie echoed.

I reached for the back door and wrenched it open. We rushed out into the cold air. We hadn't even made it to Logan's car when we heard the faint wail of sirens.

"Ty drives," I said, a snap decision. We had to trust

Logan—but not completely. And neither Ryan nor Addie and I knew this city as well as Ty.

Logan hesitated, then tossed Ty the keys.

We never saw the police cars pull up. By then, we'd melted into the rest of Brindt's late-night traffic.

THIRTY-FIVE

Addie and I sat in the backseat as Ty drove, memorizing everything about our parents' message. The weight of the card stock in our hands. The glossy raise of the golden flower. The exact tint of the inks our mother had used. Both black, but the new pen must have had a wider nib: the letters were thicker, the loops of the *es* in *sweet* and *sixteen* almost shut.

Logan told us that our family wasn't captured, like Jenson claimed. Our family wasn't *cooperating*.

Our family was looking for us.

Our mom had sent out twelve cards with twelve different people, in hopes one might reach us. Logan had come to Brindt initially because of Ty's group. He'd been keeping an eye on them for nearly a week now, but hadn't made his presence known.

"It's no secret that you're involved in a resistance," he said to Addie and me. "And if I suspected the group here might be connected with you, the police probably suspected the same."

He glanced at Ty. "It struck me as odd that I'd found your place without too much trouble, yet the police hadn't."

Ty was quiet, his hands tight on the steering wheel. It was Michael, the young man who'd come to check on us, who Logan had seen calling the police. He'd used the phone at the counter, not thinking anyone was paying attention.

I knew what it was like, to feel utterly betrayed by people you thought were friends.

When our eyes met Ryan's, he shifted his hand to squeeze ours. He knew what this card meant to Addie and me. This proof that our parents still loved us.

Both of us.

But there was warning in his eyes, too. In the stiffness of his shoulders. And I understood that, too.

<This could all be a trap> I said. *<Logan could lead us anywhere. Maybe someone forced her to write this card.>* It hurt our heart to think about, but we couldn't afford to gloss over the possibility.

Logan directed us to a quiet street several blocks from the bar, parking the car on the side of the road. He turned to face Addie and me—solemn at first. Then he smiled a little. Like he knew us—like he was some uncle who'd met us in our childhood and had heard all the stories about us growing up. It was disconcerting.

"You look so much like your brother," he said.

We swallowed hard. It was something he would say to

make us want to trust him. And it worked.

"Will you come back with me?" Logan said quietly. "Back to your family?"

I squeezed Ryan's hand.

"I want to make a call," I said. "Before I decide on anything."

Dr. Lyanne answered the phone after the fourth ring. I imagined she'd woken after the first, then stared at the phone for the next three, trying to decide whether or not to pick it up.

Thankfully, she did. She kept quiet and let me explain everything, whispering in the phone booth on that dark city street. When I finished, I waited for her to say *God, Eva, you're always so rash* or *I told you it would be dangerous to stay here.*

Instead, after a long silence, she said, "We're going to have to leave Brindt anyway. Do you trust this man?"

"You've told me I'm too trusting." I looked down at the card still clutched in our hand. "I *want* to trust him. I want to trust him so badly, I don't know if I can trust my own judgment."

"Where are you?" she asked.

I told her. Within twenty minutes, she'd pulled up next to us, Marion in the front seat, Jackson and Lissa in back. Everyone was already packed. They'd checked out of our rooms at the hotel. No matter what, we were all leaving Brindt tonight.

The only question was: Would we be leaving with Logan?

Logan's apartment was a sparse, dingy place he'd rented from a friend. Dr. Lyanne wanted to know everything—how long ago he'd met up with our parents. Why he was interested in helping. Where he wanted to take us.

Logan answered our questions patiently, one by one. He'd first come into contact with our family about a month and a half ago, when they stayed at the same safe house. He wasn't hybrid himself—didn't even have any close family that was hybrid—but he didn't think that was a prerequisite for believing our mistreatment was wrong. He wanted to take us to a small town about two hours north of the nation's capital. Our family was there, hidden away.

"If we start driving now," he said, "we can reach them by tomorrow noon."

The thought was so dizzying it pushed everything else from our mind.

Logan agreed to allow us some time to think things over. But Addie and I were almost trembling from the thought of seeing our family again. Everyone knew the final decision had to be ours.

"I want to go," I said finally, quietly. "It doesn't mean you need to all come—if it isn't safe—"

"We're coming," Lissa said.

And so the decision was made.

A little later, when the others were gathered in the living room, poring over a map and discussing driving routes, Nina took me aside, down the hallway, and said, "Ty and me are going to go find our family. So we won't be going with you."

The night's events had left her solemn, but steady. Eleven

years old, and she'd already been stolen from home, cast from society, betrayed multiple times over. It was little wonder that sometimes, she and Kitty preferred to just shut away the thoughts that caused them pain.

I fought the urge to grab her and never let go. "The government's going to be looking for you—"

"The government's been looking for me for a long time," Nina said. Her fingers fiddled with a lock of hair, then were still again. "They might be looking for me for—for I don't know how much longer."

<*In the meantime, she might as well be with family. Might as well live as happily as she can*> Addie said. <*We understand that, Eva.*>

We did.

"Make sure Ty follows through on that promise to teach you the guitar," I said softly.

She laughed. Her eyes lost a little of their grimness. "I will."

I bumped our shoulder against hers, and she laughed louder. I already missed her so fiercely I had to swallow down tears. This wasn't going to be the usual kind of parting. Not like when a friend moved away, and we'd exchange addresses and phone numbers, and promise to call. I couldn't be sure where she'd end up. If she was safe. If I'd ever be able to find her again, after all this was over.

If all this was ever over.

This was good-bye without a safety net.

"Eva?" Jackson said. He'd appeared in the mouth of the

hallway. "You ready to leave?"

He hadn't spoken much since arriving with Dr. Lyanne, and his features were strangely wooden. He looked very alone, standing there in the doorframe.

"I'm ready," I said, and he nodded, turning to go.

<I want to try it again> Addie said softly. *<Moving, I mean.>*

This time, I tried to withdraw from control as Addie reached out to take it. At first, I couldn't even do it—it was like shoving against a rubber film that kept bouncing me back.

But slowly, ever so slowly, our body's reins shifted.

We—Addie—wavered.

Took a step.

Another.

Our limbs crumpled. Addie shouted as we fell.

"Eva!" Nina and Jackson cried in tandem.

I was back in control by the time Jackson caught us. The others rushed in from the living room, Ryan pushing ahead to reach our side.

"I'm fine," I said, wincing. Jackson set us back on our feet. "I tripped, that's all."

"Is it your ankle?" Ryan said. He and Dr. Lyanne had often said we'd started putting weight on it too early. "Did it give out?"

Jackson just stared at us. Addie was silent, her anxiety flapping around in our chest.

I shook our head. Tried a smile. "No. Just me being clumsy."

<Sorry> Addie whispered.

<Not your fault. And you did better than just a few hours ago. You took a few steps. And you spoke. That's something.>

<I screamed.>

<Even better.>

My smile grew at the ring of her silent laughter.

Even if everything else fell down around our ears, crumbled through our fingers—Addie and I would be all right with each other. That was no small thing.

THIRTY-SIX

We drove and drove, chasing Logan's taillights. The sun climbed the pale winter sky. Sitting in the backseat, Addie and I practiced shifting control between us while the others slept. It got easier over the hours, Addie gaining strength with each attempt. There had been little time, since her return, to focus on anything but the chaos of the outside world. The long drive gave Addie and me time to focus on each other, and ourselves.

For two weeks, I had lost Addie, but Addie had lost the world.

<*Like you feared you might, when we were kids*> she said quietly, when I brought it up. I'd wanted to make sure she was okay in the aftermath. <*Eva—*>

<*You're back*> I said. <*You're back, and we're together, and that's what matters.*>

By the time Logan pulled up in front of an enormous, beautiful house, it was high noon.

<*Do you think our family really will be here?*> Addie said.

I knew her worry stemmed from the fear we'd gained like a callous over the last year—that good things were always taken away from us. That even if we repeated forever Jackson's mantra of *keep hope*, each of our hopes would eventually fall skewered to the dirt.

<They'll be here> I said.

We were both nervous, of course. But at least our parents had spent the weeks and months and years before our hospitalization knowing Addie existed.

They hadn't spoken with me since I was twelve years old.

But I would be the one in control when we saw our parents again.

A part of me wondered if they would notice.

Ryan stood next to us as we climbed from the car. Everyone was quiet, even Marion, who kept eyeing us when she thought we weren't watching. The trees edging the walk were bare, skeletal things, fragile in the cold.

<They'll be here> I repeated. *<It'll be all right.>*

<It'll be all right> Addie echoed.

Logan rang the doorbell. We waited forever and a millennium and a day. Then the door opened.

<Mom> Addie said. The word echoed inside of us.

Mom with her corn-silk hair, pale skin, and unfaded freckles. She looked just as we remembered her.

"Addie!" she said.

And that hurt.

It shouldn't have. Or should have hurt less, because I

should have been prepared. I'd thought I was, but I wasn't.

It hurt, deep to the core of me, that my mother could not recognize me.

I didn't say anything. Mom was making strangled, gasping noises that were the precursors to tears, her face crumpling, and I thought, *Please, please don't cry.* I'd always hated to see our mother cry. Hated to know it was so often me who caused it.

She threw her arms around us. Hesitantly, I hugged her back. With only one arm at first, because our other hand was interlocked with Ryan's, gripping on to him for dear life. Then, slowly, our fingers slipped from his. I wrapped both arms around Mom's shoulders and closed our eyes and tried not to think about how small she felt in our arms.

"Addie?" a boy's voice said.

Our eyes snapped open again. Saw, over Mom's shoulder, the little boy with the mop of yellow hair and the uncertainty in his eyes.

I faltered. Mom gestured at Ryan and the others. Her eyes didn't seem to want to leave Addie and me, but she spoke to them, said, "Come in. It's cold out."

We'd heard her say something similar so many times. To houseguests. To family friends. To Addie's classmates who came over for school projects.

Lyle slipped away, back down the hall. Away from us.

One of the strangest things in the world was looking at my own mother and feeling like we were strangers. Knowing she was avoiding our eyes. That she felt guilty because of something she'd done to us—and it wasn't something small, something casually forgotten. It was a decision that had cast us apart for more than half a year, and changed all our lives. Nothing would ever be the same.

Part of me was gratified that she felt guilty. Part of me felt guilty for wanting her guilt.

All of me just wanted her to look at me. Acknowledge me.

Call me Eva, instead of Addie.

"Your dad's out, but he'll be back soon," she said, leading us through the hallway. She glanced at Ryan. Had she spoken with the Mullans at all in the months since our simultaneous abduction? Had the loss of their children brought them together? Or driven them apart the same way Addie had avoided Hally at school for years, afraid to draw even more unwanted attention?

"Are you hungry?" Mom said. "They've just set out lunch."

"I'm fine," I said.

"I'll eat," Dr. Lyanne said, and eyed the others until they all mumbled something about eating as well. Mom pointed them to the kitchen.

<They're not doing us any favors> I said anxiously. *<Leaving us alone like this.>*

But even Ryan, who usually read me so well, left with the others with only a slight smile and nod of his head.

"Do you want to shower?" Mom asked. "You've been on the road all day—"

"I don't need to shower," I said.

She nodded.

"Did Lyle get the transplant?" I blurted. It was the only thing of importance I could think of saying that wasn't *Look at me. Say my name. Please.*

Mom faltered, then nodded. Her eyes finally met ours. "He's doing a lot better. He has to take immunosuppressants, of course, but it's better than the dialysis. *Addie—*"

The *Addie* was because I'd started to cry.

Even through the blur of my tears, I saw the way Mom's throat jumped. "Addie . . ."

<*Eva—*> Addie said.

"I'm going to go find him." My words stumbled over one another in their rush to get out. I dashed our hand over our eyes. The tears, thank God, stopped. "Lyle—I want to talk with him."

I hurried down the hall before Mom could say anything to stop me.

I wasn't sure if she wanted to.

THIRTY-SEVEN

Finding Lyle was easier said than done. The house had looked huge enough from the outside, but I'd been too distracted to really take it in. Walking through it now, Addie and I got the full effect of its ornate scope, the walls hung with paintings and photographs, the rooms airy. There was more than enough room for an eleven-year-old boy to hide.

<They fixed him, Addie> I said. Outwardly, we were steady now. No trace of tears. But Addie, I knew, could feel me still shaking. She was steadier than I was. *<They fixed him like—>*

Like they could never fix us.

It wasn't fair to say. Or to think.

<We've always wanted this> Addie said.

<Of course we have. I'm happy—I'm so happy he got the operation. If—if everything we've been through since we left home was just to buy Lyle his operation, it would be worth it.>

The night Mr. Conivent came to take Addie and me away,

he'd threatened our parents with denying Lyle the dialysis sessions he needed. Then bribed them with getting him bumped up the transplant list.

<I just—> I leaned against the wall, closing our eyes for a moment. My emotions were so tangled I was helpless to decipher anything. *<I don't know.>*

Addie and I found evidence of guests everywhere. The bedrooms were filled with suitcases, the office floor covered in sleeping bags. The bathroom bore the marks of being shared by too many people. Towels hung everywhere. Tubes of toothpaste lolled about the sink, next to a myriad of brightly colored toothbrushes. Some woman's underwear had fallen behind the toilet.

Judging from the photographs, the house belonged to a family of five—a couple a little older than our parents, and three college-aged children. Were they here now? Why had they chosen to open their home to strangers?

We'd almost given up looking for Lyle when a woman poked her head out of a bedroom and said, "Addie, right? Your family's staying in that room at the end."

The door at the end of the hall was shut. I knocked the short, staccato pattern Addie had always used before entering Lyle's room.

"Yeah?" came our brother's voice, and I opened the door slowly.

Lyle sat on a bed, a worn paperback in hand. "Oh," he said when he saw us. He turned back to his book. His eyes weren't moving, though, just staring at the same stretch of text for far too long.

"Which one is that?" I asked. Lyle held up the book so we could see the cover. I recognized it from his shelf back home. "You've read that one at least ten times, haven't you?"

Lyle shrugged, still not looking at us.

"Aren't there any other kids here?" I said.

"Not anymore."

"Mom said you don't have to go to dialysis anymore." I smiled. "That's pretty cool."

Finally, Lyle looked up from his book. He shrugged again. For a long moment, neither of us moved or spoke. I didn't know how to cross this gulf that had sprung up between us and our little brother.

<Is it because it's me?> I said.

<It's not because of you. It would be the same if I were in control.>

But I wasn't sure if that was true.

<Keep talking, Eva. Sit next to him.>

<Funny> I said with a laugh. *<I used to tell you what to do when you had trouble. I—I never thought it would be this hard, knowing what to do.>*

<You know what to do> Addie said softly. *<It's just hard to trust that you do.>*

"I'm sorry I wasn't there for the operation." I sat on the edge of the bed, and Lyle shifted, adjusting to the change in weight.

"You didn't want to leave, did you?" He looked at us from the corners of his eyes.

I couldn't be sure of the depth of his question. Was he asking if we'd wanted to leave our family behind? Leave him behind without saying good-bye? Of course not. Never.

Did he know what Mr. Conivent had told our parents that night? How our leaving connected to his transplant?

Was he asking if we'd gone willingly, knowing it would help him?

We hadn't been that selfless. I certainly hadn't been. If given the choice, I would have clung to home and a family that didn't recognize my existence, rather than leave for Nornand.

"I wish I'd been there for you," I said finally. I hesitated, then reached out and ruffled his hair. He made a face and pulled away, but I caught the shadow of a smile.

He set down his book, not bothering to save the page. "Do you want to see the scar?" When I nodded, he lifted up his shirt. It was longer than I'd expected, but faded now to a shiny white.

"Did it hurt a lot?" I said.

Lyle shrugged. "Sometimes. But they gave me a lot of drugs." He smiled, revealing the slightly crooked bottom tooth Mom had always talked about getting fixed with braces, once he was a little older. Once we had the money. "I was really loopy."

"Yeah?" I laughed. Then quieted as Lyle's eyes focused

on our forehead. We had a scar there, I knew, from the time we fell off the roof at Nornand. We might have died, if there hadn't been an outjutting not too far below.

I rearranged our hair, letting it cover the scar. But not before Lyle pointed and asked, "How'd you get that?"

"I fell."

<Thank God we're wearing long pants> I said. I didn't want questions about our scars from Powatt.

"Addie—" Lyle said, and on reflex, I replied, "I'm not Addie."

I froze.

Lyle stared up at us. The silence seemed to last forever.

The surprise on Lyle's face slowly turned into a frown. "Were you there the whole time? At home? Why didn't you tell me?"

Our mouth opened, then closed. I'd expected—I wasn't sure what I'd expected from Lyle once he knew who he was really talking to. Fear, maybe? Disgust?

Instead, he sounded a little hurt.

"I was there. But I couldn't talk, Lyle—"

"Then why didn't Addie tell me? I wouldn't have told anyone. Was it because I got sick?"

"It had nothing to do with you being sick." I wasn't sure if he believed me or not. "Lyle, I'm so sorry this happened. That Mom and Dad took you away from home, and school, and . . . and everything. That you're here. That nothing's normal anymore."

Lyle looked away and shrugged.

"Eva?" he said, and it sounded so natural, so easy, from his mouth. Like he'd never stopped calling my name. "Did you really do all those things the news says you did?"

I wanted to change the subject. To steer it toward more comfortable ground. But Addie said <*Maybe we should tell him. At least some of it. He wants to know. He deserves to not be left in the dark.*>

I hesitated. Lyle waited.

"Here," I said softly. "I'll tell you everything from the beginning."

I told him the stories Addie and I had saved for him. The initial escape from Nornand in the middle of the night. Our flight from Sabine and Cordelia's photography shop. I told him, too, stories I'd never thought I would. About the girls we'd met in Hahns. About Eli and Cal from Nornand. About Sabine, and how we'd wanted the same things, but reached for them in different ways.

Lyle asked me things I wasn't ready to answer. What had happened to Jaime? To Emalia? Were we going to go save them? What about Bridget and the other girls at Hahns?

I was telling him about finding Ty and Kitty in Brindt when a knock came at the bedroom door.

"Come in," I said, and Jackson peeked inside. He hesitated when he saw Lyle.

"There's still lunch downstairs," he said to us. "But it's

disappearing fast. So unless you're okay with surviving on pretzel sticks until dinner, you should probably come down. Unless you're busy. I didn't realize you were—"

Addie's amusement was soft and sweet. *<He does get into rambling sometimes, doesn't he?>*

"I want lunch." Lyle turned to us. "Are you going to come?"

<Let me talk with Jackson> Addie said.

I wanted her to speak with him, of course. But I also didn't want it. Or I wanted it, but I wanted it to be easier, smoother, than I knew it would be.

<Don't you want me to tell him first? That you're back?>

<It's okay> she said. *<I can explain it.>*

<Do you want me gone?>

<I still can't move. Not well. If something happens . . . I don't want to be dead weight until you come back.>

I caught her unspoken meaning. If someone came in—like our parents—she didn't want them to see her like this. I glanced at Jackson. *<Okay.>*

"You go ahead, Lyle," I said. "I want to talk with Jackson for a second."

Lyle wavered, but nodded and left. Jackson closed the door, his smile confused. "What is it, Eva?" But I could no longer answer. Jackson's smile faded as the silence stretched. "Eva?"

<Careful!> I said as Addie wrenched into control. She tipped forward on the bed, barely keeping our balance. Jackson

rushed forward; Addie closed our fingers around his arm.

They stared at each other. Silence, for three rabbit-quick beats of our heart.

"Don't blame Eva, because I told her not to say anything," Addie whispered. "I—I wanted to be the one to tell you. And I couldn't. Not for a while."

Jackson just stared.

"Well, say something," Addie said breathlessly. "I'm the one who has the actual problem speaking."

For a long, long moment, he didn't. Then he grinned. A match strike.

"I knew it," he said. "*I knew it.*"

THIRTY-EIGHT

He was different, a little, with her. And she was different with him. I'd never witnessed them alone like this—well, as alone as they could be when they both knew I was there. I wondered if Vince was there. If he felt at all like I did.

Addie was awkward, still, in our body. But even with the awkwardness, I knew she held herself differently next to Jackson. She smiled more. She laughed more.

They didn't talk about Powatt, or Hahns, or Addie's sometimes-slurred words. They remembered places they'd gone together back at Anchoit. Things they'd seen. They laughed about jokes I didn't understand, because I hadn't been there.

They talked about sailing.

It seemed like they could go on forever, sitting there together with their backs against the headboard. But they were interrupted.

Lyle banged the door open. Addie jolted to our feet, then wavered. By the time Jackson took our arm to steady us, I was in control, and we didn't need it.

"There's been a shooting," Lyle said, his face pale. "At an institution. They tried to kill all the kids."

<Hahns.>

That was my first thought. My first fear.

I'd taken too long to fulfill my promise to Bridget, and now it was too late.

"It's on the TV." Lyle was already turning around again—ready to rush back. "It's another hijacked broadcast."

A crowd had gathered in the living room downstairs, most standing, a few seated on the black leather couches. Lissa and Devon were at the other end of the room, Lissa's hand pressed to her mouth.

The footage on the screen was shaky, sliding in and out of focus. At first, I didn't understand what I was seeing. Then I realized the people moving in and out of frame were EMTs. That the objects they carried were stretchers.

That on the stretchers lay the bodies of children.

It wasn't Hahns. Despite the footage's poor quality, I knew I didn't recognize this institution. It was somewhere lush and green, even in December—someplace in the southern hemisphere.

The video ended. Silence gripped the room in a chokehold.

Marion stood in the doorway, as frozen as the rest of us.

"Did you know about this?" I demanded. "Did you broadcast this?"

Numbly, she shook her head. The air seemed to have thinned.

"I'm going to find out who did," Marion mumbled and disappeared from the room.

"Addie?" It was Dad, with Mom hovering next to him. He crushed us in a hug, and it felt so similar to the one he'd given us the last time we'd seen him. Right before Addie and I had climbed into Mr. Conivent's car.

For a second, I was that girl again—the *me* of more than half a year ago. A lifetime ago.

A girl who hoped her father would come and save her, because he'd promised.

Dad released us. "Addie—"

<He doesn't know> I whispered. *<He has no idea it's me.>*

<He knows, Eva. He just—he doesn't know what to say—>

<He just needs to say my name!>

I took a sharp breath. Addie was trying to reach for me. I could feel her—hear her say *<Eva—>* but I blocked it out.

Standing here with our parents made me feel like I'd been thrown in the ocean and had forgotten how to swim.

"I'm sorry." I backed away from our father. "I—I have to know who broadcasted that footage. I have to go find Marion."

Marion was on the phone upstairs. She glanced up as we approached, motioning for us to keep silent. "Next time, give me a warning," she said angrily into the receiver, and hung up.

Devon, Lissa, and Jackson had followed us from the living room.

Our parents hadn't.

"Who was it?" Devon asked.

"Where was it?" Lissa whispered.

Marion's lips were thin. "It happened in Roarke. Late last night—or early this morning. No one's sure. There wasn't an official report. A journalist and his friend heard rumors about the attack and drove down to see. They're the ones who got it broadcasted—they gave it to my contact at the news station. He thought it was from me."

"Roarke," I said. "That sounds familiar—"

Marion nodded. "There were riots in Roarke after I broadcasted Henri's footage."

<She told us that> Addie said. *<Back in Brindt.>*

Had Henri's footage—our footage—incited this attack? Was this some madmen's way of striking back at hybrids however they could?

I faltered. *<They're stronger than we are. At the end of the day, hybrids are only a small percentage of the population. We can be crushed, if they want to badly enough.>*

<Only> said Addie *<if this is a game of brute force.>*

<I'm afraid it's going to become one before long.>

"How many dead?" Jackson said.

Marion shook her head. "I don't know."

“Did they catch who did it?” Devon asked. “How many shooters—”

“I don’t know,” Marion said.

Lissa swallowed. Her throat trembled. “Where is Roarke?”

“Far to the south,” Devon said. But what did it matter how far away this attack had occurred? The institution must have had hundreds of kids. I kept picturing the girls I’d known at Hahns—Bridget, and Caitlin, and Jeanie—fleeing—fleeing where? They’d have had nowhere to run. Nowhere to hide.

I saw them pressed against walls. Dropping beneath beds. The flash of the guns in the darkness.

“I told you this would grow beyond us.” Marion sounded almost defensive. “That other people would be willing to help, once things got started. Once they understood.”

It took me a moment to understand she meant the reporter who’d captured the footage, not the gunmen.

“And—and this,” Marion said. “This will make even more people see the truth. Make them care.”

“This shouldn’t be what it takes,” I said softly, “just for people to care.”

THIRTY-NINE

Marion called Henri on the satellite phone, catching him right before he went to bed. She wanted to send him the footage from Roarke, once she got a copy of it. She said he could use it to focus attention on the Americas.

Addie and I just wanted to speak with him. We hadn't gotten the chance to since the day he'd left. Henri seemed as relieved to hear our voice as we were to hear his. The line wasn't entirely clear, but I made out his words well enough. Addie and I had heard his conversation with Marion, knew he planned to get a piece about Roarke broadcasted as soon as they could get it together.

For a little while, we didn't talk about anything important. Tried to pretend we had the peace of mind for small talk. But that dried up.

Addie and I were curled up in one of the offices upstairs. We didn't want to let the rest of the house know about the satphone, so we and Marion had hidden away up here. She'd left, though, so now it was just us.

"Back in Anchoit," I said to Henri, "you said the rest of the world had more pressing concerns than what happens to hybrids in the Americas. Is that still true?"

He was quiet a moment. "I think people are starting to pay attention. And I think the attention will grow. Are you and Addie doing all right?"

"We feel sick," I said quietly. "Everything that's happened—we just feel sick."

The attack on Roarke plunged the house into numbed mourning. Addie and I found ourselves wandering the halls, uncertain and adrift, wanting no company but each other. We didn't hear about the vigil until the next day. Vince explained that a man named Damien had set it up. The Capitol was only a little more than two hours away, and Damien had made calls to the other safe houses within driving distance, rounding up people to gather in front of the Capitol building tonight.

It was supposed to be a vigil not only for the children at Roarke, but for all the people currently lost. The family members gone. The children taken away.

I thought of our first attic-clubhouse meeting with Sabine, when she'd laid out the plan for the Lankster Square protest. We'd called it a memorial then. We'd honored lost children with fireworks and posters, trying to symbolize a pain and horror that was otherwise impossible to express.

And here were people trying to do it again. Trying to express a story that felt impossible to tell. A story that enveloped not just the children who were snatched from their homes, but the people they left behind. The hidden pain and fear of not just decades of institutionalization, but centuries of fear.

"Damien says there are several hundred people who've agreed to come," Vince said. We were alone in the upstairs library. Both Ryan and Hally knew about Addie's return now, but they seemed to know to give us a little space. "Hybrids. Family of hybrids. Friends."

<A couple hundred?> Addie sounded doubtful. Aloud, she just said, "You aren't planning to go, are you?"

We all knew the question wasn't just directed at Vince.

Vince hesitated. He wanted to, I could tell. *I* wanted to. But gathering in front of the Capitol like that . . . it seemed like an unnecessary risk.

"They're going to wear orchids," Vince said, fiddling with an old, worn paperback. "I don't know where they're going to get orchids here in the middle of winter."

Since the broadcast, we'd learned more about Roarke in a day than we'd known in our entire lives. The area was famous for its orchids, especially a type often called the *Christmas orchid*. It felt cruelly ironic.

"Vince—" Addie started to say, but he interrupted her.

"We won't go," he said. "Jackson doesn't want to. Because he knows you won't. And if anything does happen . . ." He shrugged.

<If anything does happen> Addie whispered *<he doesn't want us to be separated again.>*

* * *

I woke in the middle of the night, soaked in the fear that we'd only dreamed our escape. That we were still trapped at Nornand, surrounded by other hybrid children, the smell of antiseptic, and the nauseating terror that came with being absolutely helpless.

<Addie!> I reached for her. Took a shuddery breath of relief when she was there. When I found her reaching for me, too.

Sweat plastered our clothes and blanket to our hot skin. I kicked the blanket away.

<It's okay> Addie whispered. *<It's okay. I dreamed it, too.>*

Addie and I didn't always share dreams, but when we had the same nightmare, it was nice to know there were fears that didn't need to be explained.

Something creaked. Footsteps passed in the hallway. I straightened, glancing around the room. Despite the awkwardness, we'd decided to stay with our family instead of Ryan and Hally, who were camping out in a library alcove down the hall. But we hadn't crept into bed until both our parents and Lyle were asleep. The three of them still slumbered, Mom and Dad on the bed, Lyle and us on bedrolls.

The clock on the nightstand read a little past midnight. We heard faint whispering, then more footsteps going down the stairs.

<They're leaving for the vigil> Addie said.

Damien had explained the plan just before dinner, when much of the house was gathered. Interested people could meet downstairs at midnight, and carpool to the city. He hoped to have everyone there by two a.m.

The children at Roarke had been attacked, he said, during the darkest hours of the night. He wanted to light candles for them during that same time.

I'd assured Ryan, when he sought me out, that Addie and I weren't going.

I closed our eyes but didn't lie back down. Damien's words echoed in my mind. *The darkest hours of the night.* Forty-eight hours ago, children locked away in a building had woken from their beds like this. Stared down gun barrels, empty-handed and terrified.

I clapped our hand over our mouth before I could make a sound. But it lived, weeping, in our throat.

<We'll go see them off.> I was half in a frenzy, the darkness sinking against us. *<Just to see them off.>*

Addie didn't argue.

I slipped out the door as silently as I could. The hall was deserted, and I hurried down the steps, following the murmur of voices. We found Damien's group gathered in the dimmed front parlor, already bundled into coats and hats. There were maybe fifteen people total. A few were still pulling on shoes.

I picked out Logan Newsome, who raised an eyebrow at

us. Damien, tall and sandy-haired, caught sight of us and said, "You'd better grab a coat. It's pretty cold out there."

"Oh, I'm not—" I started to whisper.

Then I recognized the girl nearest the door, wearing the cream-colored hat.

It was Hally.

FORTY

Hally hurried to our side and pulled us away from the group.

"We're about to leave, girls," Damien said.

"This'll be quick," Hally said over her shoulder. To Addie and me, she whispered, "I know, Eva. I know. I'm sorry I didn't tell you. Or anyone. But God knows it's not like you or Ryan have any high ground in that regard."

"It's—it's an unnecessary risk," I managed to sputter.

<Out of all the people I'd dreamed I might find down here> I said to Addie. *<Hally and Lissa were the last on my mind—>*

<Should they have been, though?> Addie said.

I'd gotten used to Hally and Lissa being a moderating voice of reason. A leash in my more impulsive moments. But once upon a time, Hally had been the one to risk reaching out to Addie. Lissa had sat in her bedroom and told us we weren't alone in being hybrid.

They'd also spent their entire lives wishing for more than what they had. They'd wanted the world to change, too, but they'd never wanted to see anything destroyed in the process.

Perhaps they'd never believed it was necessary.

"This isn't nearly as dangerous as some of the things you've done," Hally said. "Lissa and me . . . we want to do something. You and Addie went into Hahns. You took that upon yourself. And—and I know this isn't anything like that. But we want to be a part of this." She bit her lip. "It's a vigil, Eva. There have been so many tragedies pushed aside or buried or forced to be forgotten. And for the first time, people are coming to openly mourn."

I realized she didn't just want us to let her go. She wanted us to go with her.

"Ryan—" I started to say.

Hally shook her head. "He'll try to keep us from going, and they're about to leave—"

As if on cue, Logan called out softly, "Are you two coming? If you don't have a coat, I'm sure you could borrow one from the closet, as long as you bring it back."

"I'm coming," Hally said. She looked at Addie and me.

I took a deep breath. *<Addie?>*

<We want to go> she said softly. *<We've always wanted to go.>*

"We're coming, too," I said.

Damien wasn't kidding about it being cold. Most of the cars were parked a few blocks away to cast less suspicion on the safe house. Addie and I huddled in our coat as we walked, sticking close to Hally for warmth.

The streets were quiet but for the sound of our footsteps. Suddenly, Logan threw out a hand, motioning for us to stop.

We all froze. I listened. One. Two. Three seconds. Nothing but the soft whistle of the wind.

Damien resumed walking, and after a moment, the others followed. But I stopped again after a few steps. We'd noticed it, too, this time. The initial group had split into smaller ones as we neared the cars, and the soft footsteps we heard didn't match with anyone's feet.

We sensed him before we saw him.

"Lyle?" I said. "Lyle, I know you're there. Come out."

A beat. He emerged from the darkness of the trees lining the road, his mouth already set in an unhappy line.

Ours was unhappier. "Go back," I said. "Right now."

He shook his head, approaching us. "I'm coming with you to the vigil."

"You can't," I said.

"Why not?" he demanded. "Damien said there would be other kids there."

The others had all stopped, too, watching our exchange.

"He's right," Damien said. "Why not?"

"Because he's eleven years old!" I said.

Damien's eyes were steady. "Children get taken away at ten."

"I want to go," Lyle said, too loudly. The streetlight caught the whites of his eyes. Made them gleam. "If you make me go back, Eva, I'll wake everyone up."

Damien shot us a look, his eyebrows raised.

"It's not like that would stop *you*," I said irritably.

But it would stop us. And most likely, Hally. Her lips were pressed thin, her glances worried.

"It'll be okay," Logan said. "The boy wants to go. We'll look after him."

"Come on, Eva," Lyle said, the way he used to beg Addie to act out one of his stories with him, or walk to the library with him, or stay up an hour later when our parents were gone.

So I wavered, and I hesitated, but I let him climb after us into the car.

I let him come.

We drove into a peaceful, mostly slumbering city. Addie and I had never been to the Capitol before, though we'd seen it frequently on television. The president often stood in front of it for speeches, and had done so for decades.

Damien parked the car a few blocks from the mall, where we waited until the rest of our group arrived. Then we gathered by his trunk while he handed out candles. He even had orchids, though they'd wilted a little. We pinned them to our coats, the petals pink and white and velvet soft. Both Hally and I put extras in our pockets, to give to people who might not have their own.

Silently, we headed for the Capitol building. The group around Addie and me started with just over a dozen people, but other groups merged with ours as we drifted through the streets.

Despite the late hour, there were still people out walking. Groups of students on winter holiday paused in their laughter when we passed. It was, I realized with a start, officially Christmas Eve.

We didn't have signs. No one shouted anything. We just walked. The orchids pinned on some people's coats were made of fabric, or paper, but they were there.

Hally's hand brushed against ours, and I took it.

<I wish Ryan were here to see this> I said. *<I wish we'd woken him up.>*

Because it was beautiful, despite everything.

It was as if I hadn't realized how utterly alone I'd felt all my life until this moment. How my pain, my struggles, had felt like the problems of just a handful of people, easily forgotten and brushed aside. Until I saw the crowd gathered in front of the Capitol building.

Damien hadn't been lying when he'd said there would be hundreds—hundreds of people and the little, flickering lights in their hands.

It made our breath catch.

I lifted our hand. Marion's ring still gleamed around our finger. I pressed down on the little gemstone. Set it to record. It wasn't for *footage*, wasn't for Marion to show on the news. Wasn't to try and sway anyone's mind, or heart.

I wanted this recorded for the same reason I'd recorded the

stories the other girls told at Hahns. Because it was beautiful. Because I wanted it captured forever.

"Who are all these people?" Hally whispered.

Logan, who'd stuck near us, said, "Some of them must have started driving at noon, to come this far."

But they were here.

The candles were not uniform. They were tall and short and all different colors. The scented ones pillowed us in a heady garden of everything from lavender to pine trees to the smell of Christmas-morning cookies. The one Addie and I held was stubby and fat and deeply purple. Lyle's was green and tall and skinny. He held it clutched in one fist.

No one spoke. There was something powerful in the silence we carried with us.

Soon we were surrounded by the force of so many tiny flames that there was a warmth to it. I wasn't only thinking about the children of Roarke. I thought of Peter. And Hannah. And Viola. Of Bridget, and Emalia, and Jaime. Of all the children in all the institutions, and all the ones who'd evaded capture. Of the adults they'd become, after a lifetime of hiding.

If things weren't as they were, each of them would have deserved a memorial like this. But that was what battles did. Made the horror of one death into the incomprehensible tragedy of a thousand.

A wind crept through the crowd. Made the candles flicker.

We were so lost in our private thoughts that I didn't notice the commotion until Hally's hand tightened around ours, and I looked up, toward her. She was looking in the opposite direction, frowning.

"What?" I whispered. Too quietly, maybe, because she didn't reply.

And then I heard it, too—faintly. Sirens.

Her eyes snapped back to ours. I grabbed Lyle by the arm, so tightly he gasped.

"What's going—" He cut off as he looked over our shoulder. Saw, in the distance, the people stampeding. The crowd morphed into a landslide of people. Wavering at first—shifting in confusion in the semidarkness as the wave approached them. In a second, just a second—

It would break.

"Don't let go," I shouted at Lyle.

Everyone was shouting. The magic had broken. Lyle still clutched his candle, but as I pulled him toward us, we saw dozens of candles littering the ground.

A passing man rammed into us. We stumbled.

And in that instant—that fraction of a heartbeat—we lost Hally.

Our head whipped back and forth, trying to find her again, but the crowd was too thick—too chaotic—and—

"*Addie,*" Lyle screamed.

Every atom of Addie and me pinpointed on our little brother. Someone's fallen candle had brushed against his jacket hood. Caught against the dry, soft fabric. Set it alight.

We yelled for him to keep still. The mantra we'd been taught as children leapt to mind—*stop, drop, and roll*—but that was impossible in this crowd. Dropping to the ground here could be fatal.

We wrenched off our own coat and tried to smother the fire with it.

Please, please, I thought. *Oh, God, please.*

The flames died out. It was several more seconds before we could breathe again. Lyle stood panting, his eyes wide.

"You all right?" I managed to say. When he didn't answer, I started to ask him again, louder—but then I realized he was staring behind us in shock. He was staring at something. Someone.

I whirled around.

There were three officers. They wore helmets. Dark suits that made them look all the same. Faceless and uniform.

I wrapped our arms around Lyle. Pulled him closer to us. He didn't struggle. He'd gone silent, his limbs stony.

"You can't take him," I whispered. Then I screamed it. "*You can't take him.*"

They took him anyway.

They took us, too.

FORTY-ONE

We weren't the only ones they rounded up. Everywhere around us, officers herded people toward vans and police cars. There were too many to fit. Some groups stood motionless, watched over by officers who didn't seem to know what to do with them.

The ground lay strewn with extinguished candles and trampled orchids.

"It's going to be okay," I whispered to Lyle. The officers were taking us to one of the vans—we'd almost reached it when we were intercepted by another man, who frowned at us and murmured something to one of the officers.

We exchanged hands. The new policemen didn't take Addie and me and Lyle to the van, but to a police car.

<*Where are we going?*> Addie whispered as we climbed inside.

<*I don't know.*> I was too tense to guess. Where were Hally and Lissa? We hadn't seen them at all after the initial wave of panic. Had they been captured, too?

Please be safe, I thought desperately.

They'd only wanted to mourn.

The drive lasted little more than half an hour. Instead of bringing us to a jail, they parked us in front of a house. It stood two stories, imposing with an immaculate lawn and a flag hanging from the front porch. Fixtures set into the lawn cast a low, white light, brightening our legs as the officers urged us from the car.

Lyle looked at Addie and me as if we were supposed to know what was going on, but I could only shake our head in reply.

One of the officers raised his fist to knock. He didn't need to. The door opened. The officer quickly dropped his fist.

"Come in," said Mark Jenson.

The officers stayed just long enough for Jenson to make a show of offering them something to drink. They both said they were needed back at the scene. Jenson said, "Of course, I understand. Thank you."

"The mob's taking up a lot of resources right now," one of the policemen said. "But I'll see who's available and send some more men down to secure the house."

Then they were gone.

I made sure Lyle stayed by our side. Jenson looked at both of us, calculating.

"Is this yours?" I said quietly. "The house."

Jenson walked away, toward the kitchen counter. He wasn't

even looking at us anymore. Despite the fact that it was three in the morning, he was fully dressed, black, formal shoes and everything. There was something severe about the arrangement of his dark hair.

<*We aren't so far from the door*> I whispered.

<*We'll just run into the police outside*> Addie said. <*We can't take the chance.*>

Neither of us said it, but we both understood. If we'd been alone, maybe we'd have risked it. But not when we had Lyle here. Lyle, who never should have been here at all. Who only was because of our mistake.

Sometimes, it seemed like all our decisions turned out to be mistakes.

"In a way," Jenson said in answer to my question. "It's owned by the government, but I live here when I'm in the city."

He seemed so calm. So unsurprised.

"You knew, didn't you?" I whispered. "About the vigil. You knew who we were. What we were gathering for."

Jenson picked up the pitcher of water he'd offered the officers. Poured himself a glass. "I'd hoped you might show up. There were rumors you were in the area—not all of those hybrid safe houses are as safe as you people imagine. But it's better, sometimes, to let smaller criminals continue, so we can catch the important ones. We were close, in Brindt. Very close, the city police tell me."

"It doesn't matter, you know," I said. "I'm not important.

None of this depends on *me*—you won't have stopped anything—"

"You are important." Jenson headed for the sleek sofas. Sat carefully, unbuttoning his suit jacket. "You are important because I made you important. I crafted a story around you. You helped, of course, with all your reckless behavior. I couldn't have done it with just anyone."

He sipped from his glass of water. He looked, I thought, like he did behind the podium on television. Giving yet another speech. "From the day you escaped from Nornand and attacked that man in the hallway, you've been involved in one act of violence after another: targeting the rally at Lankster Square with explosives—"

"Fireworks," I protested, but Jenson went on as if I hadn't interrupted.

"—bombing the institution at Powatt. With materials, I might add, you stole from a hospital." His eyes were steady. I struggled to keep steady, too. Because he wasn't lying. "We would have captured you eventually. But I'm glad it happened tonight. It makes for a better ending to your story."

I tightened our hold on Lyle. "A better ending?"

<*He can't hurt us*> Addie said, her voice strained. <*There are police guarding the house outside—they might think we're criminals, but he couldn't just—especially not Lyle—*>

<*Would they stop him?*> I whispered.

Jenson set down his glass. "You're welcome to sit down."

We didn't move.

He glanced up at the clock, then turned back to us.

What's going to happen to us? I wanted to ask. But I was afraid to know. Afraid for Lyle to know.

"Violent tendencies often escalate," Jenson said. The sofas were angled to face a television. He reached for the remote control. "It's understandable how everything culminated in the attack tonight. Things would have still worked if we blamed someone else. But now people will have a clear narrative thread to follow."

<*What's he talking about?*> Addie whispered.

Despite myself, I took a step forward. "What attack?"

Jenson flipped on the television. It was already on a news channel.

"The one that just assassinated the president," he said.

FORTY-TWO

Addie and I watched dumbly. Somehow, without realizing it, we drifted closer to the television until we bumped up against the back of Jenson's couch. We didn't notice until Lyle came to join us.

The president was dead. The man had been in office longer than we'd been alive, and his uncle before him. We'd seen him during Independence Day speeches, and in our school textbooks, and on stamps. We'd watched him age. Most days, of course, we hadn't thought much about him. He was the president. He and his world seemed so far away. Untouchable.

We'd loved him, though, in a way. As the face of a country we'd been taught to love. Of a country we did love, despite everything it had done to us, because it was home.

The president was dead, and though the news anchors claimed nothing was certain, they talked about the hybrid gathering around the White House. Talked about the rumors that it had all been nothing more than a distraction. A plot to create an opening for an assassination.

"That isn't true," I cried.

Jenson glanced at us. "Don't worry. We won't put all the blame on you. You are a bit young to organize an assassination on the highest office in the country. We'll say there was a whole team of people working with you. That they were the masterminds. You were only the weapon. They pointed you and pulled the trigger. Took advantage of your youth and instability. You might come out of this whole thing looking like a tragic victim."

I shook our head. "No one—there was never any plan to kill the president. Why would anyone do that?"

"Because now, we're going to need another president," Jenson said.

"The vice president—"

"The vice president will take over," Jenson agreed. "But who knows if that will last? Do you know how this regime first came into power, with the president's uncle? The Great Wars had started, and the American public was afraid. The man campaigned with the promise of safety. He and his nephew understood that if you make people fear something, then assure them you're the only one keeping them safe, you'll have them in the palm of your hand." Jenson stared up at us, almost languid. "The people are more afraid than they've been in a long time. And it's the hybrids that are the villains. They're not going to want a vice president who was chosen two decades ago, who has never been virulent about hybrids. They'll search for someone who knows hybrids. Who has been working for years to protect the people from them. Who has even been developing a cure, to eradicate them forever."

He smiled.

Jenson called in two guards to usher us into a bedroom upstairs. At least one of them was still stationed out in the hall, just beyond the closed door.

I couldn't stay still. The bedroom, despite the lushness of the furnishings, was almost worse than the tiny cell Addie and I had been locked away in at Hahns. Then, at least, we'd thought our friends and family were safe.

<How many people are in on this lie?> I said softly. I needed to know the extent of what we were facing.

<I don't know. Enough. What are we going to do, Eva? How are we getting out of this?>

The clock on the wall read half past four. It might be hours before anyone woke and realized we were missing. Until someone heard what had happened on the news.

When they did, Ryan would realize both his sisters and we were missing.

Lyle sat on the bed, watching us. He'd been silent since we arrived at Jenson's house—since we'd been captured back at the Capitol mall. But now, softly, he said, "Are we going to escape?"

I smiled at him. Said, with all the conviction I had, and some I didn't, "Yes."

I continued pacing, but slowed my steps. The bedroom

was larger than most I'd ever seen. There were two windows, but a house like this probably had an alarm system. I didn't want to trigger anything—at least not until I knew exactly what we were doing.

<Is it too high to jump?> Addie said.

We peered out the glass, trying to see in the darkness. There weren't any nearby trees to climb onto. There was a drainage pipe, though, and the side of the house was stucco. Maybe, *maybe* we'd get enough traction to be able to make our way down.

Beyond that, there was just darkness and uncertainty.

"Are we going to jump?" Lyle said. He'd slipped off the bed.

I smiled at him grimly. "It might be the only way out."

"What about the guards?" he said. "Is it like the Secret Service out there?"

Despite everything, I felt a laugh in the back of our throat. "The Secret Service protect the president. You know that from your books."

"Yes," Lyle said. "But they think you killed the president."

That quickly sobered me again. I shook our head. "Jenson's trying to make other people believe that. I don't think he'd let a lot of people know where we are right now. Or that they grabbed us in the middle of the vigil and not in the Capitol building. I don't think there will be a lot of police out there." I turned back to the window and the night. "We just need a distraction."

“Like a fire?” Lyle said.

This time, I did laugh, because why not? Laughing wouldn’t make our situation worse. “Yeah, that would probably work. I wish I’d thought to bring a lighter.”

“You don’t need a lighter.” Lyle climbed onto the dresser so he could reach the clock, then brought it down and flipped it over, removing the batteries.

“Don’t tell me,” I said. “You’ve read about this.” He smiled. I couldn’t help smiling back. “I don’t find it weird at all that we’re related.”

“I need a knife. And some kind of tinder . . .”

I held out our hand until he passed us the clock. Then I grabbed a pillow from the bed and shucked the cover off. Pressing the cloth over the clockface, I smashed it as quietly as I could. Both Lyle and I froze, listening, but no one seemed to have heard.

A sliver of the clockface served nicely to rip open the pillow.

“There,” I said, pulling out the soft fluff inside. “There’s your tinder.” I held up the sliver of glass. “And here’s your knife. What? You don’t think you’re the only one who can be handy?”

Despite my protests that he was going to cut himself, Lyle insisted on being the one to carefully cut open the back of one of the batteries. We scoured the room for something small and metal to fit into the battery and settled on a paper clip I found in the nightstand drawer.

Addie eventually persuaded me to leave him to his fiddling while we started shifting the dresser in front of the door. It was even heavier than it looked. Even after Lyle came to help, it took forever to slide it into place—especially since we were trying to be as quiet as possible.

I frowned at him as he turned back to the tinder. "Lyle, you haven't tried this at home, have you?"

"Never," he said, a bit too quickly. "Look, it's working—" The bit of pillow fluff had started to glow. Lyle blew on it and said, with what was probably more excitement than necessary or normal, "Come on, give me more to feed it."

In a few minutes, the bed was aflame.

And the smoke alarm started to shriek.

Lyle seemed a little stunned by the sudden size and intensity of the fire. I grabbed his hand, pulling him toward the window. The table lamp was heavy and sturdy—more than strong enough to smash though the glass.

I'd been right. The house was alarmed. A second shrieking joined the first, so loud that Lyle clapped his hands to his ears. I was too busy trying to clear the glass from the window.

<Who goes first?> Addie said. Her voice was calm, given the circumstances. I discovered I was surprisingly calm, too. Our heart thudded. Our blood roared. But my mind stayed clear.

Someone pounded on the door. I didn't doubt they'd break it down before long. If Lyle went first, he had a better chance of escaping the house before the guards came in. But if he went first, and he fell—there'd be no one to catch him.

<*There could be guards down there, watching*> I said, and that settled it.

Lyle hovered nervously as I edged out of the window. The fire behind us grew, spreading. We barely saw the door through the flames. Even if the officers broke through, they'd have quite an obstacle in the way.

We'd have quite an obstacle in the way if we didn't get out of here fast enough.

<*Careful*> Addie gasped as I reached for the drainage pipe. Our feet almost slipped on the sill. I retracted our arm. Looked at Lyle, who stared back at us. We could barely reach the pipe. How was he going to do it?

It was too late to go back now. I took a deep breath. Wrapped our fingers around the pipe and swung our foot out, scrabbling for purchase against the wall.

<*Just do it, Eva*> Addie whispered. <*There isn't time. Just let go.*>

So I did. I launched out of the window and clutched at the drainage pipe and slid down—*down*—down until we struck the ground. Fell. Rolled through the damp grass.

I gasped for breath. Picked ourself up. Lyle was leaning out the window. I didn't dare shout, but I waved up at him. He put his foot against the windowsill, as I'd done, but hesitated.

Something inside the house banged. Lyle twisted around. When he turned back to us, the terror on his face told us everything we needed to know.

I forgot trying to keep quiet. I screamed at him, "Jump!"

Still, he hesitated. He looked behind him again.

"Jump, Lyle—"

He jumped—

Fell toward us, flying limbs and terror, and we caught him—we sort of caught him—we broke his fall. We sprawled against the lawn, the breath knocked from our lungs. Lyle was on his feet first. He pulled us up, too.

"Come on," he gasped. "Come on, Eva—"

We ran into the darkness, past the fire trucks when they came with their wailing sirens, past the crowd of people gathering outside, staring.

We ran until there was silence in the world again, and it enveloped us completely.

FORTY-THREE

Lyle stuck close as we crept through the darkness. Soon, we were downtown, sneaking through the ghost-town streets until we found an abandoned-looking pay phone.

"Keep watch for me," I whispered, and Lyle nodded.

I called the new satellite-phone number. Then held our breath as the phone rang. Once. Twice. Thrice—

"Hello?" Ryan's voice was raspy with sleep. The sun hadn't even risen yet. He must have answered the phone on instinct, because when he spoke again, his voice had sharpened, like he'd jolted more awake. "Who is it?"

"It's me," I whispered.

"Eva?" Confusion warred with concern in the two syllables of my name. "Where are you?"

"I'm near the Capitol," I said. "I—"

I cut off. Because right then, something started glowing bright red in the darkness of the booth.

<*The ring*> Addie said.

I stared at it. The light came from under the band—what

had Marion said? The light would glow red when the memory was full.

<Oh, Eva> Addie whispered as she realized, too.

We'd taken footage of the vigil. We'd never turned the ring off again.

The raid at the Capitol mall. The car ride to Jenson's house. Jenson's words.

Addie and I had all of it.

"Eva?" Ryan's voice broke through my shock. We heard him getting out of bed, the springs creaking. "Are you all right? What's going on? Are you at the vigil?"

"I came with Lyle—and Hally. I've got Lyle with me, but I don't know where Hally is. We're—we're on Willis Avenue, right before it hits Jamerson."

"Wait right there," he said. "We're coming right now."

Lyle was falling asleep by the time the cars arrived, lulled by exhaustion and the cold air. I'd tried to get him to huddle in the phone booth itself, where it was a little warmer, but he wanted to be where we were, so we ended up sitting by a patch of trees nearby, his head on our shoulder.

I didn't recognize the cars at first. I shook Lyle awake and was ready to make a run for it when the first car slowed to a stop and Dad stepped out, along with Ryan. The other vehicle never killed its engine, the low growl muffling Ryan's footsteps as he ran for us.

"We're fine," I said quickly, reaching for him, letting him

obliterate the rest of the world for just a moment with the way his arms wrapped around us.

I didn't say anything about Jenson. Not yet. Once I started talking, there would be too much to say. Too much to explain. Better that for now, he simply thought we'd managed to escape the police.

"Where's Hally?" he said, but from the tightness of the words, he already knew my answer.

"I don't know," I whispered.

"Let's not hang around," Dad said. He came over and awkwardly squeezed Addie and me on the shoulder.

Ryan spun to face him. "We can't head back without my sister." There was a cold certainty to him. Worry about Hally and Lissa had always been one of the few things to drive him to both fire and ice.

"It's a bad night to be roaming the streets," Dad said quietly. "If Hally is still out there, she can lie low for a while. As long as the government isn't already on the lookout for her . . . You can't tell a hybrid by sight."

"But she isn't just hybrid, is she? You *can* pick her out of a crowd, just by looking." Ryan's voice had gotten too loud. He capped it with effort, his throat jumping. His eyes swung back to Addie and me. When he spoke again, the words were quiet. "We have two cars. You take one and head back with Eva and Lyle. I'll stay with the others and keep looking. We've already picked up two people from the vigil. There may be more."

“No—” I started to say, but Ryan leaned toward us. Whispered so softly in our ear I could barely catch it—“*Your family’s frantic about you, Eva. Go with them.*”

<We’d only take up another spot in his car> Addie said quietly. *<We’d be recognizable. We wouldn’t do anyone any good by staying.>*

It all made sense. But sense could be a hard thing to obey.

“Later,” Ryan said. It was both a promise and a request. He kissed us on the cheek, just briefly. A moment of warmth in a frigid night. “I’ll find Hally and Lissa. We’ll meet you back at the house.”

“Can we get something to eat?” Lyle murmured from the backseat once we’d pulled away from the curb.

Dad promised him that there would be food once we got back to the house, and Lyle fell properly asleep soon after. Then it was just Addie and me and Dad, flying along the highway, the moon a sliver in the sky.

<In a weird way> Addie whispered *<it feels like a road trip.>*

<Do you think . . .> I hesitated and turned toward the window. *<Do you think it might have been a little like this, if Dad had really come and gotten us from Nornand after two days, like he’d promised?>*

Addie was quiet, and I almost apologized for bringing up such a silly, inconsequential thing. But by then, we were both lost in the idea of it. In this darkness, we could almost pretend it was half a year ago, and Dad had flown out to Nornand and demanded we be returned home. How had he put it? *I'll fly right up there and kidnap you from under their noses.*

Funny, how I remembered the exact words after so long. Or maybe not. Maybe it wasn't strange at all to remember promises one's father made, and didn't keep.

But that wasn't fair, perhaps, to think. People made decisions as best they could. Sometimes, it seemed like there wasn't any other choice. Or that there were only bad ones, and choosing the lesser of two evils was the best anyone could do.

I'd made choices myself I wished I hadn't.

"I'm Eva," I said suddenly. Dad's eyes shifted from the road to our face. I struggled not to look away. "I—I don't know if you heard, when Ryan said—I mean, I just wanted you to be sure. In case you weren't."

Dad was quiet a long while. He'd gone back to watching the road.

"You were always more stubborn than Addie," he said finally. He turned to us again and smiled. "You liked to take risks. Liked to climb trees and go camping and look over the edge of cliffs like you didn't know you could fall." He hesitated. "I don't know if you're still like that."

For a moment, I was too afraid to speak. Frightened that if I did, our voice might shudder, or crack. But I found it in me to keep it steady, and I said, "I guess I am."

I looked up, out the window. "Pyxis," I said softly. And there it was, faint but visible in the night sky.

"The mariner's compass," Dad said. He laughed a little. "Do you remember? When you and Addie were little, you guys used to say it looked nothing like a compass. You said it should have been called the telescope. What captains looked through when they were at sea, so they could see the shore."

It seemed like half the house was awake by the time we got back, many huddled in front of the television in various states of dress. Eyes were bleary. Hair wild and crumpled. Some nursed cups of coffee. Outside the windows, the horizon held the glimmerings of dawn.

The news on the TV was much the same as what Addie and I had heard at Jenson's house. The president had been killed. Investigations were still under way. More information would be released soon.

<What do you think really happened to him?> I said as we slowly joined the others in the living room. *<Do you think someone really did attack him? Or there was an accident?>*

<He's—was—nearing seventy> Addie said. *<Maybe it was something to do with his health—>*

<We never heard anything about him having health problems—>

<Maybe it was sudden> Addie said. *<And even if it*

wasn't, do you really think we'd know? The country's been increasingly unstable for the last few months. They're not going to tell everyone the president has serious health problems.>

Marion was, of course, among the ones awake. We left Dad and Lyle's side to reach her, our hand in our pocket where the ring was cool to the touch. The news anchor had just started to talk about the inauguration of the vice president, Carson Loyde.

Hybrids hadn't officially been blamed yet for the initial attack, but I figured it was only a matter of time before Jenson spun his story.

Meanwhile, we had our own.

"We need," I said, quietly, to Marion, "to make one more broadcast."

Marion couldn't extract the video from the ring here. She needed special equipment. But we didn't have time to waste. Addie and I wanted this footage broadcasted before the government officially pinned the presidential assassination on hybrids.

<*It will be one thing to convince them to never do it*> I said. <*Harder to make them have to retract their words later and admit they lied.*>

Marion's contact at the news station, the one who'd been hacking the system to broadcast our footage, would have everything necessary to retrieve the ring's footage. We decided, in the end, to just trust him to piece everything together. Sending the ring by post would take too long. Someone would need to drive there and deliver it directly.

But first, there was something we needed to add to the video.

Marion set up a camera in the dining room. I waited as she fiddled with the camera settings. Our parents stood near the back wall, silent and watching. Jackson hovered near us at the table, but Marion shooed him out of the way so she could pin a microphone to our shirt.

There was an air of command about her I hadn't noticed before. A kind of casual assurance and precision in her motions.

Finally, she grew still, calling for quiet.

"Whenever you're ready," she said and smiled at us with real encouragement.

I swallowed. Addie and I stared straight into the camera's cold eye, but I tried to picture in my mind the footage we would be broadcasting before this segment—the beauty, then terror, of the vigil. The hysterical attempt to beat the flames from Lyle's clothes. The ride to Jenson's home.

Then we'd cut to the jump out the window and our escape.

The gap in the footage was intentional.

We'd end in this room. With this recording of Addie and me.

<Speak, Eva> Addie said softly.

So I did.

I didn't call him out by name. Didn't crush him like I could have, if I'd wanted to.

Just said, steadily, for the camera—for Jenson—for the entire country to hear: "I have the rest of the footage. The part missing in the middle. But I won't show it. Not for now. Not when we can talk."

We stared into the cold camera lens until Marion nodded. She switched the camera off. "We'll just put this along with the ring. If we can get someone to leave soon, they'll have it delivered by this evening."

The dining-room door opened. "I'll take it," a voice said.

It was Logan. He had a nasty cut on the side of his face, but it had mostly stopped bleeding. Behind him came Ryan.

I found ourself standing. Ready to ask—

But then we saw his face, and I didn't need to ask.

He hadn't found Hally and Lissa.

The footage broadcasted the next morning, Christmas Day, in the middle of a rerun of Carson Loyde's first address to the American public as president. This time, Marion had been warned, and we were all gathered in front of the television, waiting.

As vice president, Loyde's face and presence hadn't been as ubiquitous as that of the president, but we'd been exposed to it all our lives. When I saw him, I hardly saw a person. I saw the pages in our history books, where pictures of him as a young man filled the chapters about the campaign he'd shared with the last president. I saw all the early mornings before school when parts of his speeches would play on the morning news, and the dinners where his voice murmured in the background.

He was younger than the previous president. Maybe sixty, maybe a year or two under. I couldn't remember. His hair wasn't yet all the way gray. There was a slow deliberateness to the way he moved on the screen, the way he spoke.

<*What does he make of all this?*> Addie said quietly as we watched him.

For more than twenty years, Loyde had been second fiddle in a regime established around the old president. One that had been formed even before their election, during the previous presidency.

Now he was suddenly in power. And the country was in disarray.

Loyde's face winked out, replaced by our own footage. We watched tensely—we hadn't been paying attention to where the ring was pointed, so there had never been any assurance that we had any clear shots. But Marion's contact had promised us he'd pieced together something comprehensible.

We watched in silence. The vigil. The car ride. The escape. Then the footage of ourself in the dining room.

Static.

Beside us on the couch, Devon remained expressionless. Both he and Ryan had barely spoken since yesterday, when they returned to the house without their sisters.

"Now we wait," he said.

FORTY-FOUR

We didn't need to wait long. A little after dinner, the satphone rang.

Henri, we all thought.

But it wasn't.

"Jenson released me to send you a message," Hally Mullan whispered over the line.

She refused to join us at the safe house—urged us, in fact, to move somewhere else with fewer people. She and Lissa were someplace safe; they promised us. She was almost sure she hadn't been followed after being released, but she couldn't be positive. Not until more time passed. She didn't want to lead anyone back to us.

But she had called as quickly as she could, because Jenson wanted to meet Addie and me tomorrow morning, at a café on the corner of Bente and Stentwood.

"I'm fine," she assured us again and again.

We had no choice but to believe her.

* * *

Jenson was already at the café when Addie and I arrived. He'd told us to meet outside, on the abandoned terrace, and I shivered as we stepped from the restaurant's temperature-controlled room and back into the winter chill.

<*If this were a movie*> Addie said wryly <*he would have said something about making sure to come alone.*>

But there wasn't any need for such theatrics. Jenson knew we didn't dare gather in large numbers, or create a scene. I didn't doubt he'd have some kind of security, but considering what kind of secret he was trying to keep, he wouldn't want to cause a fuss, either.

Jenson sat by himself at the edge of the terrace. He'd brought a newspaper with him. A cup of something steamed near his hand.

I hesitated just beyond the door. Addie had almost completely recovered her strength. She'd offered to be in control today, for the meeting. But I'd wanted this. I'd wanted to speak directly to this man.

<*He looks so . . . casual*> I said. <*So ordinary.*>

The man who'd shown up at Nornand so many months ago dressed like he was going to the symphony—who we'd seen at Powatt in shirtsleeves and polished shoes—who was never short of impeccably dressed on the evening news—reclined against the delicate café chair in a plain, brown jacket and uncollared shirt. He hadn't even looked this casual when he'd received Lyle and us at his home.

Was he trying to be inconspicuous? He'd become such a public figure over the last few months—all part of his plan, I now realized. There were other directors of hybrid affairs, but none I—or the people—knew as well by name. Jenson had fame. Jenson also had Jaime, and the so-called cure.

<*Now or never*> I muttered, and felt Addie bolstering me as we crossed the terrace and pulled out the chair across from Jenson's table. It scraped against the floor, and I let it, dragging out the sound until Jenson was forced to look up. It was a moment of feeling powerful. Of gratification.

Then I sat down, and my boldness disappeared under the weight of Jenson's eyes. He lowered his newspaper. Folded it. I couldn't help the way our gaze drifted to the headline about Loyde's ascension. All eyes were on him, waiting for his first decisions as head of the country. Anything he did now would set a precedent for the years, perhaps decades, to come.

If Jenson didn't get rid of him, the way he planned.

"You're brave," he said. "Meeting me here like this. Or perhaps just stupid. I haven't decided."

I forced myself to stare him in the eyes. There was something almost unnatural about them—how unwavering they were. Or perhaps they just scared me, and that was why I found them inhuman. Wasn't that a mix-up people made all too frequently?

<*We're fine, Eva*> Addie said quietly, and I echoed the words back to her.

<*We're fine.*>

We're strong. We'd get through this, as we'd gotten through everything else.

"We understand you," I said. "And what you want. It provides a kind of security."

"We?" he said.

I set our hands on the table. I wished we still had our ring.

"Addie and me," I said. It wasn't as if there was any point in pretending about that anymore. If Addie and I weren't hybrid, then we wouldn't be here. None of this would have happened.

"Eva Tamsyn." He rolled my name around in his mouth, but otherwise hardly reacted. As if the idea that I wasn't Addie—that he was speaking to one of the recessive souls his program, his *cure*, sought to eradicate—didn't matter at all. "What did you want to talk about?"

"I want Emalia Foy freed," I said. He didn't react in the least to her name. "She was arrested about two months ago. I don't know where she is now, but I want her released."

"If we have her," Jenson said. "How do you know she isn't hiding somewhere?"

We couldn't know for sure, not with the way people disappeared nowadays. But if Emalia and Sophie had been able, they'd have found a way to contact us by now. They'd been extremely talented forgers, had known Peter's network well. They wouldn't have just buried themselves.

"You have her," I said, as calmly as I could. "And I want her released."

He nodded. "Fine."

I swallowed. Bargaining Emalia's release had felt easy, but promises were only promises, and this next request would be much harder. "There's an institution in the mountains of Hahns County."

"I know it," Jenson said. Of course he did. It fell under his jurisdiction.

Our hands felt naked on the tabletop. I itched to wrap them around the edge of our seat—it was more Addie's habit than mine, but physical tics sometimes bled between us. As if catching my faltering, Addie gripped on to me. Held me steady until I could do it myself.

"I want the institution dissolved," I said. "It's old—it's falling apart. You can give them any excuse you want to. But I want the institution closed and all the children freed."

"What would you have me do with them?" he said. "Despite what you may believe, not every family of a hybrid child wants him back."

He was right. I didn't want him to be, but he was. The country was changing, but not enough.

"Send them home with the families who will take them," I said quietly, and hoped that it would be enough. That the kindness of a few would stretch far enough to give each child a place to stay. At least for a little while. Until they found new homes.

Jenson nodded, his expression unchanged. I had no way of reading his thoughts.

<This means nothing to him> Addie said. *<We're right about Hahns being old and falling apart.>*

<And there's probably no love lost between him and the woman in charge> I said.

"Is that all?" Jenson said. "Because—"

"No," I said. Blurted, really. Each moment in his presence, even when he was being amiable, made me feel sicker. I wanted this over and done with. "You won't blame the president's death—whatever really caused it—on hybrids. And I want Jaime Cortae."

"Yes," Jenson said. "And no."

I fought the urge to tighten our hands into fists. "No?"

"I won't give you Jaime." Jenson leaned back in his chair. "I couldn't if I wanted to. Releasing that Foy woman? If we have her, I haven't heard about it, which means she isn't important. No one would notice. Dissolving Hahns? A bigger hassle, but as you've said, I can come up with reasons. But Jaime Cortae is the key to the future. I cannot give him up."

I tried to remain calm, but it was hard with the rush of heat his refusal sent thrumming through our body. "I can release the video. It'll destroy you—"

"Losing Jaime would destroy me," he said. "And you won't release the video. Not while I have him."

He let me sit in silence for a moment, searching desperately for something to say.

Then he leaned toward us. "I will give you Emalia. And Hahns. A gift, of sorts, for your cooperation. I won't blame you for the president's death. But don't think you have the upper hand. The world is not on your side, Eva. It never has been."

"The other countries—" I started to say, and his face darkened. He laughed a short, brutal laugh.

"This is not the school yard, Eva. Countries do not play games for marbles and pennies. Do you think those other nations are purely altruistically interested? That they'll be happy to just step in and help out, then go home again when you don't want them anymore?" He stood. "You think it's a good thing that you're cracking this country open, leaving it weak and exposed. You think change can only be for the better. But you're playing with a fire you don't know how to control. And you'd better be careful before everything burns down around your ears."

FORTY-FIVE

Two days after our meeting with Jenson, four days after the first announcement of the president's death, Marion heard through her sources that Hahns had just been shut down, the children sent away. There was no way of being positive Jenson had kept his word about actually sending them home, but Marion assured us that it seemed to be true.

We'd received no word about Emalia and Sophie yet, but Hally had joined us at our new lodging, an isolated cabin Marion managed to rent under the guise of a tourist.

There had still been no official decree for the cause of the president's death. The reports—and there were so many reports—all claimed that investigations were under way, that as soon as all the facts were straightened out, they'd release them to the public.

The delayed information whipped the country into a frenzy of theories. People clamored for the truth, and in the absence of an official story, created their own. Hybrids had done it. Foreigners had done it. *Foreign hybrids* had done it.

"It's all going to explode," Marion kept saying. The situation worried her; I could tell. Because the instability truly concerned her? Or because she liked to be in control of the storytelling around her?

"What do we do now?" Hally said, looking from Addie and me to Devon, then Jackson. "Send Jenson another message?"

We were gathered in the foyer, sunlight catching the dust in the air. I could see the strain on everyone's faces. We were exhausted like we'd never been exhausted before. The months of worry, of fear and stress and torment, had taken their toll.

"It won't make a difference," Jackson said. "We have nothing new to bargain with."

"We're not *bartering*," Addie snapped, then pressed our fingers to our forehead. Said, quietly, "Sorry. You said *bargain*. I just—"

Jackson wrapped his hands around ours. Lowered them, gently, from our face. He and Addie looked at each other a moment, silent in their understanding.

I'd asked Addie about her and Jackson. Where they stood with each other. And I'd understood when she said she wasn't sure.

I like having him near, she'd said. *That's all I know for right now.*

The truth was, we all had much bigger things to worry about. I hoped one day for the luxury of worrying about the everyday things. The non-life-threatening things.

"We need something to break the stalemate," Devon said.

* * *

Addie and I tried to focus on what we could. Jackson and Vince were the best at getting people to relax and lose themselves. They cracked jokes, talked too much, and got even the most dour-faced in the cabin to smile from time to time.

This stalemate, however tense, was also a time of forced rest. With everyone cooped up in the safe house, there was no excuse to avoid anyone for long. It was mend fences or put up more walls, and as far as our family was concerned, Addie and I didn't want the latter.

We used to eat primarily with Ryan and the others, but we made a point now of searching out our parents and Lyle for some meals.

One night, Mom said, "Eva, want me to get more carrots for you?" as if it were the most casual thing in the world.

And it was. Or should have been, and I struggled to overcome the swell of emotion I felt at the sound of my name. The feeling of her recognition.

Addie understood. Perhaps not perfectly, but better than most.

<She's waiting for an answer> she said gently, and I made myself nod. Made myself say, "Yeah, that would be great, thanks," and smile without looking like an idiot. From the way she smiled back at me—hesitant, then stronger, then wavering again—she knew a little of how I felt, too.

Things were a little easier after that. Slowly, bit by bit, our family fit back together again. We'd never be exactly the same as we'd been before, but I found myself coming to love our new whole.

Then came the morning Addie and Lyle were bickering about something stupid—spilled cereal, splashed milk—and the television in the living room burst into static.

We froze.

Turned.

And saw—heard—the missing footage from the night of the vigil. Jenson's voice explaining his plans. A brief shot of his face as he moved to the couch.

Our only bargaining chip for Jaime. Now lost.

The stalemate had broken.

There was only one person who could have broadcasted the footage. Addie hurtled through the cabin until we found Marion seated by the kitchen window.

"Why?" Addie demanded. We were so furious our body seemed to burn from the inside. Our face flushed, heat ripping through our veins. "Why'd you do it, Marion?"

She was calm. Or tried to be calm. But I caught the flicker of discomfort on her face before she hastened to wipe it away.

She spoke softly, but steadily. "Because it was the right thing to do. It's been too long, Addie. And I kept telling you—things were going to explode. The hybrids were going to take the brunt of the damage. You must see that. And Jenson is dangerous. By delaying this footage, you were giving him more time to plan—to come up with some scheme that would leave you with no cards, instead of one."

"We have no cards now," Addie cried. "Jaime—"

"He wasn't going to give you Jaime," Marion said. "Please, Addie, I know it's hard to accept, but this—"

Addie squeezed our hands into fists. Never in our life had she been prone to violence, but I felt the whirl of it in our blood. "This wasn't your choice to make!"

"Was it yours?" Marion said.

I wanted to scream at her. Force that calm from her face. Make her understand the horror of what she'd just done, because she didn't—she didn't understand—

"Addie," Dr. Lyanne said softly. She took us by the arm. We hadn't even noticed her approach.

Addie tried to speak—started to explain—but one look at Dr. Lyanne's face, and we knew it wasn't necessary.

Dr. Lyanne had, in some ways, left Nornand because of Jaime Cortae. Had begun to doubt the rules and treatments for hybrids because of him. Had stolen him away to safety, then had him stolen back from her.

"Come away, Addie." Dr. Lyanne's fingers tightened around our arm, the only betrayal of her feelings. Her expression was granite sharp.

She pulled us away from Marion, who was still seated, cold sunlight shining on her stark features.

"It was the right thing to do," Marion called after us. "You just care too much for this boy to see it."

We trembled, but we did not turn around. Did not reply.

* * *

The broadcast shattered everything. I'd known Jenson had built himself up as a hero and protector in the public's eyes, but I'd underestimated just how well he'd inserted himself into the country's heart. Mark Jenson; his plans; his cure—they'd comforted a country in desperate need of comfort and assurance.

Now all that was destroyed, right as the new administration was taking its first, wobbling steps. I thought of what Jenson had said that day on the café terrace. How we were playing with a fire we didn't know how to control. Just because we hated him—just because he was so wrong about so many things—didn't mean he was wrong about everything.

Jenson was ripped from his pedestal. That much was certain. The new president publicly condemned him. Everyone, it seemed, scrambled to distance themselves as much as possible from him and his fall, fearing for their own reputations in this tumultuous time.

But what now? That was the question on everyone's lips. Jenson was gone, and whatever plan the government had to blame the old president's death on hybrids was shaken—possibly never to recover.

But what would the administration do next? What would *we* do next? As much as Addie and I wanted to just sink into our fury at Marion, we both knew it was a waste of time. Anger could not change the unchangeable. We would have to act.

But this time, the first move wasn't to be ours.

President Loyde announced a speech to be given at the Capitol mall. One open to the public, and broadcasted live to the country. He promised to address the nation's fears and concerns. To finally clear up the confusion and controversy surrounding the old president's passing. To show us that there was no reason to give up hope. That though Jenson had proven to be corrupt, it didn't mean all his programs were bunk as well.

He promised to show us, in person, the boy who had been cured, and who represented the future.

FORTY-SIX

"I want to be there."

Addie and I said it again and again over the next few days. To our parents. To Ryan, and Lissa, and Jackson, and Dr. Lyanne. To Marion, we said it only once.

She was the only one who didn't argue against the idea. Who said she might be able to get Addie and me identification saying we were her intern, or something, and get us into the press area nearest the podium. We'd have to be disguised, of course. But like when we'd hidden in plain sight at Hahns, the press corps was the last place anyone would think to search for us.

It would still be dangerous. Our parents attempted to convince us that while *someone* ought to be at the mall for the speech, it didn't have to be *us*. But the suggestion withered as they realized we'd never accept that. Realized, too, perhaps, that Addie and I were beyond their control now.

Ryan and Lissa tried to convince us not to go alone, but we all knew that a gathering like this, when tensions were so high, was the last place for anyone who could be misconstrued as foreign, or other. If it wasn't safe for Addie and me, it was ridiculously dangerous for both of them.

"I have to see him," Addie said to Jackson and Dr. Lyanne. "Who knows when we're going to get another chance to be this close? To—to possibly learn something that might help a rescue later? I know I won't be able to do anything—I won't *try* to do anything. But I want to see him, and not just on TV."

And I want him to see us.

That was the unspoken second part. We hoped, even with the disguise and the distance, Jaime might look and recognize us, so he'd know we hadn't abandoned him. We were still coming for him, even if it took a little longer.

We arrived at the mall just after nine, about an hour before the speech was supposed to begin. The crowd was already enormous. People thronged the security lines, and beyond that, the mall itself. Everyone was eager to see, and hear, and know. I understood the need.

People were waiting to be told what the future would bring. What they were supposed to be doing. What effect these past few months would have on their lives, and their country.

"Stay close," Marion whispered to us. Her eyes met ours, but only for a moment. Ours was an uneasy understanding, an even more uneasy peace. Marion had worked quickly, getting us the promised ID, making sure we had a credible backstory in case anyone asked, and telling us how the setup for the speech was expected to go. Perhaps she was trying to make quiet amends, or show us she'd always been on our side.

The security check for the press corps had happened before we ever reached the Capitol mall. Our heart had pounded as we went through, certain the security guard would recognize us. But he didn't, just waved a metal detector over our body and motioned us through when he saw we weren't carrying any bags or purses.

The rest of the press corps jostled around us, checking cameras and video cameras and microphones. Their badges glinted in the morning light. No one paid Addie and me the least bit of attention. According to our ID, we were Dana Stevens, intern. Security hadn't allowed us to wear a hat, but the short, dark-colored wig made us into a different person.

The area around the podium was still empty, the president not yet due to arrive. Addie glanced behind us, to the rest of the crowd. Restless, aimless energy poured from them, some talking to one another, others staring straight ahead, or up at one of the giant screens situated around the mall. The screens were black for now, but I could imagine the new president's face towering over us.

He must realize how tenuous his new position was. Was he frightened of this mob of expectant people?

Then Addie whispered *<There they come.>*

The small group moving toward the podium consisted mostly, it seemed, of security. We couldn't even see the president at first. Some of the guards split off from the main group, situating themselves at intervals from the podium.

The crowd quieted, little by little. A few clapped. Then the clapping grew, and spread, and became a roar that reverberated in our chest.

"Thank you, and good morning," the president said. He smiled a little. Not too widely, but not too hesitantly, either. His suit was gray, the material textured and heavy. He looked, I thought, much the same as he'd looked when he was vice president. More like an elderly college professor than the head of the state.

The next few minutes were a bit of a blur. He talked about the tragedy that was his predecessor's passing. The decades he had served the country. The good he had done for it. The years they had known each other, and the kindness and fortitude of heart he knew the man had possessed. He didn't, despite his promise, say what had caused the ex-president's death. Perhaps he meant to address it later. Much of the crowd, I was sure, was waiting for an explanation.

The only words Addie and I waited for were Jaime's name.

And then, finally—finally—we heard it.

Jaime Cortae.

It was mixed in with something about hybrids and the cure and the future of the country. About how Jaime was proof of—of something. We heard it mostly as a buzz of sound, because Jaime was walking toward the podium.

He moved better than we'd ever seen. There was only the smallest hint of a limp—none of the sailboatlike swaying he'd suffered from back at Nornand, when we'd first met. Someone had cut his hair, tamed the mess of brown curls. Maybe it was our imagination, but he looked different. Taller. It had been months since we'd last seen him by the side of that highway.

<*Oh, Eva*> Addie whispered.

We weren't the only ones staring at Jaime. Every screen had cut to his face, blown it up so it towered over the mall, copy upon copy. His eyes looked glazed. His hands were shaking. Nerves, anyone else might think. But we knew Jaime. Knew the damage the surgery had done to his body.

I was so enraptured that when Addie said <*Eva!*> I didn't react at first. It wasn't until she called my name the second time that I heard the frightened urgency in it. Snapped back to the here and now.

And realized what she'd noticed out of the corners of our eyes.

Two men had appeared at the edge of the crowd. One stared at Jaime. We'd seen them before—there was something *wrong* about them, something that made our stomach clench, our blood roar.

<*The officers*> I said, the realization a wrecking ball. <*The ones who brought us to Jenson's house the night of the vigil—*>

It was all I had time to say. The first man rushed forward. His hand was buried in the inside pocket of his coat—

"Jaime!" we screamed.

His head snapped toward us.

We ran. Rammed through the reporters separating us. Sent video cameras crashing to the ground.

The security guards had seen the man. They made for him, too—but Addie and I were closer. Reached the man first.

Together, we tumbled to the ground. The gun clattered against the pavement.

The guards were on us in a moment. Arms ripped us away from the man. Forced us still. Scooped up the gun. Someone jabbered into a radio.

"Jaime," we said breathlessly. "Where's Jaime?"

Then we saw him. He'd frozen halfway to the podium. A guard was headed for him, but he darted away. Ran for us. We tried to grab him, and when we couldn't, he grabbed on to us instead.

He was breathless, but he smiled so wide, and for a moment, all else was overwhelmed by the joy of having him here in front of us. Of knowing he was all right.

Then the rest of the world came crashing back.

FORTY-SEVEN

We froze.

The cameras had caught everything. Blown it up larger than life and multiplied it across the mall, on screen after screen.

The two men who'd tried to attack Jaime proved volatile prisoners. They shouted and twisted. It took several guards each to subdue them.

<*Why?*> Addie kept saying. <*Why would they want Jaime dead? Why would Jenson want him dead?*>

A handful of seconds lasted forever. And in that eternity, Addie and I made eye contact with the president of the Americas. With the man who now led our country.

Then a guard grabbed Jaime by the arm. Another two took hold of us. Between them, they pulled us from the mall, out of the blinding sunlight, and into the darkness of a waiting van.

Things happened very quickly. Then very slowly.

The drive. The hustle into what seemed to be part of the

Capitol building—we saw too little of the exterior to be sure. The march through the lush hallway. The search for weapons and recording devices.

Then—and now we did protest—they took Jaime away again.

That was the fast part. The slow part consisted of Addie and me getting locked into a small sitting room, the door shutting in our face and remaining shut no matter how we pounded or shouted.

Eventually, we gave up. We didn't doubt we were being watched.

The very design of the room spoke of wealth, stateliness, and tradition. The carpet was thick, the chairs heavy, polished wood. An oil painting of some battle I was sure was meant to be the initial Revolution against the hybrids hung on the wall.

We sat down on one of the chairs. Stared at the painting. The walls. The door.

<*If Jenson couldn't have Jaime, he didn't want anyone to have him*> I said. It was the only explanation I could think of for his men's actions today. <*If he couldn't use Jaime as a way to secure power over the country, he wasn't about to let the new president do so.*>

Addie gave a sharp, disbelieving laugh. <*What happened to everything he said about the importance of keeping this country together?*>

In the end, Jenson was as irrational and human as anyone.

We sat in that luxurious room, waiting.

Time passed. An hour? More?

Then the door opened again, and the president stepped inside.

I was so shocked I almost fell off the chair.

He looked older in person. He studied us as we studied him. He'd shut the door behind him, so we appeared to be alone, but I didn't trust that. There were certainly cameras in here, watching everything. The guards posted outside would be listening, too.

"Addie, isn't it?" he said. "Addie Tamsyn."

Here was the voice I'd been hearing on the television and the radio my entire life, addressing me directly.

Only, he wasn't addressing me.

"It's Eva," I said quietly.

Unlike Jenson, he did react to my correction. But he suppressed it to just the slightest tightening of his mouth.

Addie and I had been conditioned to find the sight of him comforting. Assuring. Even as I looked at him now, I saw a certain grandfatherly quality to his face. He had a son, I knew, a young man who was probably looking to join politics himself.

If things went well, he might even become the next president. The role had passed from uncle to nephew the last time.

"Eva," he amended.

"Where's Jaime?" I said. My interruption seemed to surprise

him, but like his reaction to my name, he bit it down. I supposed when you'd been in such a public office for so long, you got good at remaining outwardly calm.

"He's fine," he said. "You don't need to worry about him."

I couldn't help my laughter. "Someone tried to kill him today."

"That's been taken care of." But for the first time, he seemed uncomfortable.

I found myself saying, "But next time? You can't be sure there won't be a next time. Jenson had his secrets. Who else in this administration has an agenda they're not telling you about?"

"Everyone," he said with a slight smile. "I'm not naive, I assure you. This administration wasn't built out of loyalty to me."

His ready admittance surprised us.

<*Maybe we aren't being recorded in here*> Addie said hesitantly. I wasn't sure what that meant for us. For this conversation.

President Loyde settled into one of the chairs across from us. I fought the urge to back away.

"I've been hearing about you for a while, Eva," he said. "Ever since that stunt you pulled at Powatt."

"It wasn't a stunt," I said automatically. "And we didn't mean to hurt anyone. We just—"

"I meant how you ran into the building to warn everyone."

His voice was surprisingly gentle. I didn't trust it. I couldn't. "It was a brave thing to do. Especially for people you don't even like."

I wasn't sure how to respond to that. "That's not what all the broadcasts said. On the news, I was just a monster."

"I wasn't in control of the news." He shrugged, an almost cavalier motion. Then he grew serious again. "If I had been, perhaps I would have made the same decision. We need villains, Eva. Especially when the country is already in turmoil. Especially when you're trying to keep control."

"But it's all lies." I couldn't keep the fierceness from our voice, however much I recognized that I should be careful. I could feel Addie biting back a warning. "You can't support a country on lies. Jenson fell because he was caught in one. And right now, this whole government is full of them. The truth behind the vaccinations—all this about the rest of the world being shattered and ashes . . . about hybrids being mentally unstable . . . maybe it's lasted for this many decades, but it won't last forever. With the way things are going, it might not last another year." I'd run out of breath. Had to pause to inhale.

And realized that he was actually listening to me. Actually looking at me and taking in my words, and maybe they were nothing new to him—certainly nothing he hadn't considered himself. But he was still listening.

It was a strange feeling. A year ago, I'd been utterly voiceless. Invisible. A ghost.

My words, which once echoed no further than the space between my mind and Addie's, now had the ear of the most powerful man in the country.

"I only have so many choices." He spoke slowly, calmly. "And all of them come with consequences."

"Help us," I whispered. "Help the hybrids, and you'll have our loyalty forever. And maybe we're not a huge part of the population, but we're not insignificant, either—"

He smiled wryly. "I've come to see that."

"And you'll earn the respect of the foreign countries, too," I said. "They'll see you as an ally, not an enemy."

"I wouldn't go that far," he mused. "But I can believe they'll like me better than my predecessor."

I straightened in our chair. Made sure to look him right in the eye. "You'll go down in history as the man who brought truth to the American people. Not just another liar. Another puppet who might, one day, trip over his own lines."

He was still smiling by the time I finished. "You have a way with words, you know. And certainly, a passion behind them."

I said, "I appreciate the ability to speak."

After a long moment, he nodded. He stood, and we remained seated, staring up at him. What did this mean? What had any of this meant?

"So what's going to happen?" I said, and for the first time, he laughed. A low, quiet laugh, but a laugh all the same.

"I don't know," he said. "But something different.

Something like nothing that's happened before."

I didn't know what to do with my sudden hope. How to control it.

"You'll have to stay with us for a little while, I'm afraid," he said. "But I'll have you and Jaime put together. So you won't be alone."

"I'd like that," I said. "I'd like that a lot—thank you. But . . . I'm not alone."

"No, I suppose you never are." His brows knit, then softened again. Something like a smile touched his lips. "Right now, I wonder if I'm jealous."

He turned, as if to make for the door, but I called out, "Wait—how did the old president die? It wasn't hybrids."

"Two days before your vigil, he had a stroke," President Loyde said. "He was in a coma—recovery uncertain. Only a few people knew. It was bad timing for a weakened president. The story within the administration was that he'd simply gotten a bad case of the flu. After he died, the planned story was that a hybrid had poisoned him through his saline drip." He seemed lost in thought a moment. "What did he really die of? Stress. Age. Life."

"Is that what you were going to tell the crowd today?" I said.

He was quiet a moment. Then shook his head. "No," he said slowly. "It wasn't."

He turned, once again, to go. I stopped him a second time.

“Are we in the Capitol building?”

His eyebrows raised. “Yes, we are. This is a corner of the eastern wing. I suppose no one really pays much attention to it. Not much historical significance.” He suddenly smiled a little. “Until now.”

FORTY-EIGHT

He kept his promise about Jaime, and for a while, that was enough to keep us happy. We were housed somewhere in the city—the van they piled us into didn't allow much in the way of sightseeing, but we didn't drive very long.

There, we were allowed to live in what basically amounted to the world's most comfortable prison. Jaime told us he'd been kept under similar circumstances for the past few months. Only they'd moved him from place to place, surrounded him with specialists who worked him through physical therapy, tried to coach his speech. We were relieved there'd been no more surgeries.

They let us know nothing about the outside world. We were allowed no television, no radio, no telephones. We weren't even allowed on the first floor, and all the windows on the second were made with reinforced glass, in addition to being alarmed.

We stayed there a little more than two weeks. Later, the others would fill us in on the missing days. How the uproar about the attackers took up most of the public consciousness at first—who they were, what they'd wanted. Eventually, they'd been tied back to Jenson. Blaming Jenson for the attempted attack gave the people someone to hate and fear other than the hybrids. And it paved the way for the president to start blaming him for other things as well—the overblown reports of hybrid crime. The exaggerated stories about Addie and me, and Peter's underground.

Public belief is at once a powerful and delicate thing. From what we heard, the president knew it. He worked carefully, but quickly in this liminal time when his administration was still new, and could be separated from the previous one.

A few weeks into the new year, he told the country the truth about the rest of the world. We were released on the same day. In the chaos, no one noticed a girl and boy ushered back into the city streets. They sent a guard with us. For our own protection, they said, however obvious their true intentions were. For the moment, it hardly mattered. All we cared about were the looks on our family's faces when they met us at the door. The way Hally hugged us and wouldn't let go.

The way Ryan kissed me later, when we were alone, and it was night, and the stars looked like a map of possibilities above us.

Emalia contacted us on a still Saturday morning, tripping over words in her rush to say she was in Renwert, a few hours away—yes, she and Sophie were fine, no, she didn't want us to come get her; she'd meet us someplace in the middle.

She sounded different than when we'd last known her. I wondered if I'd still recognize in her the willowy woman who'd dressed in pastels and looked like the dawn. Perhaps Addie and I had never given her enough credit beneath the appearances, and the woman who returned to us, months after she left that day to send Henri off, would be the same person. Just peeled back to her core.

Dr. Lyanne brought her back to us, and we greeted them with bone-crushing hugs. She seemed a little distant, a little lost. Dr. Lyanne must have told her about Peter and Warren's passing during the drive here.

"Go upstairs," Dr. Lyanne said, extracting her from the rabble of people who wanted to see her. "When was the last time you properly slept?"

Emalia gave a faint, trilling laugh. "Ages."

By the time the biggest changes came, though, Addie and I had left what we hoped was the last safe house we'd ever have to live in. Our family hadn't decided where we wanted to stay yet, though we knew we didn't want to return to Lupside. We'd just gotten back in touch with Mr. and Mrs. Mullan, and were waiting for them to fly in to meet us, when the news broke.

We'd known it was coming. The news had covered little else but the talks leading up to the decision. But now, finally, it was official.

Tomorrow, the hybrid institutionalization system in the Americas would be obsolete.

"It won't change everything," Devon said. We'd gathered in front of the television to watch President Loyde announce it in front of the Capitol. It felt utterly *right* to be here, the six of us together, for this moment. Ryan and Devon. Hally and Lissa. A year ago, it had been the six of us together, too. "But—"

"It's a start," Hally said.

And Devon smiled.

<*Think about all those children going home*> Addie said. There was a note of something like wonder in her voice.

I could imagine it. The first steps out into a warming world. The children who'd been locked away for months, and the ones who'd managed, through sheer tenacity, to survive for years.

What was more, I could imagine the simultaneous sigh of relief from the hundreds—thousands—of children around the country who were approaching their tenth birthday and hadn't yet settled. The dissolution of the institutionalization system wouldn't save them from the fear and contempt of their peers, the sideways looks from their teachers, maybe even the growing hesitance of their own parents. But at the very least, it would save them from being ripped from home and shut up in concrete boxes, to languish like refuse until expiration.

The other things—the tolerance, the fading of the hatred and the fear—would come later. I believed in that.

EPILOGUE

There were traces of our old house in our new one. Our parents hadn't taken much when they left Lupside, but some of what wasn't sold had been put in storage, so the strawberry-patterned curtains went up in the kitchen windows, the mantelpiece filled up again with our old pictures, and Lyle, digging through the cardboard boxes, unearthed a few of his favorite books.

<It's good, I think> Addie said once, when we were still moving in. *<That it's not the same. I don't think it could be the same.>*

I liked the new house, with its small but neat lawn. The worn stones of the walkway. The way our room faced east and lit up in the morning.

I liked how the Mullans didn't live too far away to visit. That Jackson and Vince knew where they'd be able to find us, when they were finished traveling the country a bit—enjoying their new freedom. That Dr. Lyanne and Jaime and Emalia and Kitty and Henri all knew our number. That speaking with them was as easy as picking up the phone.

I liked the fact that we were only a few miles from the coast. Some mornings, we spent hours at the edge of the water, waiting for it to get warm enough for swimming. Our parents had bought us a paint set, a sort of late birthday and Christmas present bundled together. Addie took the kit to the beach, and filled our bedroom wall with canvasses of the waves. Of squawking seagulls, and abandoned sand castles, and children digging for shells.

I wondered, sometimes, about Sabine. Cordelia. Christoph. If they'd managed to find peace, wherever they'd ended up. If they'd ever found home again.

It was a while before Addie and I returned to school, but by then, we'd managed to catch up with the rest of our class, so we started junior year in the fall with a school full of people who at once knew and didn't know who we were.

President Loyde made history as the first American president to make an official trip overseas since the start of the Great Wars nearly a century ago.

Addie and I made a few new friends at school.

There was talk that we might travel one day, too. Henri wanted us to come visit him, and it was no secret that Addie and I going overseas would be seen as more than just a private affair. But for the moment, nothing was certain, and we were happy to stay where we were. There would be time for traveling in the future. There would be time for so many things. Anything we wanted.

"Eva?" Mom said one afternoon as Addie and I arrived home. Lyle, who'd just started middle school, wouldn't be home for another few hours.

"Yeah?" I called back, and she appeared in the hall with the cordless phone.

"It's for you." She looked hesitant. Ryan or Hally called frequently enough, asking for me. But judging from her expression, it was neither of them.

Who is it? I mouthed as she handed us the phone.

We still got calls, relatively frequently, from reporters wanting to interview us, or people furious at everything we'd done, everything we stood for. Our parents tried to shield us from those calls, when they could. Our number was supposed to be unlisted, but people were diligent and relentless.

"Someone named Bridget?" Mom said, and I immediately pressed the receiver to our ear.

"Hello?" I said, as Addie whispered <*Ask her where she is—*>

We hadn't spoken to Bridget since the night we escaped from Hahns. Had never known what had become of her.

Bridget's voice was quiet, but steady. "For someone who was so famous, you're hard to get ahold of, you know?"

I laughed, and saw Mom's shoulders relax. She gave us a hesitant smile, and I smiled back.

"How are you?" I said. "Where are you?"

"Home," Bridget said. "It took a while, but I'm home."

I looked around at the new house, the rougher edges of it

beginning to wear away after months of our living here. At the crisp autumn world beyond the windowpanes. At our mother as she motioned she was headed back upstairs.

"Yeah," I said softly. "So are we."

<*Eva?*> Addie still says, sometimes, when we wake from dreams. When slumber peels away, and she reaches for me in the haze of another day's beginning.

<*Eva?*> she says, like she did when we were children.

And I answer <*Yes. Yes, I'm here.*>

Because I am. And I always will be.

ACKNOWLEDGMENTS

It is insanity to think that we have come to the end of the Hybrid Chronicles—the story I first began in my last year of high school and am now completing months after graduating from college. Writing this series is inextricably linked with my college years, and the people who have mentored and aided me during this process have also been my mentors in life.

I am forever grateful to my editor, Kari Sutherland, and my agent, Emmanuelle Morgen. Kari, for your incredible notes and suggestions, which guided me through each revision. The series is so much stronger because of you. Emmanuelle, for teaching me things I didn't even know I needed to learn about publishing, and for always being only an email or phone call away when I needed help.

I owe the biggest thanks to everyone at HarperTeen, who received these stories as words on a screen and transformed them into (and I might be a little biased here) the most beautifully bound books. Special mention, of course, to the lovely Alison Lisnow, who rocks my world as my publicist.

Thank you to Whitney Lee and all my other foreign agents. I've always loved to travel, and seeing my books on shelves in new countries continues to be the biggest thrill. I am very grateful, also, to my film agents, Jon and Michelle at CAA.

Savannah Foley and JJ, I owe you both infinite amounts of baked goods for setting other work aside to read through drafts of *Echoes of Us*. Amie Kaufman, even being on different continents and in utterly different time zones didn't keep you from helping me brainstorm the first outline for book three. You're awesome like that. :)

It's been a fantastic journey, guys, and I am grateful to everyone who has helped give me the opportunity to take it.